PROVENANCE

JANE MESSER

PROVENANCE

VINTAGE

A Vintage Book
Published by
Random House Australia Pty Ltd
100 Pacific Highway, North Sydney, NSW 2060
www.randomhouse.com.au

Sydney   New York   Toronto
London   Auckland   Johannesburg

First published in Australia by Vintage in 2007

National Library of Australia
Cataloguing-in-Publication Entry

Messer, Jane, 1960.
   Provenance.

   ISBN 978 1 74166 536 9 (pbk).

   I. Title.

   A823.3

Cover and internal design by saso content and design
Typeset by Midland Typesetters, Australia
Printed and bound by Griffin Press, South Australia

10 9 8 7 6 5 4 3 2 1

Australian Government

Australia | Council
for the Arts

This project has been assisted by the Australian Government through the
Australia Council, its arts funding and advisory body.

AUTHOR'S NOTE

Provenance is a work of fiction. While I have drawn on real events and places and everyday practices relating to the years the novel encompasses, and have sought the advice and first-hand experiences of those who were adults at the time the book is set, the novel's characters resemble no one but themselves and their author. Many of the places in which I place the characters are genuine, while others have been modified for the benefit of the fiction. I trust that where I have invented a town or without warning have moved a river, the reader's journey has been enhanced.

For Michiel, with love

As the saying goes, 'The hottest kiln produces the finest china.'

June Dally-Watkins, *The Secrets Behind My Smile*

But one does not interrogate, no matter how tactfully, a couple so newly formed. They were at an age, after all, when everything looms larger than it is, when nothing can ever, as we say, simply arrange itself.

Colette, *Earthly Paradise*

The disproportion in their fortune was nothing; it did not give her a moment's regret, but to have no family . . .

Jane Austen, *Persuasion*

Call everyone noble, none is low born . . .

Guru Nanak, *Guru Granth*

1960

CHANCHAL WOKE WELL BEFORE THERE WAS LIGHT. HE couldn't see the outlines of the men. He rolled from his cot and left the hut, slipping on his shoes and winding his turban. Around the hut washed turbans hung to dry from posts and the trees. They bathed each night as they were filthy from the work of cutting sugar cane each day, but along with the other Sikhs he'd also bathe when everyone was risen and the water had warmed and the porridge was cooking. The hut was set on the edge of the vast cane fields north of Townsville. He was one of a team of eleven, all Indians. That was how the gangs worked: Catholics with Catholics, Indians with Indians – Muslim, Hindu or Sikh. The head cutter found and chose the men for his gang.

Chanchal had with him binoculars, bird book, note-book and pen. He'd heard the *wook-wook* of the barking owl. She screamed at night and he wondered, is she alerting her mate to a catch? The book didn't say. He had seen koels, which he knew so well from India and his *Guru Granth Sahib*, the black males high up in the trees beyond these cane fields singing *kikooook . . . kikooook . . . kikook*.

But today he would watch the wedge-tailed eagles that nested half a mile down the road. Knowing of his interest, one of the Australians had told him about the nest. The cutter warned him it'd be empty soon; there was money in hunting the wedge-tails. Chanchal had seen them circling, their diamond tails distinctive, and their flight so close to the heavens they could be mistaken for a small bird. He'd counted the telegraph poles the day before, knowing it would be difficult to find the nest again in the dark of the morning. Here it was: the twelfth pole. He quietly put himself down on a rise of earth at the edge of a tall field, raising his binoculars and fixing the focus on the black blur where the pole made a *t*. The nest was huge – a yard or more across in size; made from long twigs and smaller branches and leaf matter. Nothing neat about it. And so he sat for the next hour as the light rose, waiting for movement.

There it was. A bird had shifted to the edge of the nest and was opening his black wings – great wide things. Chanchal calculated the span – two yards? With a great heavy flap the bird heaved up into the air, working hard, growing smaller, higher, further away.

He waited. The other bird didn't show itself, if indeed it was there. The cutter had told him that the myxomatosis virus was weakening and killing fewer rabbits, and that should have helped the eagles. But, there was a bounty on the wedge-tails. Chanchal made a note to the side: myxomatosis; efficacy; Punjab? He wouldn't follow this up; back in Melbourne he'd be glued to his biochemistry work.

It wasn't light enough to follow the eagle very far. Chanchal wrote his brief notes, then feeling hungry made his way back to the camp for his porridge.

2

RAFI CRAWLED OUT OF THE WAVES AND LAY ON THE SAND, chest heaving, mouth tasting of salt. She rested a few minutes, then found the start of the track past the twist of the black mangroves. Jogging through the bush, the tea-trees scratched at her bare legs and caught at her wet dress. The gravel and coarse sand on the track and then the hot road bruised and burnt her feet. But she made it home, feet and lips blistered, skin bleeding and white with salt. She showered and dressed in a rush; fixed up her face with some mascara and lipstick. She wet her eyebrows with a finger and reshaped the black lines into two steady curves and took a deep breath.

The house was silent. If anyone was to come home early she'd hear the creak and slap of the screen door. She listened for the slap as she stuffed socks into her pumps, collected together her hairbrush, a face washer, moisturiser and a block of the 4711 soap that had been a birthday present from her father, the wrapping glamorous gold and turquoise. Skirts, blouses, a cardigan, her prized jeans and her desert boots, her sketchbooks and pencils, charcoal – there was a lot to take. Too much. There wasn't much time. Her mother had already straightened her bed.

Rafi glanced at the faded print of Cezanne's plate of red apples pinned to the wall. She'd slept in this room all her life, and now she was going to leave it as she'd been herself until this morning: naive and half-formed.

From behind the venetians and the trail of the passion-fruit vine outside her window, Rafi took a look at the Bullens' yard. The lawn was brown and the leaves of the shrubs burnt and curling from salt and sun fatigue.

It was all so quiet. She thought – I have some time. They'll still be looking for me down at the beach.

Inside her parents' bedroom the light was dim, and the half-drawn blinds gave the walls that yellow, menacing colour. Only ever muffled sounds from this room, crowded with furniture, more each year; a larger bureau, this new side table with the figurines of shepherdesses and lambs. Rafi picked one up, put it down. Just more things to avoid knocking over all the times she had poked through the drawers while they were out, feeling through her father's pockets for shillings or pennies and the leftovers of chocolate bars, trying on her mother's slips. Only ever the muffled sounds of her mum's irritation, her dad's cushioned thumps. Once he had punched his pillow so hard the feathers burst out – then, laughter. She and the boys had run into the room on hearing Norma and Carlo laughing.

From the glory box behind the door Rafi took out an envelope thick with soft bank notes. Her mother didn't bank the money in case the tellers told Carlo she had opened her own account. The money was the women's secret: bridge winnings, horse winnings, a portion of the wages Rafi gave her mother each week. Rafi counted the notes. She wouldn't need to take the full one hundred and forty pounds – she'd take one hundred. Some of it was hers, after all. Ten of it was her art prize money. She wedged the money into her purse; she'd divide it up and hide it in her things later. Let them think she was drowned for a few hours; they'd manage. Once her mum checked the box she'd know that Rafi had run off.

The house was still quiet. Behind the silence there was the low roar of the waves crashing onto the Petal Bay sands.

Rafi figured she'd need something to prove who she was when she enrolled at the art school. Everything official was kept in the hallway cupboard. She found her birth and finishing certificates amongst the baby immunisation booklets and the useless ration books from the war. Why keep those still? The cupboard smelt of clean towels and vanilla.

The doors to the bedrooms were open, airing, the beds neatly made just as Norma had left them, the ribbing of the chenille bedspreads running in neat parallels, like train tracks, a reminder to Rafi to go, to go now, to go quickly, before she lost her nerve, before Rickie or her mum came home or the train was derailed or the bus broke down. She moved down the hallway, through the kitchen, the holland blinds drawn against the sun, and out the back door. It slapped shut. The sound of her going. Should she leave a note? No, there wasn't time before the bus. Now that she'd decided, it wasn't hard to leave this emptiness and orderliness. She'd always thought it would be too hard to leave — but it wasn't.

Rafi ducked under the apple tree, pushed through the corn, and climbed over the fence at the back of the garden. She brushed down her skirt, wiped the dust off her black-toed slides, and then was on her way. There were no neighbours out back to see her walk down the disused path between the fibreboard and the ant-eaten wood fences. Not one neighbour spied Rafaela Mollino hiking along with her bags. No one stopped her on the road to ask where she was headed with that duffel. Not a car in sight.

Not now, with the sun high and the wind hot off the beach, but in the evening, Petal Bay could be a pretty town, when the hot light had faded and the torn skirt of bush and the pinks and the greens of the weatherboards danced softly worn. It was a hard place to live in and Rafaela had longed for something ineffable to be said. What was it that she needed to hear or to say? If only just one other person had tried to find the words with her. No one in the town of Petal Bay or in the town after that or the next one again knew about the ineffable. Or about Art. About the dozens of paintings she had painted and the more she planned to paint.

She passed dry weeds, a pumpkin grown from a thrown-away seed, the same legless couch that had been there the past year, a nest of anxious kittens. She saw it all as she hurried, elation gathering, past the casuarinas of her small town towards the train to Melbourne.

Rafaela Ellen Mollino – born south of Townsville, always lived south of Townsville, now aged nineteen. Dark-haired, olive-skinned. 'Modigliani looks,' said her art teacher at school. 'From my dad's side,' Rafi'd said. She sat on her duffel bag, hidden behind an old wooden barrel at the end of the station platform. She pulled her skirt lower over the cuts on her shins. The scratches on her hands and arms were scabbing over in thin dotted red lines.

She snapped a geranium from the tub and plucked at the petals as decisively as her brother Luca pulled the wings from flies. He hadn't grown out of that. The petals fell in red sprinkles onto the wide folds of her skirt, made of a heavy cotton printed in creamy dots the size of pennies on the brown background. She'd sewn it herself a month ago, buying the fabric with her birthday money, and wore it tightly belted, as was the fashion. She tried to think of a word for this feeling of escape. The minutes were passing and she couldn't stop smiling. The rail tracks out of here were in front of her. Fat whole minutes of smiling until she thought, *elation*. This elation had seized her, as if biding its time all these years it had been waiting for her to say: *Now!*

Webs of sugar cane rail-truck tracking ran alongside the station. Beyond the station lay yet more fields of cane. This was sugar country. Flat and sunny. She was the only person on the platform, but she kept out of sight behind the big tub, smiling. Over there, bolted to the wall of the waiting room, was a timetable and a framed map of Australia, but she wasn't going to get up to look at it. She knew the shape of Australia, knew that twisted heart off by heart. She knew the cross-hatched lines of the train track leading the tattoo south on that map. Elation: she couldn't wait for the tap, tap, tattoo rattle of the train hurtling down to Melbourne. Where she was going to learn to paint. Tattoo – ta-ta! Sydney wasn't far enough away, no; she was going to plunge deep down the continent and the Pacific Ocean's long eastern lip to Melbourne. World-famous city – four years ago the Olympic city. Betty Cuthbert had run fast. An international city, said the news-reels – and home to artists and sculptors. She had read about Arthur Boyd's 'Half-Caste' exhibition. He was criti-cised. In an art almanac she'd found at the library she read of Charles Blackman and John Perceval and Clifton Pugh. She'd be seeing their paintings for herself soon, she knew who to look out for.

A few people had gathered on the platform. The Sunlander was coming. It arrived on time and with more than a dozen carriages. Rafi hefted her duffel onto her shoulder, ready to board. She found her place in the half-empty carriage, and slung her bags up into the metal basket above. A few latecomers boarded. No one looked as excited as her. When had she last been on a train? For outings to Townsville, a couple of out-of-town dances, and some fishing trips with her brothers. She'd hardly been anywhere.

With a blast of its horn, the Sunlander started up. They passed the stationmaster with his shrill whistle and flag. The platform ended perfunctorily with a sudden drop to gravel and weeds.

The phone had rung a few weeks ago, brittle-brittle, when she was alone at home lying on her bed thinking, and instead of some young woman asking for Rickie, the woman said she wanted to speak to Miss Rafaela Mollino, please. 'That's me,' said Rafi. 'Speaking', she then said, remembering her telephony training from last year. The woman with the adenoid voice said, 'Congratulations, Miss Mollino – you've won the Mimosa Town and Region Portrait Art Prize. And we'd like to invite you to attend the prize-giving.' 'Oh my god,' said Rafi, then apologised, and then said stupidly, 'Which painting?' though it could only have been the portrait of Rickie, not the beach which was entered into the landscape section of the competition. 'Well might you ask,' the Secretary said, 'because you were also awarded second place in the landscape section.'

There were four boys in the Mollino family, born during the war, then Rafi last of all. The three eldest, Michael, Paolo and Luca, their Elvis look-alike with his slicky hair and suedes, worked as cane cutters and at the mill. Then there was Rickie, only ten months older than Rafaela. They had been so close in age and aspect that for a long time they'd been like twins. But once he left school, Rickie had launched his own plans that had nothing to do with Rafi. He started an engineering course at night. He worked in the office at the sugar mill during the day. Rickie was saving for a car and knew young women who lived as far away as Townsville and a grazier's rich daughter out at Hughenden. He had girlfriends, and he was full of ideas, schedules, to-do lists that he got done. She had no plans, no lists. A list for her day might go: get up, have breakfast, hang out washing, draw, listen to mum complain about bridge partner, catch bus into work at noon, come home, help with dinner. Or it might read: get up, draw on beach, help mum with shopping in town, put shopping away, iron clothes for next day, go with mum to bridge night, come home, sleep. Or: ring Julie and see what she's doing, go into town to work, ask dad for a lift to Julie's, come home, help with vacuuming and dusting, prepare the vegetables for dinner. Her day might include Rickie saying in passing as he strode out the door, 'Set yourself some goals.' Then, slap of the flyscreen shutting.

Rafi's growing-up idea that she'd become an artist had worn thin by the time the Secretary of the Mimosa Region Art Society phoned her. She had become blurry and uncertain from the loneliness of living in a house that was mostly empty, from living in a town that was a shadow of what a town should be. Her brothers knew no such uncertainty.

The Secretary was hinting at ripples of discord amongst the judges about Rickie's pose in the winning painting. The guest judge, an art critic from Sydney, had swayed those doubters. Rafi drew a breath: an art critic, come all this way north, liked *her* work.

They piled into two cars to attend the prize-giving at the Mimosa Town Hall. Carlo, Norma, Rickie and Rafi in one; Paolo and Michael and their wives in another. Luca, often late, was too late to come with them. Norma and Rafi had been painstaking in their dress preparations; Rafi wore hat, gloves and stockings.

Before the prize-giving there was time to look at the other paintings and Rafi was annoyed that much of what was up on the old walls was so inept. Accidentally elongated arms; feet left out because they were too hard to draw. Murky colouring, the mistake of too much brown. Perhaps it didn't mean so much that an art critic had liked her work then?

The Mollinos stood before the portrait of Rickie. Norma said a couple of times, 'It's beautiful. I'm going to buy it.' Carlo asked, 'Why is he lying down?'

Rafi said, feeling the sweat gather at the back of her knees beneath the nylon, 'Because he's spending time with a friend. He's taking his time.' Her oldest brother Michael said, 'What?'

Yes, Rickie lay gazing at her from the cusp of his late boyhood. When she'd begun painting him the year before he still had that at-school, self-conscious look on his face. (Though never a pimple for Rickie or her; just smooth olive skin and black, black eyes.) But by the time she'd finished the painting for the show, that look was gone from her brother. His head rested in his hands. His hair was messed a little, months out of a cut. And to add to the surprise of her winning first prize, she had painted his face in the foreground, his body disappearing behind him, fore-shortened feet crossed at the ankles. He was not upright in a chair nor standing squarely, yet the judges who doubted her had not got their way. Then Rickie said, 'Yeah, I get it. She's got me talking to her, lying on the grass just having a gas.' Rafi looked at Rickie: was this a dig at her? Did he know she wished he were at home more, like before?

People came up to her and congratulated her. Her family laughed and smiled but Rafi felt a little angry about this because they'd not laughed and smiled the past year when she'd worked so hard at her art on her own. No teacher, no classes, no friends doing it with her. The Mollinos moved over to the landscape section on the other side of the hall. They stepped politely from landscape to landscape until they reached Rafi's. Her chest was tight with pleasure. There was the LANDSCAPE SECTION, SECOND PRIZE red ribbon next to it. She'd been thinking of Blackman's schoolgirls. The small figure of the girl stood near the rocks looking up the beach. You saw tormenting waves, a tumult of wind – windy as Petal Bay was day in, day out – and then up close, if you bothered to look, the girl's old dress clung, pressed to her driftwood legs by the wind. Her whole figure, Rafi's body, strained against the wind, the sea behind foaming like a mad thing. Suggestions of hair amid the seaweed. If you bothered to look.

'That's our beach,' said Norma with some satisfaction. 'It most surely is. Wind-bitten and inhospitable.' It was a trying time for her parents even with Rafi's art prize that day: their only daughter stubborn, and Carlo's trucking work not bringing in enough because he was sixty and tired and could not make it pay as well as it once had, and Norma half-mad with compulsion for her bridge games and the struggle to keep Carlo's temper in check, and the other equally pressing fight to stay the salt and sand from their fruit and vegetable garden.

Petal Bay village fringed a long beach, the houses and shop pinched between vast sugar cane plantations to the inland and the sea to the east. The sea was too rough for swimming and the wind came in fiercely off the breakers, whipping up through the banks of casuarinas that crested the dunes.

A member of the Art Society handed Rafi a glass of sherry. And another. Rafi felt a little dizzy when she accepted her prizes: a cheque for ten pounds and two certificates. A photographer crouched down near her and bang, there was a flash.

It was still daylight when they reached home again for the celebration dinner. Daylight and disappointment, for though this dinner was in her honour, said Norma, no one was talking to Rafi about her art. Not even Rickie said anything to her about her paintings.

It was business as usual, including helping her mother move the card table alongside the kitchen table so they could all fit around.

Hetty, Michael's wife, synchronised with Norma. 'I've got them,' she said holding up the tablecloths when Rafi came back from the linen cupboard saying, 'I can't find the tablecloths.' Hetty folded the napkins quickly, laid the forks and knives with speed, had the salt and pepper down before Rafi had thought of it; Hetty's parents ran a roadside cafe. She didn't daydream. She got things done – a list girl.

Paolo's wife Louise came back from the bathroom, her hair once again perfectly teased. She talked lightly to Hetty as a sister might, her white capri pants barely creased though she'd been in the car to the art show and back in them. Louise went out to the garden to share a smoke with Paolo and his brothers, out of the way of the in-laws.

'Out you go with them,' said her mother, steering Rafi by the shoulders towards the door. 'This'll be ready in a tick.'

Rafi didn't really want to stand with her laughing, confident brothers and the women. She couldn't make small talk or strike postures as Louise did, or as her girl-friend Julie could. Hand on hip, a toe pointing out, chin up, tummy flat. All these women struggling to stay abreast in the sticks. Sitting beneath the avocado tree on the bench that her dad had made, Rafi watched the others: these people were her family, yet they had nothing to do with her.

The table was loud and crowded when everyone was seated; Luca arriving with a sullen air, but kissing his father Carlo on the cheek; Norma as usual down the stove end; all of them talking at once, the whole purpose of the dinner – her – forgotten. Then out of nowhere – well, from next door – Sean Bullen appeared, shutting the flyscreen carefully so it didn't bang. He hovered.

'What are you doing here?' asked Rafi, glaring. Sean Bullen – inexplicably here to have dinner with them – was an only child of private parents, and had no idea how to behave. He was red-haired and too pale for this part of the country, and always looked a little burnt, just like the Bullens' garden was burnt and useless to grow anything.

'I invited him,' said her dad. 'Sit down, mate.'

Sean slid into the empty chair next to hers – which meant that the others had known he was coming and had set a place for him and it was just her luck not to have noticed. He never came to dinner. Carlo leant across the table, pouring tumblers of a cousin's homemade wine.

'Dad invited you?' Rafi asked.

'To our talented daughter!' said Norma, raising her glass. There was a pause in the ladling of the salads and pasta and meatballs, a brief raising of glasses, a chorus of 'Congratulations, Rafi'. Then, some eating.

'What you should be doing is family portraits and portraits of babies,' said her dad, not really looking at her. Rafi was in a mind not to answer him. 'Set up shop with one of those photographers and help with the colourings.'

'Dad, we've got Kodak now,' she said. Her father had been born a peasant, came here as a young man to work in the cane fields, so what could he be expected to know about anything?

'That'd be lovely,' said Hetty. 'When we start a family you could be our portraitist.'

'I'm talking about you earning a living, making a contribution and getting yourself ready for marriage,' said Carlo, looking at her now.

'I have a job.' But she didn't have a fella, never had had a fella, and the boy from next door wasn't going to be it, if that's what her mum and dad were planning.

'Mrs Mollino, could I have some more of those meatballs, please?' asked Louise.

'I'll have some too, mum,' said Rickie. Rafi caught his look, and he rolled his eyes in sympathy. The others chewed methodically, Sean jiggling his knee, swallowing like the world was about to end, the married couples talking amongst themselves. Luca got up for a beer. He held a bottle of Four X. 'Who's for it – Dad?'

'I'm driving.' Carlo was in a mood, but they all knew he'd be in the truck soon.

Norma pushed her chair back, catching it as it tipped, muttering her exasperation with the chair and her husband and her daughter.

Dessert was a trifle with custard. And that seemed to be it as far as the celebration went, with her brothers and the wives going out to the back porch with their beers. Rafi scraped and stacked the dishes beside the sink, Sean helping her though she didn't want his help.

'Go on out there,' she told him. She handed him a tub of scraps. 'These are for the chickens. You know how to feed chickens, don't you?'

Carlo was still at the table, picking his teeth clean with a toothpick. Rafi wanted to hurl a plate at him.

'I've started on Rickie's suit,' Norma said, unwrapping a dark cloth from a bag on the kitchen dresser. 'By the time you get back you'll have a son who can go to work in a full suit.'

Carlo chuckled. 'Hey, my son will have a tie, wear shiny shoes, have people waiting for him – he'll be a boss!'

Rafi slipped out the front door, then down the darkening street to the beach. The cool sand trickled into her sneakers as she ran down the dunes and started off towards the rocks a mile away. The sky was awash with bleary stars and dark patches of seaweed surged in the shallows. This was her beach, her sky, and she knew she had it in her to be a painter. But how? What should she put on a list?

She heard a windblown *whoo-oo*. Fifty yards behind her was a stick silhouette: Sean waving to her, running lopsidedly in the loose dune sands.

Rafi crossed her arms, shrinking away.

'I thought we might go out one weekend?' he said when he caught up to her.

This was what happened to people around here, they became desperate for any kind of romantic company.

'I don't think I can,' she said.

'Your parents think it would be great if we went out.'

'But you're not Italian or a Catholic, Sean.' This was a sorry grab. She only went to Mass a couple of times a year herself.

Sean looked at her with a frown. 'We could go and see a movie.'

'I think there's infinite choice,' she said to him, and she didn't mean choice of drive-ins. Even without a list of ideas about what these choices might be, and though she hardly knew what she was saying, she believed this statement to be true. Funny how you could discover something true from a quick poke of fear. 'We are so unsuited, *so* unsuited, it's inconceivable that we see a movie together,' she said.

Sean pushed the sand around with his foot. 'I'll ask you again on Saturday and see if you've changed your mind,' he said.

Rafi sat down heavily on the sand wrapping her arms around her legs, facing the sea. Sean turned and made his way back to the village. Once she couldn't see him any longer, Rafi started on her own way back, listening for his breath or a footfall, peering through the shadows for him.

At home she flopped on her bed and stared at the ceiling, following the joins of the particle board from wall to wall, familiar with each nailhead and faint streak of paint and dry remnant of mosquito. It had been so exciting to win those prizes. And now? Wait another year to enter a second time? Was that it? Outside, her father's truck started up. She would not go to him.

Carlo was turning over the engine as he packed his things into the cabin and kissed Norma goodbye. Even if they had argued there was always an embrace between them before he left on the produce haul. There was always a hug for Rafi. She dragged her pillow over her ears so as not to hear the engine. Why was he taking so long to leave? Was he waiting for her? Rickie was catching a lift with him into town. The others wouldn't go home this early. That was the delay probably; Rickie preening in the bathroom. Oh, he fussed in the bathroom these days all right.

The truck was still idling. She went out to the porch, planning to wave, but then walked over to the truck.

'Goodbye, sweetest girl in Petal Bay.'

'I'm not sweet.'

'Don't get cheeky,' Carlo said, annoyed. He climbed into the cabin and gave the horn a blast to get Rickie out and into the truck.

The next morning was full of argument – the first one with Rickie, for not defending her the night before.

'Have you seen him around this morning?' she asked.

'Who?' he said, chewing his toast across the table from her.

'Sean. He's following me around now.'

'He's okay.'

'If he had a sister, would you go out with her?'

'No!' he laughed, leaning back in his chair, clearly enjoying the conversation. Rickie had high expectations of himself, yet not for her. 'It's your argument, Raf. You need to make some plans. Offer mum and dad an alternative.'

'I just won two art prizes, may I remind you. I don't understand why none of you see that as significant!'

'From a small town committee. Honestly, you have to aim beyond that.' Rickie got up and went out into the garden for a cigarette, as impatient with her as she was with him. Then he was off to work and it was just Rafi and Norma at home, again.

Rafi pushed the mangle arm down hard, straightening the twist of sheets as she fed them through, water from the mens' work clothes dripping onto her bare feet, her shoulder aching by the end of that wringing cycle. The village was quiet this Friday; the sea roaring, the wind whipping round the wet sheets as she and her mother pegged them to the Hills hoist. The slap of the wet cloth against her was like the plateful of disappointment she'd had at last night's dinner. The line needed space and wind to spin and to lift the sheets and flap them into triangles and waves of dry white. She had sketched the patterns of cloth and the geometry of the grey metal of the washing line poles. She'd painted her mother bent over the pegs and the washing basket, and there wasn't much more she could do with the Hills hoist and the washing.

As they argued the two women struck at the line with their pegs.

'I'm not like Hetty and Louise, mum. I just don't want to get married until I'm much older.' They were only a couple of years older than her, but different by an ocean.

'You will, though,' said Norma with a small grunt as she bent over the basket. 'You will want a husband and babies.'

'But not now, not soon.'

'Your father will drive you crazy. He's tired, Rafaela. He's sixty and his gallstones are hurting him, and he's tired of these long drives.' Her mother's voice was weary. 'In Sicily, girls were mothers by the time they were your age.'

Rafi heard this from behind a dripping pair of blue work trousers. But her mother was also hiding, and her words came at Rafi from through the rows of her sons' and husband's shorts and yellowed underpants as she pegged them up.

'It's a pity none of you knew your grandparents. You'd realise the value of family then.' The war had stopped Norma's and Carlo's parents from coming out from Wales and Sicily. And then, by the time the country was ready for them, they'd all died.

Rafi thought her mother's eyes were beautiful. So different from her own, so very beautiful. But she couldn't *see* Rafi with them. They were large and violet blue, with barely a wrinkle. 'Can't you see me?' Rafaela wanted to argue, as her mum talked to this other-sister beside Rafi, the daughter Norma yearned for, a Hetty or Louise kind of girl. Her mother was saying from behind the sheets, 'If you don't think about getting married, soon enough it will be too late.' Rafi wanted to step in front of this other girl that Norma was talking to, the one who could be persuaded to go out with the neighbours' son, and say so loudly that she couldn't be missed or misunderstood, 'This is me, here – see *me*, please.'

She picked up the basket, now empty, and took it to the laundry.

She wanted to leave Petal Bay, but what work could she do other than sell fruit and vegetables in a shop? Yet she was smart; her finishing certificate proved that. She sewed her own clothes to her own patterns. She could cook, though nothing special, just spaghetti and roasts, casseroles and puddings. She knew how to puree and bottle tomatoes, and how to make preserves of fruit and vegetables, and when to harvest the corn and the avocado, and where to plant the tomatoes. But unless she got married these things weren't much use.

The washing done, it was time to catch the bus into Mimosa to do the shopping. Aprons off, hats on, Norma and Rafaela trudged through the village and across the sugar cane rail tracks half-buried in the sandy soil, to the highway. The yellow on the bus sign had faded and was laced with rust. Local boys had shot it ragged some years earlier. Luca had been one of them, not that any of the Mollino children had told their parents this. Now, Rafi stopped and pointed to the post. At nineteen years of age Rafi was much taller than her mother and for a moment she felt she was angrily towering over her.

'You know, Luca did that.'

Rafi kept walking as Norma argued that Luca wouldn't have done anything like that.

The morning grew hotter as they waited for the bus.

Town and sea weren't visible from the highway. Level fields of sugar cane stretched out around them, cane that grew all year round, in some fields tall, in other places low in the muddy soil. Sugar was farmed for hundreds of miles to the north and to the south. Away over in a distant field the cane had been burnt early that morning and the butts were still smoking, and though Rafi couldn't see the stumps from the bus stop, she knew that the earth over there was black and grey with ash and very dry. If a cutter wounded himself with his cane knife, if he tore through an artery or lopped off a finger, there was a lot of red.

Laid out before her in this cane was her own smouldering sense of the injustice of it all.

There was no sign of the bus. The weight of the late bus and the heat of the sky bore down on their bent straw-hatted heads. Rafi's boredom intensified. Norma's patience grew solid and thick in her swelling, stockinged feet. Rafi stared up at the few clouds, trying to make out some creature in the cirrus shapes.

'Rafi, you're getting too much sun on your face,' said Norma. 'And tuck your blouse back in.'

She was wearing a white broderie anglaise blouse over the gingham checked capri pants she'd made after seeing *Some Like It Hot* at the drive-in. The black and white checks made a point. Rafi's point right now was that she liked her blouses a little untucked. But she slid her hat forward again. The thing to avoid was thinking about her dad. He always had to have the last say and he seemed to spend the time he was away hauling produce coming up with new points of criticism of her. So she tried to guess what her mother must be thinking about to pass the time: the garden, the bills, her next game, her last win? Rafi played a passable game of bridge herself. Maybe her mum meditated, like the Tibetan monks in *Reader's Digest*, like the Dalai Lama who had just escaped to India. *Ommmm*, Rafi breathed to herself, *Ummmmmm-maa, mundi mundi*. Her lungs felt heavy and shallow. The bus was now very late.

She felt her arm squeezed abruptly. 'Ow,' she said, though it didn't really hurt.

'Stop it. I know what you're doing.'

The squeeze hurt only a little.

'Did Sean find you after dinner last night? So rude of you to disappear like that.'

The sky was all blue now. The clouds had run off.

'I won't go out with him.'

'He's a nice young man. It would be hard to do better.'

There wasn't a thing to look at now, other than each other, which they weren't going to do, or the cane, or the smoke and ash rising in drifts from the field over there, or the empty road. Insults and injury! Rafi walked a few feet away and squatted down to wait.

'You adored each other as children.'

'No we didn't!'

'What are you going to do with yourself then? You can't stay with us all your life.'

'Okay then, mum, I won't.'

Norma came over and tried to tuck in Rafi's blouse at the back, but Rafi walked off a few more feet. 'I'll go live in town.'

She should have gone to nurses' college when they'd offered it to her. Blood and guts and piss would be better than this.

The bus appeared as a vibrating chip of green. Norma slipped on her gloves, blotted her cheeks with a handkerchief and adjusted her hat. Rafi relented, tucking in her blouse. A long few minutes passed before the bus reached them. It stopped, noisy and hot and smelling of oils and long roads, its windscreen and grille pasted with insects and grit.

Half a dozen men lounged at the back, sunburnt and in need of a barber, a cane cutter's gang on their way into town, one of them clutching his trannie to his ear listening to the Townsville race calls. Rafi followed her mum down the aisle. One of the cutters wolf-whistled. Rafi barely noticed, for there was someone unexpected on the bus, a young Indian man in a brown turban, and as she stared at him he looked up from his book and caught her. Rafi quickly sat down, then she couldn't help herself and turned. He had gone back to his reading and didn't notice, but one of the cutters did and threw a peanut at her with a guffaw. They'd been drinking, that was certain.

'Just sit still,' said Norma.

Then the cutter threw a few more of the peanuts he'd been shelling at the Indian, calling out, 'Hey, darkie, you wanna nuts?' Another made a monkey sound. Rafi sat rigid, listened for some reaction from the Indian. If he yelled back, things would be grim. There'd be a fight, the driver would have to pull over and throw someone off.

'I don't like them,' Norma said quietly. At first Rafi thought she meant the men who'd been drinking. 'Why do they have to come here?'

'You came. Dad came,' said Rafi. 'He couldn't even speak English when he arrived.'

'Yes, but we're not coloured,' said Norma.

There was a strip of skin showing between the edge of her mother's glove and the sleeve of her blouse, and this skin was mottled with freckles and sunspots and it was *coloured*, thought Rafi.

'Don't stir them up. Don't look round.'

Norma hurried them off the bus once they'd reached town, hurried her down to the haberdashery to get more thread for Rickie's suit. A couple of women were arguing near the doorway, blocking the entrance.

'For the second time, don't stare,' Norma whispered as they squeezed past, tapping Rafi sharply on the cheek.

'But I need to stare,' Rafi said under her breath, touching her cheek. 'I need to stare so I can draw.'

Inside the shop was busy and they had to wait.

'Why do Indians come here?' Rafi asked, realising that she didn't have a clue. 'It's a long way.'

'There's farm work here they know how to do. And they're always fighting amongst themselves. They have castes, their own wars . . .'

The shop was boiling and the woman serving was taking ages. Rafi had looked at everything there was to look at. She'd even inspected the window display where the mannequins were brown with the sun and their chipped limbs showed a chalky white core. They wore flesh-toned girdles and, without the stockings to stretch the elastic taut along the thigh, the suspenders dangled loosely.

'Mum, do you mind if I go to the library? There's a book reserved for me there. If I don't pick it up they'll put it back on the shelf and I've waited ages for it.' She waited for it: the sigh, the hurt look. There it was. She was lying, there was no book, she just wanted to get out of the shopping. She should help, just as Norma felt she should let her go to the library but not without frowning. If her mum let her have small freedoms such as not going on with her to the butcher, then Rafi should agree to the larger demands such as getting a boyfriend, and fancying herself soon to be married.

And she was off, swinging down the hot street with the glare stinging her eyes after the gloom of the haberdashery, past the hardware and the disposals store to the library. And there on the noticeboard outside was a newspaper clipping about her winning the art prize, and a photo of her receiving the certificate. You'd have thought someone would have rung to tell her she was in the paper! She heard a step on the gravel behind her. It was the Indian from the bus.

'Excuse me,' he said. She stepped a little to the side.

Though his beard was black he looked like Omar Sharif around the cheekbones. His shirt was frayed at the collar and the fine tufts of cotton showed against his skin. There was a gleam of sweat on his neck.

'Here we go,' he said, and ran his finger along a list of train departure times and days. Rafi watched him blankly because he did seem to be speaking to her and not just himself.

'The train timetable,' he said, smiling a little and looking right into her eyes – but also looking as if he wanted her to smile at him to say 'you're okay even though you're coloured'. The timetable was quite close to the photograph. Rafi couldn't tell if her heart was beating hard because she was hoping she'd soon be on one of those trains, or because he might recognise her in the picture. And he did.

'That's you. That's you, isn't it?' He bent towards the picture of her in hat and skirt reaching out to shake the hand of the President, and glanced back to this girl here in her pushed-back straw hat and checked pants. 'You won an art prize. Congratulations.'

'Thanks,' she said. Rafi now wondered if her heartbeat was still galloping from looking at the train timetable or because this man had spoken to her. She was about to say, 'I'm actually going to art school down in Melbourne', but she didn't.

'The next train's not for two days,' he said, raising his eyebrows as if to comment on the long wait. Then, checking his watch, he walked away.

The weekend came and with it an overnight camping trip, some fashion of fun that her friend Julie had planned with a new friend of hers called Moira; the old friends Rafi and Catherine had to come along. Julie's dad drove them down to the local campsite on Saturday morning, helped them set up their tents, then left. There was no escape till Sunday evening. Rafi had tried to tell them about the art prize but Moira had snickered about the judges being old bags and what would they know. Moira was some sort of beauty consultant, and she made Rafi buy an Avon lipstick. Most of Saturday was taken up by a makeup session. Afterwards, Julie and Moira warned Rafi not to swim and were annoyed when she did have a surf, laughing about her makeup coming off.

By Sunday morning Rafi was stalled in the toilets, humming, reading the graffiti again, avoiding her friends.

She also spent a long time tidying her sleeping bag. Then Julie came back from the kiosk and said it was time for a walk up the beach.

'This is promising,' said Julie behind her hand, seeing a group of young men fishing a bit further up the beach. 'Lucky we look our best.' Julie's bathers were flowery and frilled at the hip and the bosom; she did look lovely.

Rafi dropped back as the others sauntered forward, smiling as they settled themselves beside the buckets. The three boys grinned and held onto their rods as if something was about to bite. Every now and then Julie or Catherine shrugged at Rafi to say there was nothing they could do about her being a fourth. She played with the sand around her toes. Then she stood up, brushed the sand from her legs and turned to walk back to the campsite.

'Hey, we've got someone for you to meet.' Rafi pretended she hadn't heard but the guy ran over and, grabbing her a little roughly, dragged her back by the arm to the others. Rafi wished he'd let go, she had brothers enough, and shook him off.

The four girls were made to go first, up through the grassy dunes. Long grass blades cut at their shins as they walked along a narrow track through the scrub. The khaki tent was dark inside. A tall central pole held up the canvas roof and four camp beds were ranged around the sides. Clothes and empty food tins, beer bottles and dirty plates lay about. Through the dark of the tent Rafi recognised

Sean Bullen. The fourth. He lay smoking, reading a magazine. When he saw her, he rolled off the bed and stubbed out his cigarette. She almost laughed. It didn't surprise her – who wouldn't want a secret life? But this set-up was pretty low.

The boys made a show of tidying the tent but a smell still lingered. They began a game of cards, and Rafi played along. The tent stank of beer. Sean was already drunk, though it was still morning. He kept leaning on her. She wanted to leave so badly; why couldn't she just walk out and not worry about what Julie and the girls would say to her later? But her legs were like lead.

And then Moira and her guy went to play their hands from his bed, which made the game pretty hopeless. Julie and Catherine and their guys were off rolling around on their camp beds. Sean took another beer, looking at Moira, and then at Rafi. The dress Moira had worn over her bathers was high up on her thighs.

'I have to go to the bathroom,' Rafi said.

Then he was on top of her, all arms and face with his tongue wet and flailing in her mouth like a fish. Pushing him off, Rafi wiped her mouth dry with her hand.

'I'll go with you so you don't get eaten by wild animals,' he said.

'No, Sean,' said Rafi. She'd just take herself back to their campsite.

But Julie stood up and said, 'Let's go for a swim.'

33

Lots of stumbling and catching was contrived as they made their way to the furthest beach. 'I've hurt my foot!' Julie claimed as she fell over grass on the dunes with a laugh, her blonde hair swinging. The boy Craig threw himself down and kissed her foot gallantly. He wanted to nibble her all over, he said, and this was so funny the others laughed and laughed. Then he heaved her into his arms and staggered into the foamy shallows. Julie screamed. Sean turned on Rafi, trying to scoop her up, but she dodged him and sat herself down. He collapsed onto her, grinding his head into her lap, and immediately fell asleep, the sun blaring at them, the sea so close. Rafi was dumb and paralysed with the humiliation. She needed shade; her head hurt with the sun and Sean's head was high up on her thighs. Moira's cleavage was reddening. Rafi licked her lips; her lipstick was dry and thin. From behind them, the cicadas droned fiercely. She thought about the train, closed her eyes and saw the long train at the quiet station, it would be there in a few hours taking on passengers. She saw herself boarding it, stepping up that big step. Her list, what was on it? She hadn't even made a list of things to do! What to do now? Get this fat head off her lap.

She stood abruptly and strode down to the water, not pausing to throw off her dress. She plunged through the breakers, diving down into them, swimming hard to meet the next one. Past the foam she flipped over for a breather.

The sun dazzled the slip of water between her white dress and the air. The sea was a smooth pan of blue and she was a strong swimmer. But then she heard Sean's panting breath and, treading water, turned to find him alongside her, laughing drunkenly in the deep. Before she could dive away he had his hands on her waist.

'Get off!' she said, working hard to stay afloat as he pulled at the straps of her dress, yanking at them, giggling. He dunked her and she sank beneath his weight, kicking at his legs, trying to back away from his grabbing hands. He had her waist again, he was unnaturally eager, and she went down under the water once more.

When she surfaced in the splashing, his splashing, she hauled air in then pushed down hard on his head to get him away. He sank under the water. One of the others was coming into the water after them. Rafi didn't look back but swam, dread of being taken back onto the beach driving her overarm, past the two beaches flecked with families and bouncing balls and striped umbrellas until she was at the far end of the Cap Head beach. She swam into the surf and let the waves catch her and surge her forward, slow and exhausted, into the shore. Truly, she was that girl in her painting, alone with her dress pinned to her legs. She stood up shakily, the bright flat sand shimmering around her, making a list in her head of all the things she needed to do in the next hours to get on that train to Melbourne.

3

ALL HIS FAMILY HAD COME WITH HIM TO DELHI FROM Ludhiana in the Punjab and stood by the train at the station right up to when he boarded it. Over a dozen farewelled him: his father Bani, though he was not well with his heart medications needing some new adjustment, his mother Aparna, his sisters Nilima, Susheela and Sarla, and their children and their husbands. For he was leaving Ludhiana for London, and he was the first to leave – but he would come back of course, he promised, and work for the rich soils of the Punjab, and remember their friends in Ludhiana and his family. He would be good, and bring credit to them; he would become a great scientist, and be virtuous and successful.

He would come back and marry a lovely Sikh girl, boasted his father Bani.

Chanchal had promised so much. Wittgenstein had written, 'Everything that can be said, can be said clearly,' and this was tantalising to a young science graduate. But the 'can' was a problem, because there was also cannot or will not, and Chanchal couldn't confess to his dearest family, *I might not come back*. He knew he was going to London to study biochemistry and then who knew, a PhD, but did he also know he would return to Ludhiana? What he knew and what he could say clearly was very little indeed.

The women had cried that he was going so far, to London, Britain, so immeasurably far from them. He was saddened that his mother Aparna must cry for her only son, whom she'd protected through Partition in Amritsar, hiding with him for hours in a neem tree that Bani had lifted them up into. Shushing him, patting, shushing him when he cried he was so frightened, holding him tight when he fell asleep so that he didn't fall. Their father had locked his sisters in a room in an abandoned house, then sat down to pray, waiting for the worst to come.

It was hot on the station platform. Soot and steam and the scents of blackened ghee from the stalls burning fires for kulcha and paranthas drifted over them. His beard prickled with the heat, while his father seemed to be breathing with difficulty in the saturated air and with the crowds pressing upon him.

That last hour in Delhi in 1957 was what Chanchal thought of when he remembered leaving India.

Two years later, on leaving London for Australia, when he'd been chosen for the Colombo Plan scholarship, only a few biochemistry friends had come to say goodbye at the docks. Chanchal was subdued and they were all a little embarrassed to be parting for good, joking that he was going to the land down under and how would he keep his turban on if upside down, and not to get hit by a boomerang and to tell them if there really were kangaroos in the streets. When it was time for Chanchal to embark, his few friends got out their streamers. Waving from the deck, Chanchal observed how weak these paper ties between boat and land were; streams of red, green, blue, yellow; all the streamers broke and sank into the ocean. He was very glad of the widening sea between him and London. He was ready to reform.

Now on this train, the Sunlander, just over a year after leaving London, he was pleased to be alone in a comfortable cabin after weeks of cane cutting with his friend Vikram Kirpal and the other Indians. Though the two summer months with the other Sikhs and Hindus in his gang had been a sabbatical indeed from the people of Melbourne. Chanchal knew he was resilient enough; but Melbourne, what a shock to the system. Compared to Ludhiana and London its footpaths were empty. It was as if the citizens were all hiding in the mountains or their kitchens anticipating their own Partition. But no, in Melbourne there was nothing to fear, nothing to dread.

Having boarded the Sunlander, he laid his things out in the cabin. He placed on the bench his notebook and his shabby copy of Waris Shah's *Heer Ranjha*, the poetic tragedy he'd kept with him since first reading it as a fourteen-year-old, his *Guru Granth* wrapped in cloth, playing cards, the *Courier-Mail*, pens, a pad of airmail writing paper (his letter to his mother Aparna being overdue), a bag of apples and passionfruit, and a *New Scientist* he'd picked up in Townsville. The cabin was spotlessly clean and the sheets sumptuously white and stiff with starch. He ran the water on and off from the drinking spout, and opened the gleaming closet door and put his few things away inside. He lifted then drew closed the small rectangular blind to the train corridor.

The train was soon passing through panoramas of cane, visible from the wide cabin window, and in the distance rising hillsides of banana plantations. Then there were breaks in the fields and the forest came close. He liked the white-trunked gums with the dancing limbs, the way they snaked up against the bright blue sky, but not the hairy coarse-barked trees – though their timbers were probably highly useful.

He and Vikram had earnt a packet of money cutting cane and they'd shared a lot of laughs, and Chanchal had his *Birds of Australia* and had taken himself off in the very early mornings away from the fields to wherever there was a tree or shrubbery, and was particularly pleased to have seen the barking owl ascending from the cane with prey and not just heard its screams; also the grand wedge-tail, chestnut-breasted mannikins and plum-headed finches. Near Mimosa he had sighted a striated heron riding driftwood at tide.

He thought – Must write to ma and pa about this. He liked this country.

4

WITH EACH NEW TOWN AND LEVEL CROSSING RAFI FELT herself striding away from what her family thought she should be. The Sunlander stopped and started, until it rattled over the river near Bowen, the last of the towns that she knew. The water was brown and low and scattered with mauve water lilies. Birds had made nests in the square braces of a set of electrical power poles. Long twigs and leaf fronds stuck out from these nests. The train passed a woman in tan jodhpurs holding a stock gate open. A seagull raced alongside, then swooped up and away. All that was familiar when she was low down on foot or in the truck appeared different from the quickening height of the train: hillocks of trees, the dips down into stock dams, the flat of the cane fields.

A strange man with fly-away hair and a dog moved to a seat behind her.

'Keeping on time, eh?' he said, leaning over the back of her seat and startling her.

'I hope so,' she said. She had to turn around in her seat to see him.

He held the dog up above the seat. 'This is Misty.' She was a fine, gentle-looking dog.

The new couple across from her were kissing. Rafi watched them surreptitiously. Perhaps they were honeymooners. The girl wore a gold band on her wedding finger, but they weren't laughing and Rafi felt there should be lots of laughter and rambling, intimate conversation on a honeymoon. Only from novels and reproductions of paintings in the town library's art section had Rafi detected a vision of sensual love for herself, but what she saw across the aisle was not it. She could see the boy's tongue, the red underside of it as they kissed, and it looked like a dead eel from the creek at home after locust spraying, like those stupid boys and that stupid Sean this morning. She was hours ahead of them, though she'd need to be careful when she got to Brisbane because by then they'd know for certain that she'd left home. Every peasant bone in her dad's body would be shaking with fury when he returned to find her long gone.

She glanced again at the couple. The girl's face was smooth and, floating over her sun-brown skin, lighting it, was a downy layer of hair along her cheek near her hairline. Rafi thought – How would I paint that?

Then a young man in ragged jeans but with a scrubbed-up nicely look to him came up the aisle, saw them, and winked at her. With a jolt the train sent him forward and he was gone. The ticket collector arrived and punched holes in her ticket, wrote something on his clipboard. He was too quick for her; she didn't have a chance to ask when they expected to get in to Rockhampton, where she planned to change her Brisbane ticket for a Melbourne ticket.

Rafi opened her sketchpad. She drew the passing trees and their flickering sun-shot shadows as the evening came down. She drew the couple: their twisted torsos and inter-locked arms. They looked as though they were grasping in need and fright, like Albert Tucker's wartime harlots.

Everything was changing and the land proved it. With evening the tilled fields outside were almost purple. On a small lake black swans studied the cold green water for fish. She recognised cows she had seen in photographs, bone-hipped undulating Brahmans the colour of dust. The mid-season fields of sugar cane were burning, the bright fires low in the leaf trash. The colder high air sucked at the fierce orange sparks, and seas of sweet, cloying smoke floated loftily above. The train gathered momentum.

Restless, she left the carriage, purse in her bag. In the shaking gangway she smelt the peculiar pungency of burnt sugar mixing with the train's odour of coal and metal.

She walked up the long aisles of seats, past the second-class cabins with their sliding doors and six seats on one side, the windows of the train on the other. People were reading, playing cards and dozing. A boy strummed a guitar. When she came to the first-class doorway a sign said that only first-class ticket holders were allowed through.

Past this door the train was quieter. Coloured prints of anonymous bush landscapes decorated the walls. A hand-tinted photograph of the Queen hung alone, reminding Rafi of her father's suggestion at dinner the other night. A door to one of the sleepers swung open. Rafi looked in. Framed by the wide cabin window, wattles in yellow flower streamed by outside. The cabin was snug and compact, the wood trims honey-toned and the chrome fittings shiny. No wonder they had a picture of Her Majesty outside.

Then she saw him, the Indian she'd spoken to in town, again in a white shirt but this time with a blue turban. Perhaps he was a prince or a sultan or a maharaja. Whatever that was. She'd not seen him get on, but here he was, disappearing into a cabin a few doors down. His eyes slid over her before he shut his door, she was sure of that. She walked stealthily to his door and watched for the slightest movement in his corridor blind, but it was down. She'd been well and truly snubbed.

She went back to the buffet car.

'What's your cheapest meal, please?' she said to the serving lady who was flipping idly through a magazine.

The woman studied the pastries on the metal heating trays. 'You can have an old pie for nothing. Nothing wrong with it.'

She passed Rafi the pie and the tomato sauce bottle. Rosella, rosella. The sauce was black around the rim, but sweet and red on the pie.

'You wouldn't know it was old,' said Rafi as soon as she was done.

The woman chuckled. 'That's good – here's another.' Fine lines ran from the woman's blue eyes. She probably had kids somewhere.

Each small conquest such as this one, being given a pie for free, and the big one of boarding the train with money, ticket and bags, reassured her she'd know how to live in the city. The train was protecting her while she prepared herself for what was to come, practising for big city life. She had a mental picture – of getting off a green tram outside the National Gallery of Victoria, wearing her broderie anglaise top untucked, her checked pants and a straw hat, carrying straw bag, sketchpad in hand. Another picture – a cafe with men and women milling about, paintings on the walls, someone strumming a guitar, she is talking to – ? Another artist.

With the evening deepening into night, drinking and smoking started up. The tables in the buffet car filled. At the toilets the mothers queued with their children, toothbrushes and washers in hand. By the time the lights in the carriages stuttered off nearly everyone in her car had drawn their tartan blinds. But Rafi couldn't get comfortable in her seat. Her skull knocked against the window frame and she dreamt uneasily of doors banging shut as she ran and ran through a house with yet more rooms. The sweater she was using as a pillow came loose. Waking, she pushed it back, but it slipped again. Somewhere in the black the train stopped. Rafi woke in a panic that they'd reached Rockhampton. She should have asked when they would get there. Eager for a hint, the sound of an explanation, all she could hear were the hoots of an owl. Mice, flight, moonlight, she couldn't sit like this any longer. With the train stopped, her feet rapped loudly on the metal flooring of the gangways. She walked faster and faster past the heaped passengers, almost running while they slept unawares. She was awake and afraid. A runaway. In a vestibule she turned to the wall and shed some tears. She had no idea where she was or why the train had stopped. She walked through another dimmed carriage. Her hand brushed against a shoulder. She was about to apologise but the man didn't stir. She came to a woman with a big shock of blonde hair. Louise had hair like that, thick and stiff with hair spray.

The young man who'd winked at her back near Bowen was smoking a rollie by the open door at the next gangway.

'Cows on the track,' he said.

It was dark by the open door, with the clouds over the stars. The train's headlamps lit up a small herd of dairy cattle in front and alongside the train. A few rail men milled around talking, unfussed by the delay. She was about to jump down when he offered her his hand. She could get down easily by herself, but she wanted to touch him, she wanted his friendliness. Now she understood it; the need for men who weren't your brothers.

There was a rustling, of foxes or wallabies. Where the field edged into the trees she thought she could see the watchful heads of wallabies waiting for them to leave. She rubbed a hand across her cheeks to wipe away the tight feel of her tears. The homely smell of cigarette smoke wafted around her.

One of the rail men searched in the gravelly grass and found a stick. Back with the cows he tapped their haunches, calling 'git up' and 'huh'. The cows ambled across the rails, hoofs thudding on the sleepers. The wind moved the clouds aside, and Rafi turned her face to the sky. The black bowl of night was rinsed with stars.

'They don't always stop for cows, but just keep on going and pick them off later.'

The jackaroo, or that's what she called him to herself, didn't say anything to the Indian who'd spoken. He finished his cigarette and climbed back aboard. So she was alone with this other one. He stood waiting for her to join him in conversation, dark-skinned against the dark.

'You were reading the train timetable at the library last week, weren't you?' she said. 'A couple of days ago.' Perhaps she was mistaken, and he hadn't seen her near his cabin; otherwise why would he be here now talking to her?

He looked at her closely and gestured for her to come to the lit doorway near where they stood. 'But yes, you're right, I recognise you now. I couldn't see you clearly in the dark. You're the girl who won the prize.'

He was making fun of her. She thought – He mustn't have seen me in the corridor.

He held out his hand. 'Chanchal Singh,' he said.

'Rafaela Mollino. Just call me Rafi.'

They shook hands. His skin was surprisingly calloused.

There was a short horn blast, loud enough to make the last of the cows skip off the tracks and down the slope, their white moon-udders shaking. Rafi laughed softly.

'Cows are sacred in India, is that right?' she asked as they stepped back up onto the train.

'Yes, no one will kill a cow.' He paused a moment. 'They play havoc with the trains sometimes.'

'So it's just dairy cattle that you have then?' she asked.

'Yes, and the problem is that when a cow is too old to provide milk, she might be let out to wander the streets and towns if her family can't afford to keep her, so many cows are sick or starving. But protected.'

She thought he must be in his mid-twenties. He was not that dark and looked a little Afghani; there was an Afghani hawker who had come in from the desert once selling tools and kitchen utensils. Others she'd seen pictures of in *National Geographic*.

'What's the turban for?' she asked touching her head.

'I'm a Sikh and it's what we men wear.'

'A seek?' she said.

'S–i–k–h,' he said.

The train gathered speed as they leant against the

walls, the vibrations of the wheels quickening, not saying much. She remembered reading that under the turbans the men's hair was uncut. Long black hair thicker even than hers was intriguing to think of. She wondered, did he unwind it and brush it nightly? And felt his eyes slide over her.

'How far are you going?' he asked.

'Melbourne.' She'd said it; she'd told him. They looked at each other. His eyes were soft. Or possibly just tired. You'll like me, she thought. I'm different from the others who won't be interested in you because you're different too.

'And you're stopping in Brisbane?' she asked.

'No, getting off at Coffs Harbour and then I'll take a bus to Woolgoolga.'

Rafi shook her head, she didn't know the town.

'I've an uncle there with a banana farm whom I've not seen since I was a boy. And then I'll go back to Melbourne University and take up my thesis again. I'm in biochemistry.'

She didn't tell him he was the first person she'd met who was at university.

'I'm going to art school.' Now she'd told him that too.

This animated him. 'That's right, you won those prizes. That's really something. What do you paint?'

'Everything. The country, landscapes, people. And I love working with charcoals and pencil. Always have. My family think it's a waste of time.' Rafi stopped. She wasn't going to let on she'd run away.

Chanchal longed to close his eyes. He needed to go back to his cabin but thought it was somehow impolite to leave her here.

'That wasn't your gang, coming into town.'

'Not at all. Another man turned up at ours, some loose arrangement, and I decided to leave early and visit my uncle instead.' He yawned; put his hand over his mouth.

'You're tired,' she said.

Chanchal looked at her gratefully. 'I am. I might call it a night.'

'Night then,' she said.

'Night, Rafi.'

Making her way back down the train to her carriage, gusts of wind swept in and the dark clanged with wheel rhythms, shaking her back and forth, rousing her. She found her seat again and tried to doze as the train accelerated or stopped, every station an unfamiliar name. She couldn't rest, so she rose again and went in search of the guard. She found him in his room, his jacket hanging on a hook, an enamel cup of tea beside him. She smiled courteously, conscious of how dishevelled she must look.

'How much further is it to Rockhampton? I need to change my ticket.'

'It's the middle of the night,' he said, getting out his book to check her seat and ticket. 'What do you want to change it for?'

'I'm going on to Melbourne now.'

'Change it at Roma Street station in Brisbane when we terminate Tuesday morning. You get your transfer by tram to South Brisbane for the New South Wales connection. You've got four hours in Brisbane before you leave; that's more than enough time to sort it all out.'

'I have to change trains?'

He laughed. 'Yeah! Different rail gauge widths, girl.'

She hadn't known the continent was fractured by rail gauges, those planks of wood and steel at spacings that didn't fit from one state to another. All the while, she'd imagined crossing the border to New South Wales, the train soberly clanking past a man in a uniform standing attentively beside an official hut – imagined his curt wave to her, a salute to the train – some acknowledgement surely?

There were no such huts, laughed the guard. 'Then you've got the Albury change for Victoria.'

She'd tripped over the simplest of geographies.

When Rockhampton was ten minutes off, the guard came to her carriage, not for her but for the wiry little man with wispy hair and the dog, tapping him on the shoulder to say Rockhampton was next. The fellow gathered a few things together, the small dog snuffling with muffled yelps. Rafi thought she might as well take a look, and went to wait with him in the vestibule.

'I've got a hearing problem and my mate Misty helps me along, you see,' he said quickly.

'Other dogs have to go in the luggage car, but I can keep Misty with me.'

'I see,' she said, wishing another question would come to her. He was watching her keenly, and sounded as though he began every conversation this way.

'Is it very difficult being deaf?' she asked loudly.

'Like I say, you can get used to anything.'

She wondered about that. He must have once had his hearing.

'Have you always been hard of hearing then?'

He nodded, his hair falling over his face. 'They don't know. It might have been there at birth. Maybe when my father belted my mother when I was inside her. Maybe he hit my ears?'

He grinned at her triumphantly.

'That's terrible,' she said. Her father's threats of a spanking with the belt when she was a kid were nothing to this. He'd then thrust his hands in his pockets and stomp out to the garden.

'Misty is a sweet dog,' she said.

He opened the door before the train had fully stopped and jumped down into the warm air of Rockhampton station, Misty leaping ahead. The station was dark. It didn't look as though the ticket office would have been open anyway, and now, thoroughly tired, she returned to her seat and slept.

Early in the morning Rafi washed thoroughly at the

metal basin, and changed into a fresh skirt and blouse. She'd only slept a few hours but was alert. She smiled into the old mirror with surprise at her triumph. She had the rhythm. At each town people swept on and off the train like fish and weed swilling in and out of rockpools back home. The flat cane fields were thinning out. The hillsides were thick with bagged fists of bananas.

She had lived by the same beach and fields all her life, but now in only a couple of days she'd be somewhere else completely.

5

Chanchal was one of the first off the train at Roma Street station. He made his way to the tram stop and though the queue formed promptly, Rafi wasn't part of it. He stood in the late afternoon sun, a hand over his eyes, as the other passengers swelled past. He hung back, then boarded, and the tram took them to South Brisbane station for the New South Wales leg. He liked Rafi and she'd said she was going on to Melbourne, so she should have been catching this tram. So where had she got to?

And here the new train was about to leave and Chanchal was worried she'd miss it. Three hours had passed since they disembarked at Roma Street. She was a young woman on her own. Was she lost? Not for three hours. He should have been friendlier yesterday, gone and found her in whatever carriage she'd been sitting in. Chanchal went in search of a guard, but the man didn't know anything about the passengers; he was there to help people board the train and to get it out of the station.

Chanchal stayed on the platform until the train was pulling out, then went to his cabin. He opened the newspaper and tried to settle on the news. He read that Australia was claiming a portion of Antarctica; the Reserve Bank of

Australia was soon to be official; preparations for Australia Day celebrations in Brisbane were well under way – this was interesting – Australia shared the same day as India's Republic Day: 26 January; Australia was sending a large team to the Winter Olympics in Squaw Valley, USA; Comalco Industries was to mine bauxite at Weipa; heavy rains in northern New South Wales threatened farmers with severe flooding. He'd have liked to be able to get hold of the *Guardian* or the *Economist* – and thinking of London, about which he missed very little, he did find himself longing for the curry puffs at the local Muswell Hill cafe where a dinner of chips, two eggs and a cup of tea cost one and threepence and they knew not to give him bacon or sausages.

Chanchal threw down the paper, opened his cabin door and looked out into the aisle in case Rafi was there. How dumb not to have said hello the first time he'd seen her. He hoped that wherever she was, she was safe. He sorted through his books, again looking at the pad of airmail paper, thinking – Must write; not now.

Chanchal had been almost in love with a married woman – Veronica. She wasn't writing to him in Australia and he didn't want her to. But each time he saw the pad of airmail paper not only did he think – Must write to ma and pa, he thought of her, and then of the men in the novels she had given him when he fled London, and he thought – They're fools, like I was. But not anymore.

V for violin, *V* for the sweet cleft between her legs, *V* for vivacious and much that was vexatious. No *V*s at all for virtuous. He had been in his professor's London university lab, where he worked most days, sighing deeply, half-sitting on the rotating stool that he swung back and forth to the question: what should he do? He remembered that night exactly, when he had figured he was too far from Ludhiana and that he'd lost his bearings and that without his family close by, the constraints on him were negligible. His turban protected him from nothing, and certainly not her.

The radio was tuned to Professor Julian's preferred channel, BBC 3. Veronica, Julian's wife, was one of the strings Chanchal was listening to, live from the London Symphony Orchestra. It was evening and he was working late. Chanchal imagined he could single out her bow from the others. Her thrilling bow. The BBC chap introduced the concert but Chanchal already knew the music well. At the boarding school he had attended for a couple of years in Shimla in the Himalayas, the choral singing of English favourites such as 'Danny Boy' and psalms had been the sum total of their music education. But when he returned to the Punjab in the summer holidays, his parents took him and his sisters to concerts of Mozart, Tchaikovsky and Beethoven and to ghazal and raaga recitals in Amritsar. So to Veronica's surprise the foreign student, Chanchal Singh, was familiar with much of her repertoire.

Chanchal knew where she sat in the orchestra; as the couple's guest he attended the concerts regularly with Julian. Afterwards they met up with her in the green room. That was how the affair had begun, bubbling up out of one of her post-performance highs and his being daunted by all the London chatter and laughter. He had felt that her elation had a little to do with him and was awed.

She had been boldly girlish and imprudent though she was already thirty. In an overheated cab to a dinner, her hand fell on his knee. At only twenty-two, he was so much younger than her that he had to defer. She affectionately tweaked his beard, and tapped on his turban as though it were a hard hat. He raised his hand in gentle protest; immediately he looked out the window, pretending to help his professor give directions to the cabbie. He began to feel hot around his neck and under his turban, his hair prickling, and averted his eyes. The street lights were startlingly bright through the sooty winter air. As the cab edged its way through the night traffic Julian talked on, oblivious to her game of détente. Both talkative, Julian and Veronica were used to interrupting each other.

They did not have children or even nieces or nephews; she and Julian gathered his students together for dinners at their place with others from her orchestra. She was right to say he must miss his family in Ludhiana. He did. On his own, to pass the time when not at the lab, he took his binoculars into the Alexandra Palace grounds and Hampstead Heath, and walked. Shimla was as cold in winter.

Lab nights: with half an ear he listened to the rumble of the centrifuge's motor. When it was done and the separations documented he could go home. The hallway was empty; though scattered throughout the building there were other young men working like him. Now Maggie the cleaner was approaching with her whirring polisher, gliding over the grey-flecked floors, louder and louder. An ageing Scottish woman whose knees were as crooked as a bird's wing, she ignored him; paid stiff homage to the professors. Shrugged off the lecturers and demonstrators. She worked in castes. Maggie passed by in a loud whirr of sound and wax. A violin welled.

The British in India were one thing; here in London the British were everywhere and Chanchal wondered how it was that they had come to rule so widely and then to leave so conspicuously. Wittgenstein could be used to make sense of the nonsensical Partition that had on the one hand almost killed his father with worry, and a million others with axes, knives, fire, abuctions, well-drownings, while it had also made their city richer. Did any Indian understand why so much hatred had flowed between people who'd lived amongst each other for decades, if not centuries? Was it not because of the paucity of language to express experience? The British surely were culprits here, in India with their maps and separation documents. Wittgenstein said, 'A picture held us captive. And we could not get outside it, for it lay in our language and language seemed to repeat it to us inexorably.' And the picture was pillage and killing.

The violins soared, and now they were quiet and stalking. He would like to have believed, but could not honestly bring himself to, that it was Veronica, the highly strung string-plucking back-row violinist, who orchestrated his longings. But he knew that he was just a horny young bugger even if he was a Sikh.

With Veronica's busy orchestral schedule they didn't have much time. She didn't let the affair encroach. They began with a chance encounter outside the chill room (had Maggie passed them by that night, sniffing her dislike?). Later, a rendezvous conducted by her. She gave a complicated arrangement of excuses to Julian, of late-ending rehearsals and rowdy dinners he'd not enjoy – stories Chanchal wanted to know little about. She settled the play of their intimate arrangements at the outset by giving him the corner tab from a box of condoms. That was what she called them. Looking at the tab of blue, Chanchal assumed she used them with Julian. She explained he was to hand the stub over the counter at the chemist shop. That way, if he was shy he needn't say anything. She assured him the chemist in such and such a street was used to students.

For their first assignation he bought a new pillow and pillowslip from a manchester shop up the road. His Muswell Hill bed-sit signalled everywhere his limited manhood: the walls undecorated, the bedspread spare and thin, the new pillow an absurdity of plumpness, his bookshelves and desk a dark unrestful brown.

He lived miles from her and Julian's neat townhouse and she preferred this game of roughing it, of later adding to his meagre collection of crockery with a mismatched piece from her own place or a Selfridges' sale, not realising that he was then to place her gifts amongst those from his own family.

But on this first night, she knocked at his door hesitantly. He had warned her his landlady might pounce. Women weren't allowed in the boarding house.

'There's a dance up near the Odeon,' he offered wildly. 'Do you like dancing?'

Up the long Muswell Hill they strode, past the tattered hedges that bordered the parkland of the dilapidated palace that Queen Mary, former Empress of India – London abounded with these taunts and ironies – built in her husband's name.

'It's absurd,' Chanchal said stiffly, waving an arm towards the palace grounds, 'what the English and the Indian share, this ostentation and decrepitude.'

'Yes,' exclaimed Veronica, but then she seemed unable to think what to say next, or was too puffed to say it.

Youths meandered between the dance hall and the Odeon and a nearby laneway. Inside, the hall was dark and cavernous. Veronica hid her handbag in the stiff folds of her leather coat. Boys and girls hung about the walls. Girls heavy with false lashes danced at their own pace and patterns beneath the revolving mirror ball. Chanchal and Veronica gave in to each other on the dance floor, breath on each other's cheek, glad to have made it this far. This was the modern part of it, thought Chanchal, of his life, of this move to London.

'Bad, mad, glad,' murmured Veronica.

Chanchal ventured a kiss, trembling from head to foot.

'Not always the lady violinist,' she whispered.

They skipped down the hill towards his room. Halfway, they crossed the road to the palace parklands, the swifts and terns silent, and against a woodland tree he kissed her wildly. He was frantic when she put her icy cold hand on his bare skin – he was a kid, he couldn't help it – and she licked her finger and said with a smile in the dark, 'Let's go back to your room.'

Later, when Veronica had tiptoed out, pleasantly flushed, to return home to her husband – that ugly fact of their betrayal – Chanchal lay on his bed wanting more. Still, of her. Her scent was on the new pillow and here was a fine golden hair. He wanted encores from *V*, she had such fine strong hands and a soft mouth. *V* for violin, *V* for the sweets she brought with her.

A few months later he was uneasy – no, he had been uneasy from the start. Each week he grew uneasier. He twirled the lab stool faster and faster, pushing his foot against the floor to propel it. He decided. He was just twenty-two years old and there were at least that many reasons to stop the affair. One, it was simply wrong to make love to his mentor's wife. Two, to anyone's wife. Three, it was not so hard to tell right from wrong. Four, it was against his religion. Five, his parents would be distraught. Six, and so on, though it was too painful to continue. The worst had been numbered.

The force of family was with Chanchal. A picture of his mother would rise, the thought that this was the same woman who'd held him in a tree all night long while the *goondas* tore through the houses looking for Muslims and any girls they fancied; for Ludhiana was a Hindu and Sikh city and so the Muslims had fled the killing for Pakistan, while the Hindus and Sikhs of Lahore had fled to cities like Ludhiana.

So his mother and his father, who'd never recovered his health, if they were to find out what Britain had offered him, how ashamed they would be. Then there was Veronica's small family of two. Such a small family was very fragile. Spinning harder on his stool Chanchal feared he could not stop. The centrifugal force of their illicit embraces would separate them all.

Chanchal wanted to act graciously and honourably in life, though it went against some of the weave of his nature, a nature that was impulsive and not always benignly so. His affair was the most fiendish example of this. Not only did he not want to do harm, he wanted to do good. That was what his science was for. The *Guru Granth* taught that an honourable life was practised through work, and science was Chanchal's work. He reminded himself of this daily.

When Chanchal tried to end it with Veronica, she said, 'Loosen up.'

They were at a pub far from where anyone knew them. Tucked into his turban, fitted blue shirt and tie, with a half-empty glass of lemon squash, Chanchal imagined what she might mean. Her fingers needling at his tie, his buttons, his zip. Asking him to take his *kara* off so she could playfully slide the bracelet up and down her smaller, but strong, lady violinist's wrist.

So here was a bit of a shock as he stumbled through his worries, attempting to explain to her his twenty-two reasons to stop. Veronica, who had been so *entertained* by his culture, was now saying she didn't want to know about his family or the tenets of Sikhism. 'Oh, grow up,' she said impatiently. 'Do what *you* want to do, not what you've been told to do out of a book!' She was keen to get on with the post-war sexy part of the twentieth century. She didn't want to be a sympathetic ex-lover.

When she heard that Chanchal was taking up a scholarship in Australia, she took it he was abandoning her, though he said it was for his career and country: the scholarship came with a bond, to return to India and work there for three years.

Days before he was to set sail, Veronica upstaged him again by arriving unexpectedly at his rooms.

'I won't come in,' she said, standing in the hallway, speaking quietly. Her hair was slightly wet from a drizzle outside, and Chanchal's eye was caught by the way the droplets could be thought to clump and by how lovely her pale, humid skin was. He could allow himself to think this because he was leaving.

'You'll need something to read on the boat out,' she said, handing him half a dozen books. Her voice was gentler than he remembered. 'Do you think you can find space for them somewhere?'

On top was *Birds of Australia*. Chanchal looked at her gratefully – what out-of-the-way speciality bookshop had found this for her? Then, *Come in Spinner* and *My Brilliant Career* and *The Tree of Man*, by people he'd never heard of. And a sheet of paper with the lyrics to 'Waltzing Matilda'.

'This is very generous of you,' he said.

'Ghastly song, but you'll need to know it,' she said with a laugh. Then, 'I am so jealous,' and with her sentence half-done she stepped back as if to go.

'Of what?' he asked. Did she think *he* was having an affair?

'Of you going, of course. I'd love to go to Australia.

I loathe England. Write to Julian, will you, and tell him what a fabulous department it is down there?'

Chanchal looked at Veronica in surprise. He couldn't imagine why she didn't like England. Well, actually he could. The winters, the insipid food, the lack of light and cheer and colour. But she had never complained.

'You're really very lucky,' she said. 'You will do great things. You have a fine mind.'

She leant towards him and kissed him lightly on the cheek. He thought he had probably loved her a little, or even more than a little. Then she went, her shoes clicking her haste down the draughty stairs.

6

ROMA STREET STATION WAS CROWDED WITH MORE PEOPLE
than Rafaela had ever seen before.

This was the big stop, the platform thick with families
and friends meeting passengers, taking hold of their bags,
sharing hugs and handshakes. She gathered her things
together methodically and looking out the window noticed
Chanchal making his way down the platform. He was easy
to spot, in his blue turban. She started down the carriage
to the vestibule out of which people were still disembarking. Then she saw Rickie. He was zigzagging through
the crowd, craning his head, pushing through the dense
bunches of family that were in his way. She crouched
down, pretending to look for something on a seat. She took
another quick look out the window and saw the back of
Paolo's head. They must have driven straight down here.
Right on time. How'd they known she was on this train? It
struck her that her going was not so simple. She was going
to have to think – think, Rafi – very hard about how to
avoid getting caught and taken back to Petal Bay.

Rafi dodged her way through the carriages, away from
the exit end of the platform, her legs hitting her duffel
bag, up the train and into a bathroom. She slid the bolt.

Huddled against the wall she listened, head thumping noisily. How had they known it was this train? They must have asked at Mimosa station and the ticket seller must have remembered her. Or maybe Luca and Michael were looking for her in Townsville right now. So maybe they didn't know she planned to get off here. If they didn't find her now, they could think she'd left the train at Rockhampton or Bundaberg or any of the other big towns. So perhaps then they'd give up. Go home.

Not able to see through the frosted window, she listened carefully to the blurred sounds from outside, trying to pick out their voices. The platform quietened. She checked her watch; it had been twenty or so minutes. They might even be on the train. There was a clanking; she knew that sound. It was a metal bucket, the foot-lever being pressed down to squeeze the mop. They had that same bucket at home. It could only be the cleaner knocking on the door. Trying the handle now. Rafi flushed the toilet.

'Sorry,' she said, tripping over her bags to get out of the little room. 'I've been sick. Tried to clean up, though,' she added. The cleaner, a tall woman with steel-grey hair, said, 'Right dear,' before propping the door open with the galvanised bucket.

Rafi tried a door on the track side, and it opened. She strung her duffel and handbag across her shoulders and climbed down. Across the tracks there were brick huts and pigeon-shat alcoves. She could hear their cooing. Hidden from the main platform by the train, she climbed up to a short platform and ran towards the first turn around a wall. She found herself in a maintenance area. Single carriages were parked on the tracks, with hoists, coils of steel, a forklift. No one was around. Empty wooden pallets were stacked at one end and she hid herself on the far side of them. She checked her watch. Another ten minutes passed.

She'd wait an hour here, then catch a tram or a cab to South Brisbane station.

But what if they were on their way there? Damn. She'd have to make her way to another town! Rafi didn't know what the next town was after Brisbane. She put her head in her arms, and thought – I have less than three hours to figure this out.

With a start, she heard some voices. Three old Aboriginal men in greyed pants, paper-thin shirts and broken boots. Looked like stockmen with their bowed legs. They hadn't noticed her or, if they had, they weren't showing it. They sat down to play cards on the other side of the pallets. She could hear them talking about the game. One of them gave a sort of groan, and a moment later appeared on her side of the pallets.

'What you doing?'

One of his eyes was white and blind-looking, the film over it opaque like barely cooked egg white.

Rafi thought a moment, then said, 'Waiting.'

'Where you want to go?' he asked, looking at her ruminatively.

Good guess, thought Rafi.

'I want to get on the train to Sydney, but I don't want to get on here in Brisbane. Do you know the name of the next town that the train will stop at?'

The other two men came around the pallets. The first one introduced himself.

'Clay,' he said and, nodding, told her the others were Albert and Tom.

'Rafi,' she said, squinting at them, standing up, brushing the grit from her pants.

'We got a car,' said Clay. 'You got any money?'

She hesitated. Should have thought harder in the last ten minutes about what to do next. 'What's the next town I could catch the train to Sydney from?'

'Greenbank's the place,' said Clay. They discussed whether or not they wanted to go to Greenbank. Rafi thought – Should I get in a car with them? She felt sick with fear; told herself they were just stockmen, they were old, it would only take a half-hour or an hour.

They led her on a wily route, picking their way over the tracks and through a fence and down a street to a rusted old sedan. Its seats were torn and the tyres half-flat. All the while as they travelled south, they laughed and exclaimed at her predicament. Every now and then one of them threw her a question. They shook their heads in disbelief when she said she'd hid in a toilet. They stopped at a petrol station and she gave Clay some notes to pay for a tank. She kept her eye on the other cars to see if Paolo and Rickie should pass. But why would they? If they'd not seen her at Roma Street or Brisbane stations, why on earth would they drive further south? They wouldn't.

Coming into Greenbank, the men pulled up outside a pub. They wanted her to go in and buy a few bottles.

'Right,' she said. She hadn't bought beer before. 'Wait till I fix my makeup.'

'You pretty enough,' teased Albert, roughly pinching her cheek as she slid out of the car.

Inside the dark pub, the slouchy men at the bar and the tables turned to look at her approach the counter, listening as she nervously asked for six bottles of Pilsener. She hoped she sounded convincing. At least not like a complete idiot. Better that none of them went outside and saw who she was with.

'Greenbank then,' she said, handing over the beers. Each small conquest!

Soon enough they were in the town and found the station. She gave Clay a few pounds as arranged. He caught her eye and winked. Waving from the car, he turned and drove off. Rafi checked her watch. She had an hour till the train came. Time to buy herself a seat to Melbourne and find some new corner to hide in. The fault lines that had opened beneath her at Roma Street station, ready to swallow her up, were heaving closed. She was on track again.

7

SEAN BULLEN IS STRUGGLING WITH THE WATER. IT'S NOT funny anymore. He forgets to open his eyes. He can't tell up from down. She's gone. There's nobody to hang on to. Sky and sea swing up and down. He swallows and yells and fights with the water, then there is a thundering sound inside his ears and distant noises – of voices. Of splashing. Then there is nothing.

His friends are still breathing hard, though he is not. Struggling to bring him drunk with seawater and beer back into the shallows. How to get him breathing again? Craig and Frank argue as Craig pulls open Sean's mouth, pushing his fingers in to pull out seaweed, then starts on the resuscitation. They're not sure what to do, but Craig just does it. The other boy, Rob, vomits into the sand.

Julie runs up to the headland along the path and can see that Rafi is still swimming. A smudge of white dress and black hair in the ocean. Then she runs through the bush to the campsite to find a phone, to call an ambulance. Moira and Catherine can't keep up with Julie, she runs so fast. They fall back, exhausted and scratched, too scared to speak.

8

An hour or so out of Brisbane, when Chanchal had resigned himself to the fact that Rafaela had disappeared for her own good reasons, all of a sudden here she was, swinging black-haired and brown-limbed and laughing into his cabin, challenging him to guess where she had been.

'I don't know!' he said, getting up from the floor where he'd been playing a game of patience. 'I looked for you at the tram,' he said diffidently.

'You didn't see me wave down the Sydney Limited at Greenbank?' She looked very pleased with herself, whatever had happened.

'Are you going to tell me why you got on at Greenbank and not at Brisbane?' he asked.

She laughed and shook her head. 'No. Can't tell you. Doesn't matter now.' She examined his cabin. Chanchal watched in some surprise as she sorted out how each of the cabinets opened and closed, shutting the wardrobe quickly and with a smile of embarrassment because, of course, his clothes, boots and dirty socks were lying inside.

'What car are you in now, then?' he asked.

'Number four. It's okay. A little full.'

The train was hurtling along with the rain whipping at the window. Chanchal began to tidy away his cards, then shuffled them when Rafi suggested a game.

'Tell me about your family,' she said.

'Tell me about yours first.'

'Oh, they're boring. Four brothers, all older, a mother and a father. None of them interested in anything I'm interested in.' Rafi pulled her skirt down a bit lower over the scratches on her leg. 'My mum and dad want me to get married and they thought they'd found a suitable boy but he wasn't at all suitable. Turns out he's a bit of a drunk!'

Chanchal frowned. 'My parents are very happy to have found husbands for their three daughters.' He didn't want to be talking about marriage, a topic his mother had begun mentioning in her letters. 'So,' he said, 'Melbourne. How are you going to go about enrolling?'

She paled. Frowned a little. 'Turn up, I think. I have funds for my first year and I'll get myself some work and somewhere reasonable to live. Isn't that how it's done?'

'I think so. If you get stuck I'm sure there's someone I know who could help. Here,' he said, going over to a bag on the floor, 'do you know this book?' He pulled out *The Getting of Wisdom*.

'Henry Handel Richardson! Oh yes, I know it,' said Rafi. 'I love this story,' she said, holding the book to her chest in a girlish way, 'though, the thing is, none of my friends ever borrowed it from the library and I'd feel so sad about that. I read it and thought – I am the only girl in this town who knows this story.' She looked at him closely. 'You do realise that the writer is a woman.'

'I thought that might be the case,' he said with a laugh. Rafi was very direct in some of her statements.

And then it was clear – he wanted Rafi out of his cabin. She was exciting feelings in him that had been gone for the past year. That were best gone.

But she'd spied another book, and touched it in the expectation he would show it to her. So he did.

'This is *Heer Ranjha* and it's a story that to Punjabis – I am from the Punjab region – that to us is like the story of *Romeo and Juliet* or *Tristan and Isolde*. We all know the story, can remember lines from it, we sing it . . .' The language was to the Punjabi what Shakespeare and Chaucer were to the English. He could feel himself reddening. She'd have to go.

Rafi leant over the page he'd opened. He'd need to explain. 'This is written in the Urdu script.' She was tracing over the calligraphy in which the letters were balanced above and below an invisible line. Her leg touched his slightly, and together they moved away from the other a fraction.

Should he warn her to be more careful?

'And you can actually read this?' she asked.

'Sure. I learnt Urdu at school. And Hindi, Persian, English and some Latin.' He read a few lines to her in the Urdu, then closed the book and stretched as if to say, 'Phew, am I tired! Think I'll have a nap!' Chanchal thought – I'm not going to ask her another question or suggest a game of cards. I shall just sit here politely.

It worked, for in a minute the girl was up and graciously excusing herself.

But once she'd gone it was hard to settle. He pulled the blind down against the wet glass of the window. How ungenerous he was. She had little money, and no companion to travel with. Was sitting up the whole way. So Chanchal debated – invite her to dinner? If he didn't leave soon she might have eaten already.

Feeling highly visible, Chanchal walked down through the train to her carriage.

9

BACK IN HER OWN SEAT, RAFI LOOKED THROUGH HER BAG.
She'd bought a book at one of the stations, but she didn't
feel like reading, so she reached for her sketchpad and
slowly flipped through the pages, studying each imperfect
drawing. The train was moving too fast to draw what was
outside, and anyway there was thick rain and it was hard
to see much. Rafaela closed her eyes. To plan her evening
in: wash, read a little, have dinner, read. Attempt sleep.
Tomorrow – Sydney.

Freshening up in the bathroom, she was shocked to
see how lank her hair was, and it wasn't the pitted mirror.
Her hair was filthy. She stripped off and sure enough her
bra straps were soiled. Her skin tingled as she rubbed
and splashed herself all over with the water. One choice
of temperature: cold. She bent over the basin and
squirted shampoo on and somehow managed to wash
her hair, hitting her head on the tap only a few times.
Someone knocked while she was rinsing her hair out. Tell
the truth, she thought. 'I'll be ten minutes,' she called
out. I can do this: when I don't know what next to do I
just have to think, something must be done, a decision
needs to be made. Think, decide, then do it. That's the

list. Rafi took out her old Sunset Pink lipstick. The one
Moira had forced her to buy had been left with all her
other stuff at the campsite. Done, she thought, just as
the same passenger banged rather more loudly on the
door. All of a sudden she remembered her blue striped
costume, the one she'd been wearing when she swam off.
She'd left it wet on the floor in the bathroom at home.

Approaching her carriage, she was surprised to see
Chanchal waiting in the gangway. He looked surprised to
see her, too. Or unprepared to see her looking a little
damp.

'It occurred to me you might like to have a meal in the
dining car,' he said. 'My treat. Seven o'clock?'

'Thank you,' she said. Of course, yes. First dinner date
ever. Apart from dates with Julie at the local milk bar,
which surely didn't count.

She made her way to the dining car five minutes early.
The waiter asked, 'Booked under what name?' What was
his name? 'Chanchal,' she said, realising she didn't know
his surname, only his Christian name, which wasn't
Christian. The waiter paused. 'The Indian chap,' she said.
Indian, the waiter knew.

Seated, she traced patterns in the white tablecloth;
admired its whiteness and its starch. Beyond the train the
land was dark with rain, except for the fast stab of inciden-
tal highway lights; a flock of white galahs huddled in rows
on a wet grey gum. She looked with purpose past her

reflection, waiting eagerly for his company and the food. She was starving.

And then Chanchal was seated and the waiter came and offered them the menu.

'Curried prawns, by golly,' Chanchal said with a grimace. 'What would you like? You probably need a three-course meal after the past few days.'

'Are you going to have the prawns?'

'I don't think so. How good do you think they'd be?'

Rafaela shook her head. 'Let's not try them.' She could feel herself frowning. There was so much to choose from and she wanted to choose something wonderful, like the steak with a green pepper sauce or these *vol-au-vents* with cheese and peas for entrée. The cheapest meal was probably more appropriate. Then Chanchal said, 'Order whatever you like. What do you like?' and she said, wilting, 'I don't know.'

'I think you do know.'

Rafi blushed and told him her order.

When the waiter came Chanchal repeated her order and asked for the *vol-au-vent* and the curried prawns with rice and vegetables for himself.

Rafi leant forward and whispered, 'Why the change of mind?'

Chanchal whispered back, 'Because I don't eat meat and there's nothing else to have.'

Rafaela thought about this. 'Religion?'

'Yes,' he said.

'Do you drink?' she asked.

'Water, yes, otherwise I would die. And alcohol on special occasions.'

He was the most educated person she'd ever met. He was a grown man and must know a good deal about the world and its people. Rafi thought – What are we going to talk about now? What do I know? She panicked. Couldn't speak. She straightened her fork and knife. But he could speak. He was telling her about his favourite foods from home and how he'd learnt to cook roti and dhals on his little stove in Melbourne and that in the whole city there was only one shop for Indians – not too far away – run by the Bharanthi brothers – where he could buy the flours and the spices he needed.

Here she was, still young and naive. But doing her darnedest to make her way, as if she was drawing a finger line through the dusty map of Australia, down the eastern lip to Melbourne. As if it was going to be that simple.

'To a great trip, and a brilliant career in art,' he said, toasting her after ordering a quarter carafe of the house red.

So she was an occasion. Rafi raised her glass a little and carefully clinked it against his. Thank god he knew how to have a conversation. She surely did not.

The timing was fortuitous, for most of the passengers had eaten and were still awake though the lights had been dimmed. The guards came through explaining that the Richmond and Wilsons rivers had flooded and the track was underwater in places. They were to evacuate the train at Linden, taking their luggage with them. They'd be put up at the railway's expense in local hotels until the waters subsided.

Like the others, Rafaela left the train with her things then stood, waiting for what next, on the wet platform. She was ready for flood or fire. She'd tied her hair back and changed into her jeans and desert boots. Cars and buses idled nearby, waiting to ferry the passengers to the hotels. Their white and yellow headlights shone through the drizzle. She saw Chanchal standing with the other first-class passengers and waved. Then she was led off with her group to a bus. Through the rain she could smell soaked grass and silt and sour wet wood and thought how wonderful – to be gone, to be somewhere new. To be here.

She didn't mind a day's delay. She thought – If Rickie and Paolo try driving they'll bog the car, if they haven't turned back already.

The publican dropped the etiquette of the women's lounge to ease the crisis. Children were put to bed, others allowed to roam, and in the crush everyone wanted a drink to pass the time and ease the awkwardness of bedding down with strangers. In the open bar and away from the confines of the narrow train people mingled and shouted drinks, sharing memories of other floods and train mishaps, fretting over waiting families and missed connections.

Rafaela took it all in. She thought – I belong to no one. There was no parent or brother to answer to; for once she was at the centre. Then Chanchal found her in the bar and they stood together, the crowd swirling past on their periphery. He bought her a lemon squash and another for himself. This time she insisted on giving him the money for it.

'I don't often drink,' he said almost apologetically.

'Neither do I. This is fine.'

Other passengers gave them sidelong glances, but in the busy disorganisation of the room no one asked any questions. Rafi and Chanchal each noticed but chose not to mention it to the other.

A few people took themselves off to their rooms, and there was a lull in the noise when Chanchal said, 'It's stopped raining but we're surrounded by water.'

'Let's go outside, see what's happening.'

The pub's porch and the footpath across the road were soiled a wet brown. The moon was round and yellow through the haze of clouds.

'A crazy moon,' said Rafi. 'Such a bright yellow.'

Chanchal thought about this.

'One of my sisters used to choose her sari each morning according to what mood she was in and she had a very strict idea of what colour suited which mood. She was often cranky in the mornings, and then she'd wear green or brown and we'd know to keep away. A good morning was a yellow morning. It was quite funny.'

'When did you last see her?' asked Rafi. The moon caught her eye again and she thought – We're looking at the *same* moon.

'Three years ago,' he said. 'It seems longer. Then sometimes shorter than that.'

She stifled a yawn, glad that tonight she would be sleeping in a real bed. They went back inside and Rafi took her key and collected her bags from the hallway. A few men watched her as she went out and up the stairs; she could tell their eyes were on her.

Two other women were to share the room with her but they were still downstairs. The sounds of the party rose up and she wondered if Chanchal was down there or in his room. She claimed the bed by the window and unpacked what she needed for the night, taking her purse with her to the bathroom. There was a bath and though her towel was still damp, Rafi filled the tub. She'd wash her hair properly with hot water. The water softened and relaxed her, and she put her head under, her black hair floating lightly. Breathy bubbles flew to the surface and she thought uncomfortably of her struggle with Sean. How she'd closed her eyes when he pushed her under and how, opening her eyes, she'd seen so many limbs she and Sean were like an octopus. She sat up to get rid of the memory. Sank down again. There was something she wanted to think about. Chanchal. How long his hair must be when he unwound it at night. She saw his hands on her bare waist – she burst to the surface, wakeful. With a jolt she felt the enormity of her undertaking. She'd forgotten tonight what she was doing. When had she been away before? A school excursion. A night of camping a few miles from home. If she were to go back – imagine the fury of her father and her mother – she couldn't bear to think about it. Was there anything she should be doing differently? Should she not have left at all?

Rafi thought – Love is meant to begin somewhere else, in some quiet secure place of the heart. But what do I know? Did thinking about Chanchal mean that she loved him?

After the other women had lain down, loneliness filled her bed. Instead of their even breaths, Rafi wanted to hear the banana leaves brushing against the fence and the rustle of the passionfruit vine as Rickie pushed past late after a dance. The swish of the casuarina leaves in the wind. All the familiar scrapings that accompanied her to sleep in Petal Bay.

She turned to look at the room. The walls were covered with a wallpaper of apple-green bamboo leaf. The wallpaper was curling apart at some of the seams. When she was young she'd do drawings of the shadows in her room and Rickie had liked these drawings so much he'd pinned them to the wall beside his bed in the room he shared with Luca. She'd drawn strange cats and big-headed dogs.

Fears were keener in the night.

In the morning they were told that the train wouldn't be leaving until the next day at the earliest. Roads and a bridge were flooded. Buses couldn't get them through. Patience was required. There was disgruntlement and milling about. Rafaela found Chanchal talking to another passenger, an older man. She waited at a distance until the gentleman withdrew to line up with his wife for their breakfast.

'That's John Bolton. He's a bigwig at the CSIRO,' said Chanchal a little excitedly. 'Told me he's just come back from California to direct the Parkes Observatory.'

'How do you know him?'

'Well, I don't, but I saw a photograph of him in the paper last week and thought I'd introduce myself.'

So confident, thought Rafi. Exactly the way she'd need to be in Melbourne. She could only count on these lessons from him for a day or so. He'd be getting off at Coffs; she'd head on to Sydney.

They took their eggs and bacon outside to the veranda where the sun was warming the wet boards in a break between storms. She let him put his bacon onto her plate though it was too much for her. She threw some over to a stray dog. She thought, standing on the steps with him – This is what I want, to have a friend to speak to. But she wanted him more than that – didn't she?

Her brother Rickie liked a crowd. She'd never been able to drag him from a picnic or a dance. Here, she was Chanchal's choice. He did like her, she could tell. They watched the wet earth steam with the morning sun. She pretended not to notice the graze of heat from his breath near her neck and the pressure of her arm against his as she reached for his plate. This was it, this was what a real friendship felt like. Or the beginnings of one.

Words like want or love or others of piquant warning, 'I have a train to catch, a city to find,' sloped off. She thought her feelings weren't visible. She couldn't see his frown, didn't feel his desire.

'Let's go for a walk,' he suggested. 'Bring your sketch-book.'

She ran up the stairs to her room. This was the first time anyone had asked her to get her sketch book. They left the pub, walking quickly. He had his binoculars and *Birds of Australia*; he liked to watch birds, he told her.

Everything was changing, and the land and him beside her proved it.

The sagging bitumen was freckled with puddles and holes and the street was shiny with water. Who knew how long before the next downpour? They headed up a hill to see what they could from the crest. Looking around her and not at the footpath, Rafi accidentally bumped into him. His arm against her shoulder was briefly solid, and though murmuring sorry she ever so lightly brushed alongside him again.

A thin old man in trousers that bagged at his ankles came out on to his porch to see what they were up to. He glared at them.

'Good to see the rain has stopped for a bit,' she called out good-naturedly.

He grumbled his assent and shuffled back inside, the screen door tapping shut behind him.

They paused at the crest, then ran as hard as they could down the hill until it flattened out to a long stretch of boggy fields and in some places wide plates of brown water. Across the flood-lake were hundreds of ibis, cranes and seagulls and other birds that Rafi didn't know the names for but guessed Chanchal did, or would find the names for from his book.

A rivulet of water ran alongside a dip and turn in the road, tinkling with a small sound. On a hump of soil that hadn't been washed out, yellow creeping buttercup was flowering.

'Being an artist, you must need to be very observant,' Chanchal commented as they walked. He stopped, and looked through his binoculars. 'Have a look at this,' he said. 'There's white ibis and black ibis together.' She looked where he told her to, and sure enough there were two kinds of ibis. 'And over there, near that tree? There's a darter. You see these birds in India as well.'

'You must need to be observant, being a scientist,' she said.

He jogged a few steps ahead then walked backwards to look at her. As she came up beside him he caught her hand, kissed it and dropped it again, then stopped walking to look through his binoculars. He thought, heart pounding – What on earth have I just done?

She'd felt his beard more than his lips. As though he hadn't kissed her, she said, 'I like the idea that it rains a lot in Melbourne.'

The road declined languorously.

'I'll have to stay with my relatives in Woolgoolga at least a week,' he said. 'A couple of weeks, I should think. Then back to my thesis.'

'What is your thesis about?'

'I'm studying the way that animals like sheep, ruminants, convert the cellulose they eat into energy. The cellulose is in the grass,' he added.

They walked further, picking their way through large puddles of water. 'Let's find something half dry to sit on,' she said, 'and I'll do a sketch.'

'Then I'll be going back to Melbourne and we can meet up again?'

'Yes, I'd love to,' she said. 'I won't have an address until after I arrive, though.'

'There's a hotel near Spencer Street station that a lot of people stay at when they first arrive. It's called the Grand, or something like that.'

They reached a bit of a gully and could see then how high the water had been. The tree trunks were still sodden and wet, and in the shrubs and lower branches of trees the leaves were shawled with spiders' cobwebs and insects. Sitting down on a wide felled tree, Rafi opened her sketchpad and asked Chanchal if she could borrow his binoculars for a moment. She spent some time really looking at the wading birds then drawing a part of the bird – a beak or the pattern of feathers. 'What's that very black one over there?' she asked. Chanchal took back his glasses and said after a moment, 'I think it's a black kite.' She looked at it again.

'It's rather fierce-looking, isn't it.'

'It's a raptor; a bird of prey.'

She drew; he made his notes and read aloud about the various birds. Then he sauntered away, to calm himself, to take in the wide fields around them. He thought – I shouldn't be feeling this intoxicated. Rafaela was still sketching when he came back. From out of her pencils and a white page, with mere lines and black smudges, she was creating an image of the floodplain and the birds, and the grey and cloudy sky.

'Could you do a drawing for me?' he asked, handing her his notebook.

'Sure,' said Rafi, noticing that on the page he'd opened the book at, he'd already written the date and where they were and a two-word note, 'with Rafaela'.

He lay back along the wide felled tree, wriggling to find a comfortable position while she drew for him, glancing at him surreptitiously. She knew that this day, 'with Rafaela', wouldn't be forgotten by her.

She noticed her pants were getting damp. He'd be wet all down his back. She glanced at him, saw he'd put his hands over his eyes to block out the sun. His turban, the blue one, hadn't shifted. She wondered again how long his hair was. Did he brush it out at night? Was that the sort of thing a Sikh wife did for her husband?

'It must be anarchy up there,' he said.

'Where?' she asked. Not, what's this word anarchy mean?

'Those webs are very beautiful and intricate.' He was looking up at the trees. Then he looked at her through his fingers. She kept her eyes on the trees and the birds and the paper in front of her.

'It's very brave of you to have left home and to be going to Melbourne.'

'You think so? It's the only thing I could think of doing, actually.' She was thinking that Chanchal's list of possible plans must be long. He'd have a big list.

'Yes, brave,' he said.

She was afraid and euphoric. The sun would be gone in

minutes – look at that gathering sheet of darker cloud – but just now it poured through the leaves and the heavy webs and a loud horny burst of cicadas started up. Did he know about cicadas?

'The cicadas want to mate,' she said. He was a scientist. A naturalist, perhaps.

She felt *herself* with him. 'You'll be soaked through at the back,' she said, reaching out a hand – to do what? He had it in his before she could bring it back. He closed his hand around hers and then they embraced. He sat up and put his mouth against her hair near her neck and she let her hair fall and stay fallen so she couldn't see him.

He'd be getting on that train tomorrow so she wasn't going to be stupid today. 'I think it's about to rain,' she said. Chanchal didn't say anything for so long she began to worry.

'Are you okay?' she asked, standing up.

'The train might not leave tomorrow after all,' he said. 'Wouldn't that be good? Ah look, it's starting.' He put his hand out to catch some of the drops. Neither of them hurried, though. He looked at the small sketch of an ibis that she'd done, its head down towards the water. 'This is wonderful!'

'No it's not,' she laughed as they began to walk back.

In the pub, platters of sandwiches and wedges of fruit cake lay out on the bar. The news was that there might be a further delay. 'Let's not get back on the train straight away, even if it does leave,' said Chanchal quietly. 'We could stay here a few more days. Do some hiking if the rain eases. There's a circus setting up. There's even a cinema here.'

Rafaela looked at her desert boots. They were soaked through and rimmed with mud. His leather work boots were muddy and sodden. Here they were, the still life of a woman and man.

'Maybe,' she said. 'Let's see what happens tomorrow.'

10

From his truck that first week Carlo scours the ditches, the thickets of lantana and grasses alongside the highways, looking for her. He drives south and north, looking for his daughter. He is afraid he will find Rafi lying twisted in the long grass. Her black hair tangled. Her legs warped. Her back broken. Her jeans ripped. Her honour gone. Her breath taken. Her mouth full of gravel. His daughter dead.

He approaches a milk bar in Bundaberg and prays to God and to her, 'Please, I want to see you in here.' The girls inside are not his girl. The sweetest girl in Petal Bay. She must be all right, like these girls, wherever she is. People are good. He has to believe that, but his faith waivers. People are not good. They rape, steal, mutilate, stone. Though he'll kill the boy who took her. Norma says it has nothing do with boys.

IT PROMISED TO BE HOT IF IT DIDN'T RAIN. VAPOUR ROSE FROM the rain-soaked streets and paths and from the wooden walls of the shops and cottages lining the street. Chanchal was already up and out on the porch when Rafi appeared.

'Have you been up long?' she asked him, squinting as she came out of the dark of the pub into the grey glare of the street.

'A while. I went out early. I saw a darter take a fish, then it flew up into a eucalypt and swallowed the fish, head first.'

'I'd have liked to come.'

'You'll need to set your alarm then,' he said, smiling.

Chanchal heard some people talking about which town the circus was headed to when it left, something about whether they'd be there to see it. Everybody was waiting on news of the train. All decisions depended on the weather and the train.

'Is the circus opening tonight?' she asked him brightly.

'It is, even in the rain they're saying. Shall we go?'

'If the train hasn't left. It doesn't seem fair to have everyone stranded here and then for them to miss the circus.'

Chanchal walked off the porch and over to a lamppost, taking his mug of tea with him.

She followed. 'Why do Sikh men wear turbans?'

'We don't cut our hair for many reasons. Some say it is because, centuries ago, Sikhs lost their heads defending their beliefs. The *dastar*, the turban, is a symbol of dignity and, well, it keeps the hair out of the way. All Sikh men wear it, and some women, though more often they wear a loose scarf.' He showed her his steel bracelet. 'This is the *kara*; it's a symbol of restraint. I also have a *kanga*, my comb, and there's the *kaccha*, which are shorts, but I don't wear them. And there's the *kirpan*, the sword. And *kesh* is our hair.'

Rafi looked at his turban, which today was maroon. An ugly colour, she thought. 'And the different colours?'

'Some colours you wear because you like them, others have meaning. The royal blue is often worn by the *gyanis*, the scholars. White is popular, it extends the wearer's aura.'

He brushed his hand along the tips of her fingers. 'Let's take a walk,' he said. Hands-off was the way. To not be impulsive – which was near impossible the way he felt. Or was it wrong to be too careful? Chanchal wanted to take this girl in his arms and tangle his fingers into her hair and feel her breath on his lips. And more. The common English words that came forward weren't right.

'Let's stay a few more days even if the train goes today,' he said again. 'When we get back maybe they'll know what is happening with the train.'

As soon as they were out of sight of the last house, he took her hand. It was warm in his. There was a turn in the road and he embraced her and felt her pressing herself against him and he thought that, though it wasn't literally true, she felt closer to him than anyone had ever been.

'You're part of me, Rafaela,' he said. 'Do you understand what I mean?'

When she looked at him her eyes were large like black moons. It was as though they were each pouring themselves into the other without boundary, without hesitation. He remembered her voice from the other night saying 'a crazy moon', and said, 'I love you.'

Her moon eyes filled with tears. 'Don't make fun of me,' she said.

She felt herself flushing and pulled away.

'I mean it.' Chanchal thought – I mean it, while she thinks I'm an idiot for saying it.

'But you're going to Woolgoolga.'

'We'll meet up in Melbourne.' But how could he wait that long? How could she? He could feel this was right between them. 'So let's not go right away, Rafi. Let's stay here a few more days.' If they arrived in Melbourne too soon the city would separate them somehow.

She walked away, arms wrapped around her sides, but he quickly caught up with her and took her hand in his again.

'Is your hair long under your turban?' she asked.

'Yes it is.'

'Take off your turban then, so I can see,' she said.

Chanchal was shocked. 'Not here. I couldn't.'

'Later then?'

He smiled, couldn't help but smile. She was a girl after Heer's bold heart, that was for sure.

'Later. So there is a "tomorrow"?' – What song was that? There'd be many with that refrain he guessed.

'There is, Chanchal,' she said in a voice that was at once sober and playful. She shivered, and he took both her hands and brought her up against him and kissed her slowly on the mouth and then he knew she was Heer and he was Ranjha; romantic if not so tragic. It was right, that's what he knew. It could be right, even if with the appearance of wrong.

He remembered Wittgenstein. 'The object is simple.' The picture of his love for Rafi was the fact of it. Explanation wasn't necessary, even if others would want it.

'I love you,' he said. 'That's a fact.' He could feel her heart beating hard against her skin and his skin, they were so close, and feel her fine waist, her shoulderblades beneath his hands.

'Don't make fun of me,' she said again, frowning, turning her face from him. He kissed her neck.

'I'll buy you a ticket for a first-class sleeper, all for you, when we leave. First class right through to Melbourne.'

She laughed at his tactic – a cabin to herself!

'Let's stay a few days. Don't you want to?'

'Of course I want to.' Rafi breathed in deeply. 'Of course.'

'I have money. I'll pay for your accommodation, and the new ticket.'

'It's not the money,' she said, though it was a little. No, it was the delay. That was it. Melbourne. But a few days' delay – since Chanchal wasn't going to be in Melbourne for a couple of weeks there was that much less of a hurry for her to get there.

'We will be friends, won't we? In Melbourne.'

'Marry me, Rafaela.'

'Now you really are making fun of me,' she said and walked off and hid behind a tree.

He found her and said, 'Yesterday I fell in love. I want us to get married. I decided years ago that I would choose my own wife.'

Yesterday? Leaning against the damp tree, Rafi looked to the ground, shaking her head, hiding her smile. Yesterday. Now this was turning into nonsense. And this nonsense was confusing her because it had seemed simple, there'd been the straight and simple way of things – of reaching Melbourne, finding a place to stay, enrolling in art school.

Now it was raining again, harder and harder.

A car passed; they barely noticed.

'Take off your turban then, if you love me,' she said.

Chanchal shook his head. 'I couldn't do that here.'

'Where then?' She looked at him and he saw her desire. Yet she didn't know he could see it. He thought – She's a crazy moon girl.

'Let's find somewhere,' she said, looking around them. A barn would do, or something like that.

They walked down another street, away from the paddock where the circus was at last setting up its tents and rides, and found a dilapidated house with a back porch and overgrown shrubbery. A FOR SALE sign lay rotting in the overgrown lawn.

Chanchal breathed deeply, heard a cricket strumming during the break in the rain and the burst of the sun through the ribbed clouds. Her look was provocative, but she hardly knew what she was asking. They sat on the porch, damp and dishevelled, their shoes muddied again.

He said as kindly as he could, 'I'm not going to take off my turban and I don't want you to say another word about it.'

She nodded. 'You're right,' she said. 'I was being too cheeky.'

The rain was heavy for an hour or two and they went back to their separate rooms to dry off. Rafi told Chanchal she was ringing her family to say she'd been delayed by the rain; she wouldn't tell him she'd run away from home. While it rained she lay on her bed and worked on a cross-word, and dozed. The heavier the rain, the more it hurtled down, the more certain she was that her brothers had turned back home and that there was nothing from them that she needed now to worry about. She liked the sound of the rain belting down on the roof.

Chanchal lay on his bed and read pages at random from Waris Shah. He thought – If she doesn't marry me how can I be honourable in my intentions? He couldn't settle, remembered, 'drawing up breath, drawing down breath, the necklace of sweet basil, all these I have . . .' Songs, *rags*, Rafi's sweet neck, this too-tight necklace of desire. He would purchase two rings.

Chanchal asked downstairs then went off in search of the town's hock shop. Inside, he found two rings, one a little scratched, the other broader and flat. They were gold, but a different gold to the brighter Indian gold, much duller. Hers had a small ruby at its centre, a gypsy ring the pawnbroker called it, but Chanchal paid for them gladly, and taking the little velvet bag with the two rings inside, walked back through the rain toward the hotel. He thought about his older sister Nilima's marriage, of her walking around the *Guru Granth* the four times with Kirpan; and remembering his family, Chanchal's steps through the town slowed. As well as the traditional arrangements, his parents had arranged for a piece by Handel to be played on the gramophone. Chanchal had looked about him as the families and guests had silently listened to the monumental *Largo*, saw his teary, giggling younger sisters, and his mother's eyes closed with emotion or perhaps in prayer, and the serious face of his father, and most of all the round, young face of his sister Nilima, ecstatic and frightened. Chanchal remembered realising during the ceremony that Nilima would not be coming home again, and the shock that he too was to grow up and leave.

He had the rings for when he and Rafaela needed them and, like his sister, felt both uneasy and joyous. Then, uncomfortably, he remembered some words Veronica had whispered: 'Mad, bad, glad'. He was soaked through when he reached the hotel, but drank down a lemon squash, carefully ignoring the stares, before returning to his room to dry himself off.

It was more a funfair than a circus – no lions or bearded lady, though sitting alongside each other on the hard benches, surrounded by half the town and the train's other passengers, they did see clowns and ponies, and a trapeze act. Families and friends swapped stories of the flood and their animals and the mud; some even laid out picnics on the wet ground or ate from the backs of their cars.

The train was to leave later that night.

The crowds fanned out, chattering across the trampled grasses, clutching their blue strips of ride tickets and creamy, melting ice-creams, screaming as they soared gloriously higher on the rides. The scarred ducks fell back from the blows of the popguns, and kewpie dolls were paraded by little girls too young to know their other meaning of love gone wrong. Stragglers at the edge of the wet field fell about laughing and intoxicated. The piebald pony bit its keeper but not the child riding it. Chanchal kissed the inside of Rafaela's wrist and with that she laughed and pulled him over to a darker corner. The night-time laughter pealed towards them until Rafi's mouth and cheek were raw from his beard. She said, 'We have to stop.'

After supper, the passengers gathered their bags together at the hotel and went to the front veranda to board the buses.

Chanchal and Rafaela thought that their absence from this gathering would go unnoticed. But with each hour their story was catching burrs of gossip, seeding itself as it passed from passenger to railway man to shopkeeper, and postmistress, wholesaler, farmer. With the rain lifting and the floodwaters falling and the bridges and byways opening up once again, the story of a girl and an Indian travelled.

12

One of the men who had stared at Chanchal in the hotel bar was Bob Carmichael. A cutter from up north, he'd thought. They're good. He'll be useful. The Indians worked hard, harder than most, and this one looked strong enough. Or he might be a farmhand from one of the banana plantations. Because of the flooding, Bob Carmichael hadn't been able to keep the young fellow he'd hired to fix the fences and care for the stock while he was down in Sydney. The boy had left as soon as he'd arrived, back to his parents' farm to help with moving their stock to higher ground.

Bob asked the bartender, 'What's the Indian doing here?'

'No idea,' the guy said. 'Came off the train when we had all them passengers here. And he's stayed on.'

Bob nodded, thought – Perhaps I should talk to him. He got Chanchal's room number from the barmaid, Evie, and walked around the back of the hotel and up the stairs to the rooms the men had been put up in.

He knocked and Chanchal opened the door, broad and bare-chested yet still in his turban. The room was stinking hot. Bob cast his eyes around while Chanchal put on a shirt; three metal beds, a couple of small bureaus with some books stacked on top.

'Bob Carmichael,' he said, extending his hand. 'I'm wondering if you're after any farm work? I have some fencing that needs doing.'

Chanchal nodded cautiously, thinking – This could work if Rafi came along too.

'I can do fencing,' he said, though he'd never built a fence. But he could learn. He was keen to learn any new farm skill.

'And we have a small herd of cattle. There's not a lot of work but it needs doing now and the men around here are all off at their own places, because of the flooding.'

They talked about the work for a short while, then Chanchal asked if he could ring Bob later with an answer. There were a few family issues he needed to sort out before giving a firm 'yes'.

'I'm in town for another couple of hours,' said Bob. 'Does that give you enough time? I'll come back around three and if you're interested we can drive out there.'

Rafaela sat on the steps outside, hugging her knees, frowning as she thought it over when Chanchal suggested they go out to a farm a few miles from the town and work on fences. But with the train gone and the pub empty of people she felt conspicuous. She couldn't see what they were going to do here in town for a few days.

'I don't need to be in Woolgoolga on any particular day. My uncle isn't expecting me until later in the month as it is. This way we won't be apart for too long.'

'I'm glad the train has gone,' she said decisively. She would believe it. She wished, though, that Chanchal would stop this romantic talk of his. Couldn't they just be together without it?

'I love you, Rafi,' Chanchal said, leaning close to her, whispering though there was no one about. Rafi looked to the ground then let her eyes slide to meet his. 'Do you love me?' he asked.

She nodded, smiled, then scowled. 'I don't want to get married, though – not until I'm . . . about thirty.' She grabbed at an age. She felt derailed, as if it was literally true that she wasn't on track to Melbourne any more, which in fact *was* literally true as here she was in Linden being romanced by Chanchal. Whom she was falling in love with. Was already in love with.

'I'll go on my own then,' he said, disheartened. He stood up.

'Where are you going?' she said, squinting up at him, thinking – I want his hands on me. Thinking – I want to kiss him on the mouth. And – I wish I didn't have to make these choices.

'I'm getting my wallet. To buy you a ticket for the next sleeper down to Melbourne.'

'Don't do that,' she said.

'No?'

'Wait here. I'll see if anyone knows anything about these people at the farm.'

At the bar she asked the barmaid about the Carmichael farm – was it a large one? Was it very far out of town?

'Nice people,' the woman said. 'They do their own thing, of course, but that doesn't matter because you're not living with them; you'd be in the caravan.'

'What's their own thing, then?' asked Rafi.

'Bob's our local artist. He has shows in Sydney.' She spoke as though he were her son. 'His dad's an artist and lives in the Blue Mountains, if I remember rightly. And his wife writes for a women's magazine. And they have their herd and they muddle along.'

'Is that why they need help on the farm? Because they're not really farmers?'

'I wouldn't say that, quite. They're from farming families, but then they sailed off to Europe. That changed them considerably,' she said, wiping the last of the glasses dry.

'And Mr Carmichael exhibits in Sydney? Which gallery?'

'Oh, I wouldn't know that. Ask him.'

Back on the veranda, Rafi said, 'She told me that Mr Carmichael is an artist.'

'I thought he was a farmer.'

'He's that too.'

'Then we must go to the farm.'

Rafi swung on one of the posts thinking – Chanchal, kiss me now! Instead, she said aloud, 'What's everyone going to think? What would the Carmichaels think?'

'I've something to show you,' he said. 'I'll be back in a moment.' Chanchal bounded up the stairs to his room. He had considered bringing the holy book to her, his *Guru Granth Sahib* that they were to walk around the four times as the four stanzas of the *Lavan* hymn were said. They didn't need a *granthi* to marry them. But holding the book, wrapped in its old silk, it was as if the weight of it had trebled. He thought – What does it mean that I can't suggest we do the ceremony ourselves? Does it mean I know it's wrong to want to marry her? He couldn't take the book down to her, he just couldn't. He quietly left the room, but with the rings in his pocket.

'I bought two rings.'

'Let me see.' He mustn't have been teasing her after all, then.

'No, not here. At the park.' Beyond the pub and down one of the wide side streets there was a park with a grove of willows beside a pond. They sat under the weeping branches. A couple of freckled ducks skimmed over the water towards them, expecting bread.

Chanchal pulled the velvet bag out of his pocket and untied the cord. He opened his palm and showed them to her.

'I can't imagine arriving in Melbourne a wife,' she said, picking up the smaller ring with the ruby. 'What would my name be? Mrs Rafaela Singh.' She laughed at this, but Chanchal didn't. He took the ring from her and slipped it back into the bag.

'Marry me, Rafaela,' he said. She wasn't taking this seriously enough.

'Let's stop this! Give me the ring. I'll wear it on the farm.' She held out her hand, and he gave it to her a second time.

'I love you. I really, really do,' she said, wrapping her arms around him, looking at the ring on her finger. She held her hand up to the light and the sun shone through the edges of her skin, lighting it up red. She slipped Chanchal's ring onto his wedding finger, but could hardly believe what they were doing.

Kissing her, he was sure he felt some hesitancy in her; or was it just his doubts about his own impulsiveness?

'This is not quite what I meant,' said Chanchal.

'Chanchal, you have a career. You have prospects and you're going back to India to do wonderful work. I'd be in the way.' She sat up, and felt her back. 'It's all so wet still, the earth. My mum used to say, take one step at a time. Now I know what she means. Let's do this, then go to Melbourne.'

'The Carmichaels have a caravan. I'll sleep on the floor. Until we get to Melbourne.' He felt very clear in his mind about it now. He looked at the ring on her hand and the ring on his hand. He thought of a line from the *Guru Granth*: 'No one belongs to anyone; like a tree is home to many birds.' Though if he belonged to India, where did she belong?

That wasn't right either. One step at a time then – she belonged to him and he to her. 'Lie on me,' he said, pulling her onto him, her weight a certainty, the curves of her back and buttocks, her lips and eyes waiting to kiss him the most delicious of reassurances.

'Hello,' said Bob Carmichael, shaking both their hands vigorously when he met them on the street outside the pub that afternoon. So this was the artist, Rafi thought. He was brown and lean with uneven blond hair and a burnt neck. He wore a wide, plaited leather belt and his shirt sat well on him. When they shook hands Rafi watched Chanchal's hand, the strength of his grip, his dark skin and Bob's lighter tanned skin. She noticed Bob wore a wedding band. Her ring pleased her the way it knotted her to Chanchal, and him to her.

They threw their bags in the back of Bob's truck with his dog. The truck was ex-navy stock, the cabin roomy even with the three of them. They drove for half an hour or so, and all the while Rafi, who was sitting by the window, could feel Chanchal's thigh against hers; every element of her skin felt him. She thought – This is why people get married in a rush.

'Where did you say you're from?' Bob asked, after a silence. He'd hardly asked them anything about themselves so far. He was surprised to hear that Chanchal wasn't a farmer, but a student.

'I've heard of the Colombo Plan. Is it useful then?'

Chanchal assured him it was. Students from all over Southeast Asia were able to train in their field in developed nations' universities, then go back to their own countries to teach, research and work. Bob nodded in interest. Rafi listened carefully, watching Chanchal sidelong.

As he talked, he thought – Does she know that I think the Colombo Plan is just more colonialism if with a more generous face? The British generosity that knew no bounds, as long as the transference of knowledge was one-way, us to them, to those 'coloureds' who had the potential to be like the British. However, it wouldn't do to say all this to Mr Carmichael.

Eventually they turned into a rutted driveway. It wound up from the road towards a house set square in the home field's rise to a ridge of trees. Beef cattle watched as they drove past. The fields around the house were lush, though sodden in many places.

'It's so green around here,' Rafi said.

'The rain's done its work,' said Bob Carmichael.

The weatherboard cottage was wide and fronted by a veranda. A couple of tubs at the step's edge overflowed

with geraniums and pansies, and to one side of the door
shoes and muddy gumboots were thrown in a basket. Two
girls pushed hard through the screen door, followed by Mrs
Carmichael. Bob introduced them to Clarissa, his wife, and
the girls: Amelia, who was four, and Thea, who was five and
was starting school in a month. Then he went to unload
some things from the truck. He wasn't unfriendly, but
he hadn't been talkative either. Clarissa took Chanchal
and Rafi into the house, the girls following. She said to
Chanchal firmly, 'I want to hear all about India.' Rafi
thought – Aha, the people I know don't usually *want* to hear
anything new. Clarissa wore a shirt and brown slacks with
the waist pulled in by a wide red belt. Her legs were full
and shapely and she wore her shirt unbuttoned lower than
usual, Rafi noticed. Rafi could see freckles above her brown
breasts when she bent over the girls.

The girls tripped them up and interrupted, holding
Rafi's and Chanchal's hands and treating them like a
couple in an easy way. 'The girls are very excited to have
visitors,' said Clarissa, studying Rafi and Chanchal. 'Not
that you're the first by any means. We have friends
through here all the time.'

Around the side of the house there was a laundry and
loo that looked out over the cattle, and a small white
caravan.

'Is this all right?' Clarissa asked, pushing open the door
to the caravan.

Rafaela realised with a shock that she and Chanchal would be sleeping together in a very small space indeed.

As they headed back to the house, Bob called Chanchal over to help change a tyre on the truck. While Clarissa fixed tea, Rafi moved cautiously around the large living room. It was decorated with rugs and squat-carved wooden figures, and a tall Chinese-looking urn. Paintings hung framed and unframed on the walls: portraits of the girls, and landscapes, hills and fields. Perhaps these were local places. Rafi could see through a door to a study, where a typewriter sat on the desk. Tall shelves were filled with books. Papers, magazines, scraps of drawings littered the desk. Rafi stared. I want this life, she thought. I want to live like this.

Thea and Amelia ran in from the front, noisy, slamming doors, stopping when they saw Rafi standing in the middle of the living room. She smiled, followed them into the kitchen, found a seat at the table when bidden by Clarissa. She thought over the story she and Chanchal had agreed on; that they had met in Mimosa, were married, and had been on a working holiday. They would be going to Woolgoolga to stay with his uncle at the end of the month. They talked about the flooding and Rafi made certain to ask lots of questions about the area and the town, and asked was it true that Mr Carmichael was an artist; were they his paintings on the walls?

'He's an accountant some of the time, does work for

the vet and a few locals. On other days he's a farmer, and a painter when we can afford it. It's a mish-mash really,' said Clarissa.

'That isn't a Rembrandt, is it?' asked Rafi nervously, having looked for some minutes at a sketch which hung above the dresser.

'Yes it is,' said Clarissa, holding her tea in her hands and watching Rafi's reaction.

'A Rembrandt in your kitchen! You don't worry some-one will steal it?'

'Out here? No. You're the first person who isn't a friend from down south to recognise it.'

They looked at the sketch of a middle-aged man with a stomach and a coat, his face half in profile.

'It's a self-portrait,' Clarissa explained.

Rafi stood to look at it more closely. It was just a little thing.

'We bought it in Europe. It *is* a Rembrandt, the master himself, though it's no masterpiece.'

'But still . . .'

'That's exactly what we said! And then went without dinner for a few nights.' Clarissa laughed and pushed her bobbed hair back with a hand, and Rafi thought unfavourably of her own long hair that some days she still wore in a plait.

When the men came in, Amelia and Thea took it in turns to climb Chanchal's legs. It was not something Rafi's parents would have allowed any of them to do with visitors. The adults finished the pot of tea, then Bob and Clarissa led the way on a tour of the farm, and all of them including the girls walked from chook shed to hay shed, past bicycles and another shed that Bob told them was his studio. A herb garden was pointed out; a small orchard. They went down to the cow paddock and Bob told Chanchal about a cow that needed watching because she'd been lowing at odd hours. Two others were soon to calve; another tended to bloating. He showed them the water troughs and told them to change the water every couple of days. Stagnant water made the cattle prone to illnesses. The dung needed collecting. They walked along the fence lines, checking for new damage. A fallen tree needed removing. Much of the fencing was just plain old.

That done, Rafi and Chanchal were sent to the caravan so they could wash up and unpack. A couple of old burn marks studded the laminate bench top and the gold-flecked plastic walls were yellowed with age. Strips of a flowered cotton hung loosely over the windows. Chanchal stretched his arms out wide, and grinned. He could almost touch both sides of the van. When he slept on the floor Rafi would need to step over him if she got up in the night for water. They sat beside each other on the kitchen seat and said nothing. Rafi went over what her mother would say about this caravan: that it was grubby and small. And the man in it: he was a darkie and a foreigner, and she was throwing her life away with him. She thought – I'm not going to think about mum or what she'd say. It made her sick to the stomach.

Then Chanchal pushed the windows open and closed the door. The van darkened. Rafi set about hanging her few clothes on the wire hangers that rattled sharply in the tiny closet. She was nervous. He seemed older all of a sudden, and she younger. Maybe that was good; let him decide. He had lived in London, Ludhiana, Melbourne – he was worldly.

He watched her do her tidying, then reached out an arm to her and Rafi went to him and silently, at the small table, they embraced. There was no one to see them now. No townspeople or train passengers or passing drivers. This was what they'd wanted, to be alone together, skin to skin, mouth to mouth.

They heard one of the girls calling them, and Rafi rose from his lap, touching her mouth gingerly. 'That beard rash again,' she said, taking her lipstick from her makeup purse, and giving her wrists a squirt of cologne. 'You go in, while I splash some water on my face,' she said. Chanchal stayed sitting, one leg crossed over the other.

'Come on then,' she said.

'A little delay won't worry these bohemians,' smiled Chanchal. He thought – She has no idea why I'm not standing up.

'They're bohemians? Or are they beatniks?' she asked.

'Not beatniks: they wear black and listen to pop music. I think they're bohemian because they're artists and like to travel.'

At dinner – chops and vegetables, with Clarissa's apologies when she saw that Chanchal didn't eat meat and him assuring her he was most happy with the other provisions – Chanchal was asked so many questions about his studies and the Colombo Plan for Economic Development that it was a surprise when Clarissa asked how they had met.

Listening to Chanchal's answer, Rafi thought – How interesting, what a wonderful way to have met. They had met, he said, at the library in Mimosa when he was reading a newspaper clipping about a beautiful young woman who had won an art prize for portraiture. And there she was, the same girl, outside the library. Chanchal didn't mention that this first meeting had occurred only five days earlier. Bob and Clarissa were interested in Rafi now; their attention swivelled from Chanchal to her. Bob said he'd take her to the studio, and asked what media did she work in and did she have any of her work with her? Chanchal pulled his notebook from his pocket and showed them her sketches of birds, but Rafi said not to, they were nothing. The two girls listened attentively, watching her face, watching his face, nudging in close to see the drawings.

Later, as she washed her hands in the bathroom, Rafi looked at her mirrored self, looked at this face that he *loved*. She parted her lips slightly, invitingly; she frowned and turned down her mouth; appeared startled; smiled seductively; flicked her hair back.

She thought – It's Saturday and I've not been gone one week, yet it's a lifetime away. Time, she thought, stretches out, or is smaller and hurried. There should have been lots of time to meet and come to know Chanchal, but here they were, rushing through this short week. Some moments she was as elated as she'd been while waiting for the Sunlander to arrive. Others she was worried. What was time's correct measure really? She thought – The wind whips through the casuarinas at Petal Bay. How do I paint those minutes of a wind-blown walk? Can a painting convey time?

She asked Bob about his painting, though not about time, as he cleared the plates and Clarissa readied the girls for bed. 'Not doing much at the moment, I'm between exhibitions.' He said they'd talk more the following day; he'd take her to the studio. Rafi thought he seemed distracted.

Chanchal and Rafi took their leave, carrying their breakfast provisions to the white caravan.

Rafi sat on the bed wondering what she should do next. Chanchal said, 'I'll take a walk while you get ready,' and stepped outside. She changed into her nightgown and then when he came back, crossed the small space and kissed him, slipping her ringed hand into his ringed hand. She wasn't tired. 'Let me draw you,' she said.

Chanchal sat at the table fully dressed and Rafi drew a delicate picture of a young Sikh, upright, turbaned, bearded, fine-fingered hands resting on the table. The drawing was decisive: much black against the white, black beard, turban, eyes. Shadows behind him; a moth at rest in the corner.

'That's me?' asked Chanchal.

'That's you,' she said.

'Can I keep it?'

He folded the drawing carefully, and slipped it between the pages of his notebook.

The kerosene lamp at the door lit the small room, and as the night darkened moths hit out in animus rhythms on the curved glass. Foolish moths, thought Rafaela.

She went to bed and waited for him to finish his ablutions in the laundry, to return to her; then dozed as he read one of his books. She wished she'd been tucked in, crooned to, patted. Yet he was on a hard floor, uncomplaining, with only a couple of blankets to soften his bed. He turned the light off. From somewhere not far away, frogs called. She thought of the garden back home and her room – her quiet, simple room with the print of Cezanne's apples: without her to look at them they'd be growing mouldy. Then she remembered Sean pulling at her in the water and Julie's stupid laughter before that, and she squeezed her eyes because tears were welling. She could hear Chanchal shifting on the floor, and wondered – Is he lonely too?

The night was hot and the floor of the caravan cool, but hard, and Chanchal *was* lonely, thinking – I'm too far from home, yet I don't want to go home. There's nowhere comfortable for me yet. He recalled the day he left Old Delhi, the cluster of family around him; Susheela had worn a pale blue sari that day and had said she'd miss him. He recalled Professor Julian's enthusiastic 'Welcome! Welcome!' Words which ended with Veronica's dismayed look; and his friends wanly farewelling him at the wharf; and then in Melbourne Professor Turner's arch comments, and Mrs Fletcher's cool politenesses: Melbourne had not embraced him as London had. Then, as always happened when he was glum, the worst night during the weeks of Partition came back to him. On their difficult way back to Ludhiana they'd seen many mutilated people and heard wailing all about. Chanchal rolled onto his back, and to stop the memory, opened his eyes and traced the faint pattern of flecks on the caravan walls.

'Rafi,' he whispered. 'Are you awake?'

'Yes,' she said.

'Let me hold your hand.'

In the dark he could hear her shuffle across the old bed, moving the sheet and her pillow. She reached over and they found each other's hands; he only had to stretch a little way because the bed was low. He gripped her hand, and she squeezed back. He felt the ring on her finger, and thought – If only I could take her to meet my uncle. But I can't. Once we're married, I'll need to tell ma and pa. I'll find a way to console them. He could almost hear the cries of outrage.

Rafaela was tracing lines on his hand, and she felt his palm turn warm and clammy. She thought – The night's too hot for hand-holding. But kept hold of him nonetheless.

There was a tap on their door in the morning, and they woke with a start. Birds were calling, shrikes, cockatoos, warblers and parrots picking at bottlebrush flowers.

At the steps of the caravan he kissed her. She wanted to say 'I love you', to experiment, but to say the word *love* was like being asked suddenly to sing. Being adored was strange. What did she know about being adorable?

The day was already heating up. Rafi turned on the burners for the stove, placed the uneven pan over the heat and watched the butter melt before placing in a few halved tomatoes. As she broke the eggs, each yolk intact, into the frypan, she thought – This is the first meal I have cooked for him. While they were eating, one of the girls, Thea it looked like, peered at the van from the corner of the veranda, then disappeared.

'What will you do today?' Chanchal asked, getting up to go to the house.

'Not sure. Clarissa will have something for me. Or I'll find work for myself.' She watched him go: this man, Chanchal Singh, who shared a ring with her.

She could hear him at work, the sound of the handsaw cutting through posts for the fences. Clarissa did indeed have work for her: weeding in the orchard, weeding in the herb and vegetable garden. She picked grubs from the leaves of the lettuce. Dug troughs for new seedlings, and reshaped the troughs beaten down by the rain. Took the dying flower heads off the lavender. Easy work and though it was hot and humid without the rain, Townsville was hotter. Going inside, she offered to iron, but Clarissa said no.

So Rafi walked down to where Chanchal was working near the paddock alongside a stretch of uncleared rainforest, and sat on a stump while he sawed the posts and cut them to shape, making a slow pile of work for himself the next day, when he would begin sinking them. He bent, hefting the wood, the saws. Taking a rest, hands on hips, his back was straight.

'You look pleased with yourself,' she said.

Chanchal narrowed his eyes at her, put his hand up against the sun. 'When I'm working like this I'm thinking also of the Punjab and what a rich agricultural future it has. And it's a welcome change from laboratory work and biochemistry texts.'

Rafi burst out laughing, shook her head at him. 'How can you have trouble thinking of what to write to your parents, when you can say that to me?'

That was a levelling thought – parents. Chanchal and Rafi shared a pause.

'Our mothers wouldn't like us, would they,' Rafi said.

'No, they wouldn't.'

'But that doesn't mean that we shouldn't be together. What do parents know? Mine had picked out an awful young man for me. A drunk.'

A kookaburra sang out loudly from above them, then stopped immediately. Chanchal took up the saw again. 'It's not something we have to sort out right now, Rafi,' he said. 'Though won't your family be wanting to hear from you?' She seemed curiously relaxed about contacting them.

'You're right. I'll ask Clarissa if I can call later . . . When you're done, let's take a walk through the bush here.' The old fence divided the paddock from the bush. There was a rise but it wasn't so thick you couldn't find a path through to the ridge. Maybe there'd be rocks, a bit of a platform to see out over the farm from. Birds to sight.

When they hiked up through the bush later, bird and sketch books in hand, Rafi thought – I can't believe my luck! Chanchal was in front of her and he was so handsome and unlike any man she'd known before; his feet certain of a path, but gentle too. They reached a rocky outcrop. Cicadas droned all around them while Rafi sat cross-legged, sketching the red corrugated top of the Carmichaels' roof where it showed through the trees. Chanchal kept his binoculars trained on a black currawong that watched him then flew off in response to an invisible idea or subtle shift in the breeze.

'Bob told me there are lyrebirds around here,' Chanchal said. 'According to my book they'll be what's called an Albert's lyrebird. He said I should listen for them scraping at the leaves and twigs on the ground, rather than listen for their call, because they mimic the sounds of other birds.'

Chanchal picked the flower of a small boronia. The petals were a pale pink colour. There were a few of the shrubs scattered through the bushland, along with some wattles heavy with round puffs of yellow flowers.

'Do you know the names of these?' he asked her.

'I used to collect and press flowers – in a flower press – and then I'd identify them and draw them of course, and use them to make birthday cards,' she said, smiling at the memory of her past enthusiasm. 'I don't think I've ever seen a lyrebird. Around where I lived there wasn't much bush left.'

'Shall we try to find the bird then?' Chanchal lay back on the rock, after finding a space that wasn't too rugged. 'Not as bad as the caravan floor,' he said.

Rafi put down her charcoals, dusted off her fingers and lay beside him. Their hands met and they entwined fingers.

'Sorry about the floor. I'll take it tonight.'

'Never. It's fine. I like roughing it. I was so unfit when I started the cane cutting, the first day I thought I was going to pass out. I thought that for a few days. Now, look at these muscles.' He pulled up the sleeve of his shirt and flexed his arm. Rafi smiled and couldn't resist giving his bicep a squeeze. 'So strong!' she agreed.

'Before, I was a pale and weak student. Now I bristle with strength.'

Rafi laughed at this. 'You – bristle? You're too gentle for that.'

That night they ate on their own without the Carmichaels. Bob and Clarissa were friendly, but around tea time Bob took the truck into town. Something had come up, Clarissa said to Rafi. Rafi thought it best to keep out of the house. They were here to work, not to crowd the kitchen, though she was still waiting for Bob to show her his studio.

When Chanchal put out the light, and the moths ceased to butt at the windows, and he'd lain down once more, they again held hands in the dark caravan.

By the third day, Chanchal had got the hang of the fencing and was making good progress. Rafaela finished with the weeding and started on cleaning the chook and pig pens and, with a pitchfork and barrow, heaped the manure ready for bagging. She accompanied the girls and Clarissa each morning to check on the calves and the cow that had been lowing; whatever had been bothering it before seemed to have abated. The girls also had their jobs, and in the mornings went to the box by the road to collect the neighbour Peter Boil's milk and in the afternoon, the mail. Amelia was too young to do these things on her own. Rafi thought it would be lonely for the younger girl when Thea started school.

They ate in the caravan again that night, but were invited to have a beer on the veranda later, once the girls had been put to bed. Mosquito coils were lit and scattered around the chairs.

Taking her glass of beer from Bob Carmichael, Rafi felt newly adult. Here she was the 'wife', no longer merely the youngest or the sister or the child of Norma and Carlo.

Bob told them that his father was unwell, and he would be going to Sydney the next day to visit him in hospital.

'He's had some problems with his heart, which is a bit of a worry.'

Chanchal said, 'My father also has heart problems. Angina. He still won't exercise, though we've tried to get him onto a bicycle many times. He's a manufacturer of bicycles.'

'How many millions of bicycles would there be in India?' Clarissa asked.

'Perhaps not millions; thousands. And my father builds many of them. But doesn't himself ride.'

'Can you stay on the rest of the week?' Bob asked Rafi and Chanchal. 'I'll be gone a few days. Chanchal, you're looking pretty competent now.'

The next morning Clarissa drove Bob into town to catch the train south. His father's health was much worse than he had let on. He and his father were very close, Clarissa told

Rafi when she returned. 'His mother's not well either, and she's not able to visit the hospital without assistance.'

Two more days passed. At night and in the mornings, Chanchal prayed on a mat on the far side of the caravan, with the sun waning or rising to his side. He'd wait on the steps of the caravan for Rafaela to undress and wash and take herself to bed. Each night she willed him to come in earlier than he did, willed him to sit on the edge of the bed with her, to lean across and kiss her.

But no. Chanchal was doing the right thing.

On the third day after Bob's departure, Clarissa approached Rafi as she and the girls were feeding the chickens to ask if Rafi and Chanchal could stay on their own a few days while she took the girls down to Sydney.

'I think he might be going to die,' said Clarissa, quietly enough that the girls didn't hear. 'Bob's mother isn't coping at all. She's very upset. Doesn't want Bob to leave until it's clear what's happening.'

'I'm not sure,' said Rafi. 'We have to visit Chanchal's uncle. But it could be possible.'

'It's just with the flooding . . . It's hard to get help on such short notice.'

Rafi wanted to be reassuring. 'I think it should be fine. Except for the cows.'

Clarissa looked towards the cow paddock, frowning. There were the two soon to calve. 'I'll stop by Peter Boil's place on the way into town. If they do begin, go and fetch him. It's their second time round, so it shouldn't be too complicated.'

Clarissa left to pack and to write a list of things to be done while they were gone. Then she bundled the girls and their bags into the truck, telling Rafi and Chanchal to make use of the house. 'Cook in the kitchen and use our bedroom, if you want to. There are clean sheets out for you. You'll be okay?'

Chanchal said he'd take instruction from Rafi. 'She knows the routine better than I do now.' Rafi had worked with all the animals and did indeed know the basics of feeding, and cleaning their pens, collecting the eggs, shutting them up in the evenings, walking to the letterbox to collect the Boils' milk in the mornings.

'She does,' nodded Clarissa, distracted. 'I'll ring you from Sydney, and you've got Peter and Susan Boil over there. It's just for a few days. If an animal gets sick, you can let Peter decide whether to call the vet. But they'll be fine.'

She told the dog to get down from the truck; he'd jumped into the pan. Chanchal and Rafi watched from the steps as Clarissa drove down the driveway to the main road, then turned, and slowly was gone.

13

WHEN RAFAELA HAS BEEN GONE TWO WEEKS, SEAN IS STILL unconscious and in intensive care. Julie is sitting on the front steps of her parents' place smoking hard on a cigarette. Her blonde hair looks dirty. She's taking it badly, though she ran as fast as she could for the ambulance. Rickie takes the cigarette from her but then thinks better of his bullish ways, and gives it back.

They were hoping that Sean would have something to say about Rafi running away, but he's been in a coma for two weeks now.

'You might like to have a shower first,' he says.

'We're only going to the hospital,' she says back, but gets up to go inside.

As Julie turns, Rickie catches sight of the back of her knees, which are red and damp from her sitting. She has great legs.

It's another hot day south of Townsville, he thinks.

He tries not worry about her, to just wish Rafi well on her way south. When they didn't find her in Brisbane everyone had their theories, but Rickie knew she'd headed for Sydney. And he hopes that Rafi is in a better state than that stupid git, Sean.

14

'WE'RE KIND OF STUCK NOW, UNTIL THEY GET BACK,' RAFI concluded, taking Chanchal's hand and stepping down off the porch. 'When must you be back at university?'

'Mid to late February.'

They went over to the gate that led to the paddock. Skittish and wary, the cattle retreated. The Carmichaels' old dog waited beside them for her orders. 'Do you know what to say to her?' asked Rafi. 'Because I don't!' She knelt down and gave the dog a scratch behind the ears.

'I wouldn't have a clue. We're going to drive her barmy.' They continued to watch the cows.

'Clarissa said to keep an eye on their rear ends,' said Chanchal with some hesitation. 'They will swell and look wet when they're going into labour.'

Rafaela had nothing to add to this information. Thea had told them the two cows in question had their own names. Minkie and Queen Bee. Minkie was the one without the round white spot on her head. Other than that, Chanchal and Rafi agreed, they looked pretty similar.

'Come on then, let's put the chooks to bed,' she said. Behind the wire enclosure the brown hens were pecking, their small heads bobbing with precision.

Back in the house, Rafi went through the kitchen opening the cupboards to find glasses and plates and the cooking utensils. They'd agreed they'd have omelettes, potatoes and pumpkin for dinner. Finding some sultanas, Rafi decided to bake a bread and butter pudding.

Cooking for her family had been a chore, a duty. The meals were planned by her mother; it was Rafi's job to make them. But here she was: she knew what to do. Chanchal had gone back up into the bush to walk and listen for the lyrebirds, if indeed they were there. The kitchen was quiet, with only the sounds that she herself made: the clang of crockery and pots as she prepared the food. After whisking the eggs and adding some parsley and chives, she put the mixture aside to wait for Chanchal's return. It was evening. Perhaps he was saying his dusk prayers. The lyrebirds might hear him, and mimic his words, 'truth is the timeless one'; she couldn't remember the Punjabi words. She wouldn't be able to copy him as well as a lyrebird. She put the potatoes on to boil. The gas was low no matter how high she turned it. Rafi lit another match, just for the smell of it.

She walked down to Bob's shed, but the old door was locked. She peered in through a window. A heavy table to one side was covered in tubes and brushes and jars of linseed oil, and she could see paintings leaning against the walls, and another on an easel.

She went back to the house and for the first time entered the main bedroom. The Carmichaels' bedroom. The marital bed. Their bedside drawers. She shut a half-open drawer without looking inside it. A Persian carpet was laid beside the bed between the door and a pair of french doors that opened to a small porch. She stepped onto the porch, where there were a couple of garden chairs. The view over the fields was pretty from here too.

She took a deep breath in and let it out slowly. She thought – Here I am, Rafaela Ellen Mollino, living in the house of an artist, in love with Chanchal, on the way to Melbourne, no longer a child.

Inside again, Rafi took the folded sheets that Clarissa had left out and made up the bed. Lying on it, she thought of him. She thought – How am I going to get through the night with him in the caravan? She lay flat against the mattress, waiting for his return. She looked at the ring on her finger. She thought – Why should I wait? She rolled onto her front, pretended to be asleep – she was turning into a Mills & Boon heroine – he was leaning over her to kiss her, he took her in his arms . . .

She heard his feet on the front steps and leapt up to meet him in the kitchen.

His finger was on a page of his bird identification book. 'Didn't hear anything,' he said. 'I think I might have seen a rose-crowned fruit dove though. I was staring hard at a spot, listening in case I heard the lyrebird, and then realised there was something else there, quite small, with a pinky-rose colour on its head. Two of them.'

Rafi took the book from him and looked at the description. There was a coloured drawing beside it of a small intricately coloured bird. While she was looking at the page, he put his arms around her waist and kissed her neck and her ears. She read, 'They are shy birds, not easily seen among the foliage, some are migratory.' Thought – Am I shy? What do I want to do now? And turned around and kissed him fully on the mouth, still holding the book awkwardly. He ran his hands over her breasts, down across her skirt, the one with the penny-sized dots of white on chocolate which earlier she'd changed into from her work shorts. Not letting go of him, she leant towards the table and laid down the bird book. She didn't want to wait.

Chanchal abruptly left the room.

Rafi's legs were trembling. There was nothing to stop them now, with everyone gone. Did she want him to stop? That must be why he left the room? To stay at arm's length, wait out the days here, until Melbourne? She could hear groaning from the water pipes – there was air in them – and realised he was running a bath or showering.

She thought – He can't be showering in his turban. And if he comes back into the kitchen shirtless, in only his trousers and with his hair wet?

He was soon back. 'I was washing a couple of my turbans in the sink,' he explained, deadpan. She thought –

He noticed that I noticed that he ran away.

Rafi took the boiled potatoes out of their water and checked on the bread and butter pudding. Chanchal cut up the pumpkin, and found a pan to cook it in with a little oil and some spices from a tin he carried with him. Sitting at the table they complimented each other on their cooking – their first meal prepared together – then washed up, talking about the animals and what was to be done the next day. Clarissa had left with the morning's dishes still to be washed, so it took some time to wash and dry and put everything away.

Chanchal asked, 'Who is your favourite brother of the four?'

Without hesitation she said, 'Rickie. Less than a year older than me, my best friend for years until he changed.'

'Changed?'

'Well,' she paused. 'I didn't change. Rickie knows what he wants and makes plans and does what he plans. He's studying engineering at night school.' She liked to speak of him. 'Then, when my parents said it was time to get married, I decided I'd rather go to art school.'

And here she was, all of it, all of it unplanned. Not that she would tell Chanchal that.

They lit mosquito coils so they could sit on the veranda, but even with the noxious coils of smoke curling around them they were bitten. She slapped her arms, Chanchal brushed another off her leg, she blew at one buzzing near his turbaned ear. They retreated to the kitchen and he pulled her onto his lap and, unaware of the itchy swellings on their arms and legs, bitten by sweet desire, they struggled on the hard chairs to be decorous, to touch but not touch too much, not there, until Chanchal begged to leave, laughing, sad, bidding her farewell at the door, joining his palms, a brief bow. Gone in a rush.

Rafi lay on the freshly made bed in the Carmichaels' bedroom. Her rest lasted about ten minutes. She opened the french doors to see if the light was on in the white caravan. It was. Mosquitos buzzed at her. She retreated inside.

Back in the bedroom, she opened her drawing pad and roughly sketched the sight of him coming back inside with the book in his hand. His expectant look – happy to have been in the rainforest, and to be seeing her before him. She paused, remembering that look. She was loved. Truly, she was. She drew quickly, covering a whole page in black except for the trace of a telegraph pole rising up over a flat road with a shock of the eagle's nest at the join, just as he'd described. The bird's presence in reverse, white on black. She laid a piece of tracing paper between the pages, tying the pad up tightly so the charcoal wouldn't smudge. In the kitchen she washed her hands, and there she decided. She couldn't wait until they were married.

His light was off now, but the door was unlocked when

she stepped up into the caravan. She slipped almost noise-lessly onto the bed where he lay, his breathing even; was surprised to feel his hair across the pillow. Rafi touched it carefully in the dark, feeling it thicker and coarser than hers. He had slept in his turban the other nights.

This hair, which she'd waited days to see and touch, was longer than her own. She crept her fingers along it, breathing in the smell of him and, just as her mouth came close – to where she wasn't sure – he moved. His arms caught her and their hands were on each other. He rolled aside and found the bedside candle and lit it, the scratch and flare of the match like a tantalising finger on her skin. The walls of their small abode shimmered with the gold flecks. She sat behind him, ordering him to stay still, and brushed out the long black strands with her fingers. He shook back his head and his thick hair slid across his bare shoulders, uncut like a woman's, yet manly. It hung in kinks from being wound tight. She put her hands on each of his shoulders, and thought – I am undone. He turned and without apology pulled her nightgown off. No one had seen her naked since she was a child. He played with her hair, her shoulders, her breasts. She liked the feel of his mouth on her neck, his hard legs, the firm flesh of his arms when she ran her hands along them, the soft lobes of his ears.

There was the deep, cricket-chirping night all around them.

Here was their net of hair, long and dark and tangled together, their thick and slippery hair knotting together. Lying over her, the muscles of his shoulders and arms bunched thickly. He was larger than life, yet also himself, she thought. His beard grazed her belly, his lips nipping her, nuzzling. She saw colour, turquoise; the colour and shape of his hands spread hotly over her breasts. His fingers and mouth ate at her. She thought – What should I do? It can't matter, not to know. She reached below his stomach, to his – it sprang when she touched it. It was hot and smooth and dry. He drew in his breath with a gasp and when she put her lips to his she smelt the anise and other spices that they had shared. Standing, naked, Chanchal's hair was wild and disarrayed and his body taut, all of it. Rafi couldn't help but look at him, her mighty lover, and then he was on the bed again, on top of her, nudging at her until she was gasping for something, pushing at her until he found where he wanted to be. She made him cry out when she pulled his mouth to her breast. He cried out and sank with all his weight on her.

They wound their legs around each other, whispering endearments. He kissed her eyes, her face. 'Never apart,' he said. 'Never,' she said.

She needed to go back to the house, to the loo, so they ran through the humid, insect night to the house. He went inside to wait for her, black hair swinging.

Her water hit the porcelain noisily. She dabbed

herself, gingerly running her fingers up and down, fingering the sticky wetness. Her contours had changed.
Everything was changing and the land proved it. She was
plump and bruised, and wanting. Rafi slid a finger inside
herself, proud. Thought – What is this feeling? Elation
again, that's what. Whispered to herself excitedly, 'I am
no longer a virgin.'

They slept together in the house, fingertips on each
other, the sheet loosely over them, stirring occasionally to
kiss the other on his shoulder or her breast.

On waking, Rafi found Chanchal crouched in front of
the bedside drawers.

'What are you doing?'

'Looking for protection,' he said. He knew he was being
blunt, but he was uncomfortable speaking about it. 'I was
worried last night,' he said, climbing back into the bed
where she lay watching him uncertainly. Chanchal regretted opening those drawers. Poking through other people's
things wasn't something he'd normally do.

Picking up his hair and twisting it so he had to come
closer to her, she said, 'You've done this before. Am I right?'

Chanchal flinched and then spoke too quickly.

'With my English professor's wife, actually.' He instantly
regretted his words. Yet, truth was all, as in the *Guru Granth
Sahib*, and as Wittgenstein sought it. He should not regret
speaking the truth, though he was saying too much.

'A violinist? A married woman?'

How gorgeous Rafi was, and now what was this conversation they were having? He began a nervous explanation, but she interrupted.

'I don't want to hear your reasons. Were you in love?'

He took Rafi's hand; she looked so dismayed. How could he answer what he hadn't been certain of? London was a world away. It seemed completely irrelevant, but of course it wasn't. 'Sometimes I thought I was, at other times I didn't and I just felt trapped and unhappy. So, no, I don't think I was. And she definitely didn't love me.'

'How can you be certain?' she asked. Rafi was right; how could he be certain that Veronica hadn't loved him?

Chanchal looked at Rafi and without speaking asked her to please stop.

'What protection did she have, then?'

'A couple.'

'Two? What do you mean, two?'

As he told Rafaela in the blandest way what a diaphragm and a condom were, Chanchal thought that at the very least he now had to act responsibly.

'It sounds cluttered.'

Chanchal put his finger to her mouth to shush her. Too much talk! He let her play with his hair. 'Why don't you help me wash my hair today?' he said.

'You're trying to distract me. Explain the reproductive cycle. We only had one lecture at school with our mums there, and it didn't really sink in.'

'I'll demonstrate,' he said, sliding under the sheets, teasing her legs apart. But then she jerked the sheet away, leaving him naked on the bed.

Pale-skinned Veronica could never have attributed an accidental pregnancy with Chanchal to Professor Julian, even if she'd wanted to. And having known a friend to die following an abortion, pregnancy was out of the question. Hence the two methods. He wouldn't tell Rafi about all that, however.

'Did he know about you two? The professor?'

'I don't think so. It didn't go on very long and then I left to come here.'

'You ran away?' she asked in some affront.

Chanchal tugged at the sheet. 'No.'

'Is that what you'll do? Run off all of a sudden?' she asked. She seemed to be joking, but Chanchal sensed that she was upset.

Chanchal thought it would take an hour and a half to cycle to the pharmacy in town, but he'd forgotten the hills. He walked up them, leaning onto the bicycle, pushing on the rhythm of Ludhiana-London-Melbourne. He always ended up on bicycles! Now Linden. And trains. Bicycles and trains. He pushed on, his thoughts veering between the erotic and an apprehension that it was all too good to be true. Occasionally a vehicle passed, leaving behind a floating wall of dust. Pedalling over a crest, Chanchal saw before him a gentle downwards slope, tree-lined and shady. The air was so humid now he was dripping in tickling rivulets down his sides.

She couldn't be expected to buy them. With an image of her innocent shock as he'd dropped her nightie to one side the night before – when she'd said, 'No one's seen me naked since I was a child' – Chanchal felt a rush of shame and threw down the bike to sit beneath a tree. He'd put her on the train tomorrow. He'd buy her ticket in town, and lock himself in the caravan alone. He'd send her away. Miserable with this plan, Chanchal began to cycle again. The ring on his finger glinted, slipping along his sweating hands. Then the grade turned long and easy, and Chanchal relaxed, letting the mild slope carry him along, the breeze a little cooler. On the other hand, he thought, sex is international and natural, and I love her.

He heard a truck changing gears, and the straining roar of the engine accelerating. Looking over his shoulder, he swerved away from the road as sprays of gravel and dirt from the wheels hit him. There was a shrill laugh as he fell, tangled in the bike, almost hitting a tree. He rolled off, bruised and cut, with something soft and mucky on his face. 'Bugger off, you bastards!' he yelled but the truck was far along the road already. He thought – I've been speaking English for so long that now I'm swearing in it.

At last he reached the town. Looking for water, his

head pounding with the heat, he walked into the park, passing the black cannon and the honour roll. His relations had fought in both the world wars for the British; in the second as a bid for India's independence from Britain upon the cessation of hostilities in Europe. The war had been good for manufacturing, and his father's business had thrived, as had Punjabi agricultural industries with the construction of canals and other infrastructure.

Chanchal found a tap and washed his face. He looked about, and as the park was empty, took his shirt off and sat near the pond in the shade of the willows beneath which he and Rafi had lain only a few days earlier. Thinking of her rested him, but roused him too – he got up, dressed, and bought fruit and some other things for their meals, then ordered a sandwich at the pub, which he ate on the veranda alone. A man he didn't remember having met before came past and said, 'Back again, are you?' and spat liberally on the ground. Chanchal went on reading his newspaper, but thought – This is no place for me, or for her.

There were two pharmacies, with the larger one beside a general store. He picked out a packet of toothpaste. She'd been solemn when he said why he was going into town, but had mentioned she needed toothpaste. The young fellow who was serving was ringing up the item on the register when Chanchal asked for a packet of sheaths. He made sure not to mumble, using his most authoritative English, but spoke quietly so as not to be overheard.

In London this little embarrassment and expense had been his contribution.

'Just a moment,' the man said. He went over to an older man working behind the high bench and whispered. By the look of their bony noses and square necks they were related. The pharmacist came forward, the son following.

'We're all out. We're not expecting any stock for a couple of weeks.'

The older man was almost smiling, enjoying his lie. The two men stood side by side as if guarding something.

Chanchal paid for the toothpaste and left.

In the second pharmacy, Chanchal hovered, sorry for the pale-haired woman who said good afternoon to him, because her shoulders were so bent with timidity. She smiled, and Chanchal smiled back. The shelves were barely stocked. Price stickers were crossed out and many of the wrappings around the items had faded.

'There's a few things that I'm after, but I'd like to know if you have any sheaths. Condoms?'

'Yes,' she nodded.

Chanchal thought a moment, grabbing at a generous figure. 'Six packets then, please.'

The lady went behind the counter, unlocked a cupboard, counted out the packets, put them in a paper bag and sealed it with tape. Chanchal chose a bottle of the 4711 cologne that Rafi liked, a pumice stone, and a bottle of nail polish; he didn't want to return to her with just one gift.

'The other shop wouldn't serve me, you know,' he confided to the woman.

She looked at him sympathetically, but didn't say anything.

The ridge of rainforest behind the house was dark when Chanchal reached the turn-off, its shadow leaning over the fields. He dismounted to walk up the drive. There she was, reading a book on the veranda. She was beautiful in all ways and he kept his eyes on her. Look up, so I can see your face, he thought. And she did, and her eyes were swimmingly dark and sweet to see him. He dropped the bike and flopped onto the steps. She fussed over him. He felt relieved, and at home with her. His knapsack and the back of his shirt were wet with sweat. She took the groceries into the kitchen and brought him out a glass of water. He took it, and drank. She picked at his turban, at some grime. Chanchal smelt her close, touching her legs, while she asked him what had happened.

'You're covered in dirt,' she said.

'Some guys tried to run me off the road with their truck and I took a fall.'

'You've had a meat pie thrown at you, too. This brown spot, that's gravy.'

They laughed, though Chanchal immediately

unwound his turban. 'The woman who served me in the pharmacy will be telling her friends, "He was polite and well spoken, but very dirty and smelly, just as you'd expect."'

'No, from what you've told me I don't think she'd talk like that.' Rafi took the pins from his hair and shook it out. 'Do you think the whole town knows about us?'

'Yes.' Chanchal thought – I won't tell her about the guy who spat or the men in the first pharmacy. 'Why else would a truck try to run me off the road?' He would leave her to her well-meaning naivety; he didn't want to berate her about her countrymen.

'I want to see one,' she said.

'Really?'

'What do you think, Chanchal? Of course.'

Chanchal handed her the paper bag. 'I bought you a couple of little presents. And I remembered the toothpaste.'

'Six packets with how many in each?' Rafi looked at him aghast.

It did look excessive. 'A week's supply,' he joked.

She folded the bag up and sat close to him. 'The cologne is lovely.'

Chanchal stood up slowly, feeling weary and unwashed, and low about himself. He thought – I should send her on her way. 'Rafi, why don't you go down to Melbourne now, and I'll stay here until the Carmichaels get back. Perhaps it's better that you go.'

'No,' she said. 'Unless you want me to?'

'No, only . . . I just want to get stuck into these packets.' Chanchal threw the bag lightly across the veranda towards the front door. But then he retrieved it and put it on a seat. 'I need to clean myself up, and there are the hens.'

'I've done them already. Why don't we wash your hair?' He was so brazenly handsome with his black beard and long hair.

'You're sure we should stay here together?' he asked.

'Don't. You frighten me when you're this serious.'

Three days passed, but there had only been one call from Clarissa, the day after she'd left, to say she'd arrived safely. They were hot-skinned and heavy-loined and they couldn't keep their bodies apart. At night they fell asleep in a knot of limbs. Each day had its routines of collecting Peter Boil's milk from the box by the road, feeding the animals and cleaning their pens, and checking on the cattle, washing clothes and tending to the vegetables and the small grove of fruit trees. In the evening they collected the Carmichaels' mail and replaced Peter Boil's milk bottle. Grit from the road had settled on the floor of the red tin box and a spider nested at the back. They hoped for news of Bob's father and when the Carmichaels would be back. Rafi stacked the mail on the dresser beneath the Rembrandt sketch. She thought of her family. Imagined her mother doing the dinners on her own – unless Hetty or Louise had come over to help. But Norma wouldn't need help to feed only herself, Carlo, Rickie and Luca; when they were all there, which wasn't often anyway. All of which Rafi didn't want to think about a minute longer; it made her stomach tight and hard. She pulled open one of the drawers of the dresser. Inside was a long key that looked like it might fit the studio door. That was an omen, not that she was superstitious. A foretelling omen that what she was doing was right – the artist's key, here in her hand just when she was worrying about her family.

They rose at sunrise, following the birds before tending to the animals. There was a collage of sound, of twitters, high chuckles, trilled toots, an explosive *hookcoo* from the fruit dove pair, the male with his red-coloured crown and the female grey-green. They skipped out the door, Chanchal with his books and Rafi her sketchpad and pencils. She drew them on the fly: the little wattlebird, superb fairy-wren, a red-browed finch and her favourite, the grey-crowned babbler, whose beak curved down at the end finely, like a ponied eagle. She was learning the names and habits of a great many birds. On the third morning, though, she used the key she had found and went into Bob Carmichael's studio. She had dreamt that morning about being on the beach back home, that she was painting in the wind and the wind was flicking her fingers so that her brush was quick and instantaneous. Inside Bob's shed the smell of paint and oil was powerful from the shed having been shut for days. Rafi breathed it in. She studied the canvases, carefully shifting them out of their stacks to look at them one by one, trying to imprint upon her memory the facts of his paint-work, before returning them to their place. Bob's brush strokes intertwined and overran each other. Close up, dabs, squiggles and other inconsequential marks of colour made up the shapes, light and perspective – seemingly chaotic – while further back the image in all its wide drama and meaning was clear. She thought – I am on the verge of understanding it. Hills, roads, fields with heavy ridges of forest and, again and again, a partly collapsed barn's diagonal lines of silky wood. An old working barn had fallen hard to one side, half its face paralysed by a stroke of gravity and stormy rainfalls.

Rafi carried a primed board, a small easel and a box of oils and brushes outside. The cool, after-dawn air slid over her skin as she walked, light with anticipation.

Chanchal was in the rainforest hoping to see the lyre-birds. He'd said this morning they'd find a flat. She wouldn't be able to stay with him in Princes Hill. He had many plans, none of which she felt very confident about.

She went down the gully to a small forest of eucalypts and a tall flame tree, bright with scarlet flowers. The fence here was like the broken barn painted by Bob Carmichael, at angles and aged to grey, the wood-grain grizzled. She thought – The colours of things are not solid but made of shifting, moving light, just as atoms shimmy. Or a bird's wing opens to show an unsuspected shade. Just as my retina is flooded by light and my nerves carry the chemical messages to my brain. Colour is pliable and subjective.

Rafi set up her easel and worked directly onto the board, trying to paint without pencil or preparation – what Bob Carmichael called working *en plein air*, painting outside, straight onto the canvas. She wanted to paint the fence line with the shadows from the posts long, though as the sun was rising quickly everything shifted each time she looked up.

She heard Chanchal singing out her name and waved to him. He jogged down to her.

'I've just started,' she said before he could say anything about her work.

'I wasn't going to say anything,' Chanchal said, wanting to say, 'how brilliant'. He gave the fence a shake.

'I'm painting that. It can't fall over yet.' She continued to work, trying not to be too distracted by him.

'I could be here for weeks working on the fences. But I'll run out of wire.' He scuffed at something on the ground. 'What animal made these?' he asked.

Rafi took a quick look at the small glossy black pellets. 'Wallabies, probably. But I don't know that much about animals. Where I come from there's just sugar cane and rodents.'

Chanchal gave the fence post another friendly kick.

'It's exciting to think that in a few weeks we'll both be in Melbourne, getting married, and I'll be back at university and in the lab – a married man.'

He spoke with such enthusiasm that she envied him, and as robustly as she could she added, 'And we'll go to art galleries together and you can take me to your lab and show me bubbling test tubes.' But looking between her board and the fence posts she saw she'd lost the moment; that the air and the light and the colour of the wood and the leaves and the shadows were now much bolder. She'd need to begin a new board.

'Let's head back,' she said.

She thought – I don't want to get married. It was true. She didn't, though she should be wanting to very much, since, one – she loved him, and two – she'd lost her virginity to him. Why she was hesitant about his marriage talk, she wasn't sure. Hadn't he convinced her of his sincerity? But there was that other something she'd been worrying about.

'It would be bad luck to fall pregnant the first time, wouldn't it?' she asked.

Chanchal's hands were around her waist, skimming down to her hips. She liked these ambushes, her hands now full of tubes and brushes.

'Very bad luck. Highly unlikely,' he said, picking up and folding the easel.

He looked to her, as if asking was there more she was going to tell him. Instead she said, 'Let's go swimming. Let's take the bikes and a picnic.'

'In the river?'

'The beach. We'll ride to the coast. Do you have togs with you?'

'I've got some shorts.'

It took them most of the morning to cycle to the coast. The first beach they came to was a blaze of blue water and white breakers, swimmers dotted along the sands, though not so many or so close together that she and Chanchal would be conspicuous. Rafi wriggled into her swimmers beneath her towel, then ran into the water, eager to flaunt her swimming skills and to enjoy the cold after the long hot ride. She swam out past the breakers, waving to him, teasing him to come out to her. But of course he couldn't and she didn't want him to, if what he said was true, that he couldn't swim. He entered only up to his hips. Floating, Rafi recalled Sean Bullen's stupid attempts to grab her, half-drowning her. She much preferred Chanchal's temperate, Sikh way of life. What would Sean be doing now, midway through a weekday? Working at the packing mill, or skulking off with those dumb friends of his.

'How can you swim with a turban on?'

'I wasn't planning on swimming,' he called back. 'I planned on carefully paddling.'

'Don't be ridiculous.' She waded out of the water, pulling on his hand, and unwound his turban, folding it up carefully. During the past week she had brushed his hair, plaited, combed it, helped him re-wind it. She liked the way he let her touch him.

Back in the water, she cajoled Chanchal through the breakers, to trust her and to lie back in the water and float with the swell. She supported him with her arms. His hair was loose and floated around him. She kept her arms firm underneath him as he spread his arms wide. She explained how to breathe, told him to open his chest and to believe in the buoyancy of the water.

She thought about telling him how she'd swum hard and long to escape. Yes, she was a strong swimmer. She'd swum for an hour, run home, walked for the bus, hitched a ride from Brisbane to get back on the train, and now here she was in the ocean with this man, Chanchal Singh.

'Let me show you something,' she said, to give him a rest.

As she performed her backward handstand, walking on her hands, legs waving, feet flopping, Chanchal smiled, thought – She's not like anyone I've ever known. Then he dipped down beneath the water's surface, submitting himself to a mouthful of her grand Pacific.

15

LATE THAT NIGHT, CLARISSA DROVE UP TO THE HOUSE, THE girls asleep beside her. She'd rung from town, so Chanchal and Rafi had a chance to tidy the bedroom and move back to the caravan. The dog gave one excited yelp when the truck pulled up. Clarissa explained that Bob needed to stay longer as both his parents were faring badly, with his dad hospitalised and his mother poorly. Clarissa looked careworn and exhausted carrying Thea into the house. She let Chanchal peel Amelia off the seat and take her to her bedroom, the three of them whispering around the sleeping girls, the dog panting excitedly.

Rafi and Chanchal had become used to the cool of the house, and they joked as they struggled for room in the smaller bed. The caravan was hotter than ever. It took a long time to settle as somehow, though they'd showered, they'd brought sand from the beach into the bed with them.

The next morning everyone was up early for the inspection of the animals. Thea and Amelia pulled their gumboots on as soon as they'd breakfasted and were waiting on the porch when Chanchal and Rafi emerged from the caravan.

'The girls are getting big,' Clarissa observed of the two cows. They walked through the paddock quietly, Chanchal carrying the hay.

Later in the morning, Rafi looked after the girls while Clarissa drove back into town for groceries. Chanchal was finishing off another section of fencing up near the rainforest and the boundary of Peter Boil's place. When Clarissa returned, she asked Rafi to stay with the girls and make them some lunch. She went into her study and closed the door. To do what, Rafi had no idea; a newspaper assignment that needed finishing? Rafi had wanted to ask what Sydney was like, which galleries were the best. She'd have to wait; she might not even get the chance before she and Chanchal had gone. After all, they were free to leave now.

Rafi finished the laundry that she'd started, hanging out the Carmichaels' clothes from the trip to Sydney. The girls kicked a ball around and washed their dolls in an old tub on the grass.

'Thea, Amelia, let's see what Chanchal is doing,' Rafi said. It was easy to locate him by listening to the sound of his sledgehammer as he sank the pickets. 'Better get these dolls out first, so they don't drown.' She fished them out of the tub and laid them down to dry.

When they found him, Chanchal pulled off his gloves and sat on the grass to rest while the two girls ran laughing around him in circles, getting dizzier and dizzier.

'Should we ask for our pay and a lift into town?' Rafi asked.

Chanchal thought it was probably better that Rafaela established herself in Melbourne alone, just as she'd intended in her dare-devil way. Again, Chanchal was reminded uncomfortably of the books that Veronica had given him, stories of disobedient daughters and outspoken women. Rafi wasn't as frightening, but she didn't need him interfering; in all likelihood she'd have her plans all sorted out by the time he got there.

'It's a pity I can't have more of your swimming lessons in sunny Woolgoolga,' he said, limply. That small town on the coast he'd yet to see. Chanchal tried to recall his uncle, whom he'd not seen since Partition when he was ten years old. So much had happened to him between the age he was now, twenty-three, and back then, that he had no memory of Ajit, or of Ajit's wife who had been murdered that August in their village. Like thousands of other Sikhs, Ajit had left India for good after that.

But by the time Rafi had meandered back to the house with the girls, stringing out the afternoon as long as she could to give Clarissa more time to herself, Clarissa had got off the phone from Bob, who'd called to say that his mother Betty had fallen and broken some bones.

'What's the saying? If it doesn't rain, it hails? Storms? Or something. Could you stay on a few more days, Rafi?'

Clarissa was beautiful, thought Rafi. She must have people say yes to her all the time.

Clarissa and the girls again set out for Sydney the next morning, Thea and Amelia reluctant this time to leave Rafaela and their toys and the animals.

'At least she gave us our pay,' said Chanchal resignedly, as they waved goodbye. 'And I have you.'

'And I you!' she returned, tingling with the thought.

16

CHANCHAL'S MOTHER APARNA IS SITTING WITH HIS FATHER Bani in their lounge room. It is winter and though the heater is on, the room is not quite warm enough. She rises and goes to a small decorated table to one side. The *Guru Granth* is placed open at a page and Aparna reads to herself from the evening prayers: 'The world is sunk in doubts and vices, but the enlightened can swim across.' Oceans divide her from her son. She doesn't know the names of these oceans.

The post has come and again there is nothing from Chanchal. She wishes that his letters would arrive in a more timely way because now that he is in Australia he is beyond her imagination. It is hard to reconcile bushrangers, convicts, Anzacs, kangaroos and koalas, with Melbourne University, and a place called Princes Hill where he lives and which has nothing to do with royalty, but in fact borders a cemetery. Her son struggles with his letters; that's clear from each uninformative missive that he has sent over the years. It has been a month and his last aerogram was from Queensland, where he was cutting sugar cane. He wrote that when the koel birds sang he thought fondly of his ma and pa.

She wants to lean over to Bani and say – For all we know he's died of an injury already! But Aparna doesn't say a word. He'd tell her not to worry, but then he'd fret.

She puts down her glass of tea and picks up the photograph of a young woman from Delhi whom Bani's brother has recommended. The girl looks nice, but less vivacious than her own daughters. Still, beauty is in the eye of the beholder, and as soon as she hears from Chanchal she'll send him the photo and the girl's particulars.

17

THE NEXT MORNING, SITTING ON THE LOO, HER FEET ON THE cool cement floor, Rafaela thought hard about her dates. She was late. Her undies were clean. The white cotton stretched between her legs was clean and smelt still of sunlight. She thought – I can't cope with this.

Chanchal was set on chopping lumber, so it was easy to suggest that she ride the bike as far as the bus stop they'd found and go into town alone.

She dressed carefully, with a sense of foreboding, buttoning her broderie anglaise shirt up neatly. She wore a broad hat and put gloves into her bag. She thought – Mum would be pleased to see me wearing a hat and my shirt tucked in. But the thought didn't appease her anxiety.

She pedalled, then hid the bike behind some grasses and waited for the bus in the mud-brown bus shelter. Her mother wouldn't appreciate Chanchal's colour. She was against tanning, and all foreigners who weren't Italian like Carlo. She would not like Chanchal at all.

Still, Rafi was looking forward to going to the newsagent to see if they had any of those small boxes of oil paints that some places stocked. She thought she'd also stop by the train station and see about the train times. But first, the library. Coming in from the bright street, the large room was dark and the book titles hard to read. Or was this only her gloomy impression, expecting that the books she needed were hidden? Then her eyes adjusted and she saw the librarian, a very large woman with spectacles. She sat to one side of the room, behind a desk. The window alongside her was half-covered with drawings done by the local primary school kids. Father Christmas. Snowmen. Pine trees decorated with red Christmas balls. That's what Thea had to look forward to, and what Rafi remembered being told to draw at Christmas time.

'I'm waiting for the boy to come back to fix the globes,' the librarian called out.

What Rafi wanted was a book on marriage. That was the word she thought would be right, the polite cue. There are these books, she thought, that tell you things you need to know. The wedding day, the wedding night. Planning for a family. The priest gives them to you before you get married. Surely not everyone has to be told by a doctor? There'd be a chapter on how to find out if you are *with child*. She felt sick to the stomach.

A white poodle sat on the librarian's floral lap, panting rapidly.

'You're at the Carmichaels', aren't you?' said the woman, looking at her carefully. Rafi smoothed a fold of her skirt. 'How are you finding it?'

'Everything's fine.' She sounded like a kid again.

'Peter Boil giving you a hand?'

'When the cows start to calve,' she said. 'We're to go get him if there's trouble.' She thought – How do you know so much? Busybody. Perhaps the Carmichaels had told people in town their place was being looked after.

'They've had an illness in the family, haven't they? They're a lovely family.'

Rafi nodded, but thought – I'm not saying anything more to this nosy parker. She stretched out a hand to pat the poodle.

'Oh, don't even consider it, dear. She bites all strangers.' She said it in a kind way, though. 'Got family with you?'

'Just my husband.' Liar! She jiggled her leg, thought – Ask her now, ask for the book.

'Of course! I know exactly who you are now. You're the one married to the Indian fellow. Why would you marry an Indian, dear?' The librarian looked at Rafi earnestly, pityingly, genuinely perplexed.

'For love,' Rafi mumbled. 'Like everyone else.' She felt her cheeks redden.

The woman nodded.

Rafi thought – Her dog is old and filthy. The white poodle's hair was stained brown around his face and chest.

'Say hello to the Carmichaels for me,' the librarian said, as if Rafi was now supposed to leave the library.

'I might borrow a book first,' said Rafi. 'Do you have anything about marriage?'

The woman shook her head. 'You see, you need it, but someone nicked it. Dr Rowse is nice. You go and visit him. You know where he is, he's in Rowntree Street, three back.'

Rafi walked towards the station feeling subdued. Not for a moment did she consider turning down Rowntree Street. At the station the stationmaster searched through a pile of papers for a printed timetable to give her. He seemed to look at her knowingly. Everyone knew about them.

When she got back to the farm she was sweaty from the bike ride, but going to the bathroom saw that while she was sweaty, her period hadn't started. Perhaps, with everything that had happened the past week, she'd got her dates confused. Inside, Chanchal had left a note to say he'd gone up to Peter Boil's place with a query about the cattle. There was a Mrs Boil, but Rafi couldn't remember her name. It might have been Sally or Sarah or Susan. If Clarissa was about she could have asked her for advice.

How she missed Chanchal. Her whole body wanted him back whenever he was any distance from her. She missed his enthusiasm for her, and his certainty. But he was also annoying, the way he'd started to play at being a farmer. She thought – The reason I'm here is because of him, so where is he?

She lit the stove for tea, then unwrapped the oil paints. She couldn't just keep on helping herself to Bob Carmichael's stuff. She undid a cap: the green was startling, almost a shock in its bright severity, and worth every penny she'd spent on it.

She dabbed a smidgen onto a plate. She thought – The more beautiful the colours, the grander my mistakes will be.

Bob Carmichael had said he didn't know how far apart the two Herefords were in their cycles, but that Minkie had been serviced first, from his observations. A couple of nights later, on Peter Boil's advice, Chanchal went out again to the check on the cows.

Once back, he said, 'I think one of them has started – the one without the white spot.'

Rafi frowned. 'Which one is that? I know, it's Minkie. Queen Bee has the spot. The names have something to do with bee stings.'

Peter's list of symptoms of approaching labour had included the stringy mucus. Her tail was high and tense. Rafi and Chanchal set out gumboots and lanterns. Chanchal used a knife to cut a thick rope into a couple of long lengths, but then couldn't work out how to tie the slipknots that Peter had told him to tie for the calf's ankles if it got stuck. Rafi did the knots. Then they went to bed.

At two a.m. they woke to the bedside alarm and went to check on Minkie. From the light of the lanterns and the hazy glow of the moon they could see her flanks rippling. Hoofs appeared and then the hairy edge of a knuckle. When they crouched close to look, they saw that the hoofs were turned back on themselves, as Peter Boil had warned they might be, and this was making it difficult for her to push the calf out.

'You said he was really helpful, Chanchal. So we should go and wake him. That's what Clarissa told us to do.'

'Let's give her some hay and then we'll pull the calf out ourselves. Peter said that's what he does.'

Rafi thought – You're obstinate. What do you know about calves?

Minkie was fleshy and wet and stood there, silent, as if she didn't know what was going on. Once again the hoofs pushed forward. Rafi ran back across the paddock to get the ropes they'd dropped.

The edge of a hoof was still visible. 'One of us is going to have to put our hand in,' said Rafi, holding the rope.

'I'll do it,' said Chanchal.

'She might kick you,' said Rafi. He was being so self-important.

'Let's get her into the race then, like Peter suggested.'

The corral was up in the other corner of the paddock. Using more hay, they walked Minkie towards it. She didn't want to go into the race, though, and stopped before it. They switched her with the ropes and threw the whole bale in, but still she wouldn't move. The old posts shifted when her flanks hit against them. Suddenly she folded down heavily onto the ground.

'I'll get Peter,' said Rafi.

'No, I can do it.' Chanchal looked up at Rafi in the dark. 'Well, I think I can.'

Rafi shook her head. Thought – Neither of us knows what we're doing. We're just playing at this!

Chanchal took the rope, wriggled his hand into the birth canal and managed to slip the loop around the calf's ankle, muttering all the while, 'I think I've got it . . .' He pulled the knot tight. 'Maybe I should have done veterinary science?' The ankle came down a little but then Minkie heaved herself up to her feet. The rope dangled from the calf still inside her and Chanchal and Rafi looked on aghast as she cantered away, criss-crossing the paddock, the rope springing along the grass behind her.

'Please, *please* let's get Peter now,' said Rafi. 'You're not a farmer!'

When Peter Boil came he managed to catch her. A few grunts and she calmed down. There was nothing to brace themselves against but her rump, so the two men each put a foot on her and pulled. 'If we were in the corral we could winch the rope,' panted Peter. He looked a lot like Bob Carmichael, only a bit heavier. But he had the same warmth to him and Rafi was very glad he was in charge.

Then the three of them were needed to pull until, with a bellow from Minkie, the calf slipped out.

'She's dead!' cried Rafi, for Minkie's head was flat to the ground and her eyes closed.

'She's all right,' said Peter calmly, and carried the newborn calf to the mother's head. Minkie began to lick the calf dry and, after giving them further instructions, Peter Boil left. But once he was out of sight, the cow stopped licking the crumpled wet calf, rose, and looked to the paddock.

'She's meant to lick it dry,' said Rafi. She ran up to the kitchen and came back with salt. They sprinkled some on the calf, but it made no difference. Damp with the birth and the drizzling rain, the calf struggled to its feet to find a teat. A yellow drop clung to one.

'That's the colostrum,' said Chanchal excitedly. But when the calf tried to clamp on, Minkie jumped.

'If she'd been like this last time Bob would have warned us,' Rafi said. 'Peter will understand if we wake him up again.'

'She's just taking a while to get the hang of it.'

Rafi felt more than just a little angry with him. The calf could have died or been injured all because he wanted to play at being a farmer. She found towels and laid them over the calf. It had been born an hour and it still had not had milk.

'I'm going,' she said, and began to walk towards the

Boils' place. The house was still dark when she knocked on the front door. A woman came, and Rafi remembered her name: Susan. She had a kind look to her. Then Peter was behind her, still dressed, and they went back down to the cow and calf.

He picked the calf up and told it to suck, almost tossing the limp newborn at its mother. Obediently it struck out and Minkie stayed put.

'Seems you two don't have beginner's luck,' said Peter with a laugh, giving Chanchal a pat on the back.

Rafi turned away. She and Chanchal walked to the house, kicked off their filthy boots and slumped onto chairs in the kitchen waiting for the kettle to boil for tea.

'Do you look like your mother or your father?' asked Chanchal. He remembered Rafi getting on the bus somewhere on the way to Mimosa, and that there was a woman with her, but he'd not paid any attention to the woman, only to Rafi.

'Why are you asking me that now?' Why did she dislike him so much at this moment?

Chanchal sat back, surprised by her ferocity. 'I was just thinking about meeting your family.'

Rafi fixed her gaze on the table to avoid his eyes. 'I can't see us visiting my parents in the near future.'

Chanchal thought – What isn't she telling me about?

'You can say they don't like foreigners. It won't hurt my feelings, Rafi.' He crept a hand towards her, and she took it. 'My parents won't be happy about you, either. But we can work on that. With both our families.'

Rafi kept her eyes averted until he let go.

'Your family don't live in Mimosa, do they?' he asked.

'No,' she said. 'Out of town.' She put her tea to one side. 'Let's go to sleep, Chanchal.' Now she could look at him. She led the way to the bed, and they were both soundly asleep within minutes.

Mid-morning, as they were eating their breakfast, the phone rang. It was Clarissa. Rafi told her that Minkie had had her calf and that it was doing well. Clarissa wanted to stay another week, since both Bob's parents were in hospital now. She'd double their wages if they would stay.

'Hold on while I ask Chanchal,' said Rafi. He was already standing in the hallway waiting to hear the news.

'Can we stay another week?' she asked him.

He shrugged his shoulders as if to say, what else can we do?

After she put the phone down, Chanchal said, 'We don't want to stay here all summer!'

'No. I should have said the calf almost died and we didn't know what to do. Perhaps she'd have come back then.' At least Chanchal had agreed they'd fetch Peter as soon as the other cow went into labour.

'I need to get back to university. And I still need to

visit my uncle and cousins,' Chanchal said with some agitation. Like her, he sounded as if he'd been brooding.

'And what about my plans? It's all taking so long.'

He went to the back porch, *Guru Granth* in hand, to say his prayers.

Should I ask to join him, Rafi wondered. What does he pray for? That I not fall pregnant? Then she thought – Shut up, Rafi.

On the porch, Chanchal sat cross-legged and laid the book in front of him, opened to Japji's morning prayers.

He thought – Loving her is a good thing. Yet what I'm doing here is wrong. The few days' delay had unravelled. By helping the Carmichaels, he was neglecting his other responsibilities – he was *not* with his uncle, and he *hadn't* married Rafi to make things right for her and his family. And he couldn't concentrate on his prayers.

He heard a koel bird and looked up towards the trees. There were so many birds! Then he heard a soft footfall and here she was beside him, and so he took her hand and began to read the *rag* aloud to her.

Rafi asked him to translate some of the words. He went to the Barah Maha and read a few lines. The koels they heard each day here were present also in the book: 'The chatrik bird cries for the Lover, the koel bird sings in praise. Embraced by her Beloved, the woman savours all delights.'

'Does it really say that?' asked Rafi, surprised that a bible would be so intimate.

He continued, for she liked the poetry, though it took some minutes to think how to translate.

'Nanak says, the chatrik cries, Beloved, Beloved, and the koel is made lovely by the call.'

'Why haven't you told me that these prayers talk about birds? And this is the same bird that's over there in the trees!'

'I don't know why. There's lots I haven't told you. What haven't you told me?' He thought she might tell him what was bothering her.

But all she said was, 'What a question,' and went inside.

The new calf was up on its feet. Chanchal checked on the second cow during the day and in the evenings. They were halfway through the week before Clarissa was expected back. Chanchal was both nervous and confident about this second calving. Rafi was uninterested and wouldn't come with him to the paddock.

Her breasts were sore. She felt nauseous sometimes and only wanted to eat toast. She didn't tell him her fears and then could hardly speak for desire, once they began. No one had told her she'd *want* him just as much as he wanted her. She thought – How can I want to do what we're doing, yet be so worried at the same time? In bed, their language was free; she was a round ball of shocking colour and when she came it didn't break but flared as she rushed wet around his black shining sex. Then, early one afternoon as a cloud shadow passed over them through the windows, she said, 'I'm so ashamed.' It was a wail, unexpected and inchoate. She covered herself with the sheet, pulled it over her head and cried. She was so afraid.

Chanchal stroked her through the cloth, saying, 'Don't be ashamed, Rafi.' He thought – We have to leave. She needs to get to Melbourne soon. I'm making her miserable! With a start, Chanchal remembered her triumphant smile when she'd swung into his cabin after Brisbane. He thought – She was so happy that day.

Then Rafi came out from beneath the sheet and as they started again he hurt her a little with a thrust. Here's my chance – she thought. He would hit the thing inside her and force it out. If it were there after all. She abandoned herself, exciting him; held her breath with the pain.

But then he stopped. 'What's the matter? What on earth are you doing?'

She looked out the window but kept her hand on his beard, the black hair firm beneath her fingertips.

'Rafi?' He took her face and gently turned her to look at him.

His hair hung over her like a curtain, like a veil. 'I love you,' he said.

'Yes,' she said, fingering his face gently.

'Will you say it then?'

'I love you,' she said. 'Of course I love you!'

'And I you, more and more every day.'

How could he, more and more every day, when she was so awful, so cranky and secretive?

'Through thick and thin?' she asked.

He nodded, lips and beard brushing along her cheek, his hair tickling her shoulders and breasts.

'In sickness and in health?' She was tricking him. Only very bad girls got themselves into this kind of trouble. She felt sick in her belly.

'That's settled, then. So what's upsetting you?' he asked. He thought – Something is wrong, but Rafaela won't tell me. But then, women are moody. Is that it?

'Why are you so moody?'

'Because you keep asking me questions and talking about getting married. Hasn't it occurred to you that I didn't even want to get married? All I wanted to do was go to Melbourne and enrol in art school. I don't want to be a wife. I want to be an artist.' She sat up, hugging the sheet to her.

'And I thought all I was going to do was visit my uncle and cousins and go back to my thesis work. But we met each other. And this has happened.' He pulled on his boxers and then his trousers, flicking through his clothes for a shirt.

'Poor you,' she said.

'Be logical. We're in love, we've had sex. We want to be together.' Chanchal thought – Maybe I'm alone in this? Why can't she just tell the truth?

'Yes,' she conceded. 'We've done all that. But then you did that with the violinist too.' She flicked through her mess of clothes to find her skirt.

He looked at her, hurt that she'd spoken that way. 'Why didn't you say you were jealous? I was never in love with her.'

'I'm not jealous. I just can't help thinking that my plan to go to Melbourne, which was so simple, has gone out the window because you keep convincing me to do things I don't want to do!'

'I should never have told you about her. It didn't mean anything, really.' He shouldn't have said a word about London.

'Oh leave me alone! It's not the violinist that's bothering me,' she said. Half-dressed, she ran from the room.

'Okay, I will,' he yelled back angrily.

She ran to Bob's studio, locked herself in and sat in a corner of the hot room and cried. She heard Chanchal calling her name. After a while he stopped. Only then did she leave.

Keeping an eye out for him, she returned to the house, pulled on some sneakers and took off through the paddocks until she was well out of sight of the Carmichael farm. She sat in the shade, thinking of what she must do to herself, looking in shock at the lush hills around her.

This place had abandoned her. The short fence posts streaked black and grey were tilted like tombstones and were as wizened. She thought – I wish I was just a post, just another thing. Today, she couldn't draw these things that had been beautiful to her only hours ago. Today, she couldn't lift a pencil to draw the faded, slat-posted haysheds on miraculous and historical tilts. Deep shadows. Bundled-high clouds

Riding around the area on the bikes, they'd passed grey water towers and tanks sitting singularly in the middle of bright paddocks. She had seen rolls of barbed wire pollinating rust, and tangles of blackberry bush. Weeds, unwanted things, once wanted but not any longer. People couldn't be bothered to tell stories about broken old things. Only stories of bad girls, girls with filthy names following them down the street.

Why am I here and not in Melbourne? 'I'm a stupid thing,' said Rafi aloud. Then bang, silence.

Over there was the barn that Bob Carmichael had painted many times. She walked towards it. Twenty feet from it, the doors wide open, the barn's shonky stricken side was only half-visible. Entering, Rafi paused so her eyes could adjust to the darkness and the height of the bales in front of her. She counted them up towards the roof. They were many in number. She'd planned on this.

She climbed, digging her fingers into the matting. She felt the straw's hardness, its tight pack. Near the ceiling the smell was strong and the air hot. The floor was way, way down there. Water looked as hard as this from the high-dive boards at the Mimosa pool. She looked at the spiders' webs and the sparrows' nests matted in the roof in grey clumps. They were dusty and pocked with holes. The birds had gone from the nests. Up, down, up, down. Looking up and down made her dizzy. Rafi closed her eyes. She swayed, hoping she'd overbalance. She wobbled and her legs braced with the effort to rebalance. She wanted to break the child inside her, but rescue herself. Tricky business, she thought. To really jump she'd have to leap out into mid-air, but then she might break her neck. She thought – How do women fall down stairs, how do they do it? Twist and turn, come down crashing, legs, arms all over the shop. Hit the floor, slam, at the bottom.

The Carmichael house was single-storey.

Rafi squeezed her eyes tight, tried to let go. She needed a push.

Half-crouching she pushed out from the straw, her skirt tearing, hands grabbing. She let her arms flop, tried not to grab and waved her legs so she'd bump and fall. Her hair caught on the stiff hay and some was yanked out. She climbed again and slipped herself off the top bales fast. She did it a few times. Tufts of hay loosened. Her bruises swelled. Where was the shift in her belly, though? The gush of baby blood?

Sitting exhausted on the floor of the barn, Rafi thought

– The baby might want to live as much as I want it to die. Perhaps it's curled up on itself, arms round its head?

She left the barn, zigzagging across the green fields, dragging out the pain that every bone and all her skin felt. She crouched behind a tree and checked her pants. Not a drop. Everything hurt and reminded her of her naivety and the desire she felt for Chanchal – still. Rafi sank down amongst the cowpats and the clumps of grass, thirsty and tired. Ants were everywhere. Industrious. Purposeful. She moved away a little. She throbbed with pain. The posts, the fields around her, herself – another thing. Her hand on the ground was dirt-streaked, nail-chipped, a veiny thing that didn't look a part of her. The soil here was dry and grainy and the colour of her hand. If only she could disappear into the earth.

Rafi brooded and the ants crawled. One diverted to a dark patch, and disappeared. Rafi crawled over. It was the strangest thing, only a foot, or maybe less than a foot across. When she looked down into its blackness it was dark and cool. A very deep hole.

If she stuck her head inside, she could suffocate herself. Get her head in but not be able to wrench it out, the way it was with children and stair banisters and dogs with gates. She thought – I could choke on spiders, ants, worms, dirt, and old air all the way up from China. The last thing I'll see is nothing, just black, and my greasy hair will grow long. That's what the hair of dead people does. It keeps growing. I'll scream all the way to China down this beautiful deep hole.

China; a place not so very far from India. She didn't want Chanchal accused of beating her and then stuffing her face in a hole!

Picking scraps of hay from her hair, she decided that she didn't mean him any harm. She found a good-sized stone and dropped it down the hole, pressing her ear to the ground for the thump. She heard nothing. She'd have to come back with twine and a rock to measure its depth.

Through the early afternoon, Chanchal dug away at the earth, driving his spade down hard in simple rhythms that didn't do a thing to appease his anger. He didn't know where she'd got to, didn't understand what was bothering her, and was sick of being on this farm.

Walking back to take a drink, Chanchal saw a vehicle, a large utility with slat-panelled walls, the kind to move stock or produce in. As soon as he saw the turbaned men, he knew it was his uncle Ajit and cousins Tejpal and Uday.

'How did you find me?' he asked, walking forward to meet them, bringing his hands together in greeting. But before he could nervously bow, Tejpal and Uday grabbed him by an arm each and dragged him towards the truck.

'Let me go,' he said, trying to shake them off. He almost fell pulling away from them, telling them to stop, then calling out to Rafaela – 'Rafi, where are you? Rafi!'

'You're leaving now,' Ajit said in Punjabi, and kept saying. He waved some of Chanchal's belongings at him, his clothes already half-stuffed into his bag.

'Have you been through the house?' asked Chanchal, trying to understand what must have happened in the past hour – because where was Rafaela? Had she been here when they arrived?

'Where's Rafi?' he asked. 'The young woman, where is she? Did she let you in?' Ajit's sons had Chanchal pinned to the truck and neither of them would answer. He could feel the engine's heat against his back.

'I'm not leaving, uncle,' Chanchal said in Punjabi. 'I'm staying here. I've got a job here.'

'You've been living here with a girl you're not married to!' said Ajit, opening the door wide and gesturing angrily for Tejpal and Uday to put their cousin into the cabin.

'We're betrothed,' said Chanchal.

Tearing away from the Carmichael farm, the truck sucked the bitumen up beneath them. Chanchal was high above the road, savaged by panic, shoulder to shoulder with these cousins whom he'd never before met, wedged in the middle so he couldn't make a jump for it. When they let me out, I'm going back, he vowed. But when Ajit turned the truck onto the highway Chanchal realised they weren't likely to pull over.

No one spoke. There were no explanations or questions or accusations, and the silence between them was terrible, the truck droning louder and louder, it seemed to Chanchal, until he had to speak, to clear some of his confusion. 'How did you find me?'

'People talk. We have many friends here, you know,' said Ajit angrily. Chanchal thought – We stuck out like a sore thumb, because of me.

'We are highly regarded as hard-working honest men.'

Chanchal felt heavy with remorse. He'd been so flippant about meeting his uncle: not writing ahead to say what date he'd be arriving; speaking casually about him to Rafaela. 'I need to tell Rafaela what's happened,' he said. 'She might think I've had an accident if I'm not back soon. We're there on our own while the farmers are away.'

Ajit didn't say anything, so Chanchal tried again. 'Uncle Ajit, please, can we stop so that I can use a telephone or send a telegram?' His cousins' silence was scaring him. His uncle's silence was worse: this was his father's half-brother. What would Ajit write to ma and pa?

'Uncle Ajit, please!'

'It's no use, Chanchal. She won't be there. She's gone already.'

'Where? To Melbourne?'

'Yes, or back to her family, I don't know. What business is it of mine? She went to the station. She said she had been doing bad things and she was glad to go, that it was over between you.'

Chanchal thought – If she's gone ahead, she'll find me at the university. If she wants to, that is. Maybe this is for the best? But if Rafi hadn't gone to Melbourne, where was she then? She wouldn't go home . . .

'But the animals, the farm. We can't just leave it. There is a cow about to calve. Someone must be there to assist.'

Ajit grunted angrily. 'Tejpal can drive back and see about the cows. Now shut up!'

An hour or more passed in complete silence, until Uday asked him, 'What's this?' and touched his ring.

'You didn't marry her, did you?' Ajit asked, taking his eyes from the road to glance at the ring that his son had noticed.

Chanchal wanted to hide his hands. Everything that he had done appeared indecisive and unfinished. 'I hope to,' he said.

The men guffawed as one. He could read their thoughts – that this Chanchal was weak-willed and flighty, and not even bold enough to marry her. A 'student' exactly: unreliable, romantic, foolish. Chanchal felt their disdain.

The pressure on his shoulders and arms from sitting between his cousins held him upright. He looked only at the road, the black bitumen raging along like a long mark against his name; while they were steadfast farmers who year by year increased their land and after an exchange of photos and useful details, briefly returned home to marry good Sikh girls.

'You'll take up your studies and I'll have a letter written to Bani and Aparna about this. I'll promise to keep a close watch on you,' said Ajit.

Chanchal thought – I sound so lame.

Rafi didn't even have his address, had never asked for it. He had been a bad influence on her, making her do things she didn't want to do. Why should it surprise him that she didn't want to know where he lived? Chanchal remembered their last conversation. Her irritability of the last few days. Her reluctance to marry him. Indeed, she'd said more than once she didn't want to marry, but he'd not listened. Chanchal thought – The last thing she said to me was 'get lost'.

The house was empty. Rafi ran a bath. Afterwards she picked the wet hay out from where it had gathered in the plughole and wiped the enamel clean of the scum. Dry and naked she examined her stinging legs and arms. The bruises were coming, purple as eggplant. She had scratches galore. Her skin hurt, her heart too, but the mound of her stomach was resolute. She dabbed the cologne that Chanchal had given her on the parts that ached.

There was a field of onions planted not far from the house in a neighbouring field. Rafi walked over to it.

Foot-high stalks grew up stiff and pert, white flower balls at the top. In the late afternoon light, with the shadows beginning to reach over, she watched the field become a plate of slate green and dark purple green, like the hand-sized bruise on her flank. She didn't want to be here any longer. She thought – Bruises linger. I don't want to linger here with a thing growing inside of me.

Walking back to the dark house, she found the kitchen light needed replacing. She wondered where Chanchal was. He'd been gone a long time. She thought with a pang – What was the last thing I said to him? 'Leave me alone!' She checked the paddocks and fields where he might have been working, then went back to the house. Perhaps he had gone into town. Other than the ticks and burr of the kettle, the evening silence continued. Before all the light died, she took some hay down to where they'd corralled Queen Bee. Reluctantly she looked at the cow's back end, and was relieved to see it looked normal. She heard the faint rumble of a truck and thought hopefully – Will I recognise Clarissa's truck when it comes near? Going back to the house, she remembered that the ferns hanging in the latticed part of the veranda needed watering. As she poured, the water pooled on the flooring, splashing her feet. She swept the water across the boards to the front steps then, hearing a car's approach, looked up. But the sound disappeared, and no one came. And in that silence Rafi knew Chanchal wasn't coming back.

She went to the bedroom. Her clothes were strewn across the floor, as usual. Chanchal's things should have been folded on a chair. But the pile was gone: trousers, shorts, shirts, turbans and his canvas bag. Now she went through the house and she couldn't find his copy of the *Guru Granth* or *Heer Ranjha* or his special comb.

Then, on the kitchen dresser, she found his *Birds of Australia* and his notebook. She asked silently – Why did I say those things to you? When I love you? He'd left behind what he'd asked for from the start: her drawings. 'He's run out on me,' she said to the room, moaning it, creening, appalled. And she wished so badly that he'd left more of himself. A turban or a shirt – an explanation. She went to the laundry and threw all the clothes in the basket onto the floor and found a shirt and a turban. But no letter or note of farewell. On the veranda she found his sandals amongst the shoes. So in his hurry he'd forgotten some of his things. In his hurry to be free of her.

That night Rafaela found she couldn't sit on the veranda or in the living room to read, but only in the kitchen, with the wireless on to make some sound. She boiled water for cups of tea, the kettle clanging when she placed it on the trivet, waiting for him to come back, or for a car to pull up. When she heard the phone ring in the hallway she ran to it, only to find it had stopped. A couple more times she heard the phone ring faintly over the sound of the wireless, before she concluded she was imagining that Chanchal was phoning her. She gave the dog a bowl of milk and was glad it slept close by on the porch.

Inside the bedroom, Rafi pulled the curtains tight, afraid that someone, knowing that she was alone, would come and peek in. She collected Chanchal's belongings and put them on the bed close to her. She felt stunned, and her heart hurt. To warm it, she laid her hand over her heart, felt its fast thumping, but the physical hurt there didn't abate. It took a long time for Rafi to fall asleep.

The next morning, a turbaned man came to the door and told her, 'Chanchal has gone and he's not coming back.'

Rafaela looked at this young man who was so resolute in his demeanour. He scared her, though he was younger than her. He wore a dark brown turban and his skin was dark.

'Who are you?'

'I'm Tejpal, Chanchal Singh's cousin,' said the man. 'How's the cow?'

Rafaela thought – What's he asking me this for? 'I don't care about the cow,' she said. 'Where is Chanchal?'

'He said to tell you he's on his way to Melbourne and won't be coming back, but was concerned about the animals. Are they healthy?'

Rafi felt herself go very cold and a tremor started

through her body. She thought – Why does he keep asking about the animals and not about me?

She was aware her hand was clenching the screen door harder and harder as she said, 'The animals are fine. I'm looking after them. But why has Chanchal left like this?'

Tejpal turned away and then, when she shouted 'Why?' to him again, he looked back at her apologetically but still kept walking, and walked quicker as she moved after him. But Rafi could hardly take a step she was trembling so hard. 'I don't understand,' she said. 'Explain to me what's happened.' Her legs were slow and the ground seemed to swing. 'Why has he gone like this?' she called out.

But the young man got into his car and he wouldn't turn to face her. He kept his head bent low.

Chanchal had said he'd pay for her to get to Melbourne. He'd earned forty pounds a week cutting cane, he'd said. She remembered that he'd hidden his money underneath the bedside drawers and yes, it was there. She counted a hundred and twenty pounds out. My god, that was a lot of money to have left behind. She sat on the floor with his money in her hand and waited for her trembling to cease. He'd taken everything except the money. Did he think she was that sort of girl?

She found a bike, and pedalled away from the farm with a bag slung on her back. A warm wind blew against her and she stopped to tie her hair more tightly. She found the paddock she'd been in the day before, and walked over to the hole, the bewilderingly deep hole. Sheep grazing in the neighbouring paddock looked at her dumbly. She picked up a stone and hurled it towards them.

The hole's astounding blackness subdued her as she comprehended the absoluteness of her predicament – He has left me. I'm going to have a baby. There was no way to gloss over it. Rafi knelt and put her ear to the hole's narrow, cool depth and heard the full echo of her bereavement.

He would never see these bruises on her body. Never ask – Where did you get these? Never touch her gently. Never insist on her telling him – Chanchal, I'm pregnant. Or again say – Get your sketchbook. Do a drawing for me. See that bird? I love you, Rafaela.

Rafi emptied his belongings onto the grass, dropping the sandals down the hole first, then his shirt and a science magazine she'd found. She took his *Birds of Australia* and dropped it too down the hole. His turban: she stood up and flung the blue length of it, the yards and yards of muslin, out into the wind, and like a weathervane it held its weight, loose and flowing before quickly sinking to the ground. It was beautiful, but it had to go. Finding what this cloth had covered, touching his hair, had been her terrible seduction.

She'd keep his notebook; she had to hold onto something. She had his money, and she had his baby. She dropped the long blue cloth down into the hole last of all; her fingers simply let it go.

18

VEGETABLE PEELER IN HAND, NORMA IS CASTING OUT LONG thought-lines for her mislaid daughter in the windy evenings, fishing for the wisp of a suggestion of her girl's return. Not believing for a moment that she won't be seeing her only girl again.

Shavings of peel rise in a grey heap alongside the cut potatoes. A fine grey mist of potato spray coats the cutting board.

She's the daughterless mother, feeling the load of her lonely evenings.

She steps once again into Rafaela's room and looks at the Cezanne print. She can't imagine why her daughter liked this painting so much. She opens the desk drawer and unfolds a sketch of herself that Rafaela drew years ago. She, Norma, looks kind – she was always kind.

The room is losing the smell of her daughter, of her inks and charcoals, her perfumes, her tossed clothes. The room is changing for the worse. Norma opens a wardrobe and, taking Rafi's clothes out, hangs some of her things on the line to air. She wouldn't want them to be musty when Rafi gets back. Each day for the rest of the week Norma methodically airs what is left of her clothing, then folds the pieces away. The room recovers something of Rafaela. She tells her friends, the women she plays bridge with, what she is doing, and they understand. They take her hand.

19

THEY DROVE STRAIGHT TO MELBOURNE, STOPPING ONLY ONCE.

As they were nearing Woolgoolga, Ajit had turned the truck off the highway and driven up a muddy unmarked road. This was his uncle's banana plantation. The sun disappeared as they passed a low-slung wooden shed out the front of which ran a gaggle of white ducks. The ducks waddled to the wire fence as the truck rocked its way past on the uneven track. Banana trees clustered to the sides of the hilly drive and old palms and gums deepened the shadows. The road ended at a newly painted cottage set in a small clearing. Another narrower track led up behind it through the banana trees. Lacy curtains hung at the windows and Chanchal saw a woman push one aside. 'My wife, Neena,' said Uday, smiling when she came out a moment later. She offered Chanchal a brief *namaste* greeting and he noticed that her fingernails were painted pink.

Ajit asked her to find a car for Tejpal to use to return to the Carmichaels' farm. They talked briefly about whom she could talk to. Chanchal thought – He's right, they do have many friends. 'So Tejpal can see about the animals,' Ajit said to Chanchal. For a moment, his uncle sounded conciliatory.

Neena gave them a box with containers of food, bread and dhal, and Ajit and Uday and Chanchal resumed the journey south. Ajit had put all of Chanchal's things under his seat, so that Chanchal had nothing if he were to try to leave the truck.

At first Ajit wouldn't answer when Chanchal tried to speak of Rafaela. 'Did Rafi pack her things? Does she know what has happened to me? Won't she be worried?' he'd asked when they were driving.

Finally his uncle said, 'She went and got her belongings. She said to tell you that she understands your studies are important to you. And she feels remorse at what has happened.'

Every time Chanchal tried to speak of Rafaela they made his idiocy clearer to him. And they saw pretty quickly that the student had learnt very little about the girl. Midway through the journey, Chanchal slipped his ring off his finger and carefully put it into a trouser pocket. He thought – What an idiot I've been. She didn't even want to marry me. She was right, she just wanted to go to art school and to study. Like me.

Chanchal's landlady, Mrs Fletcher, had three children. The boy, Nicholas, was playing out on the footpath when Ajit drew alongside the house in Princes Hill. He ran back inside crying, 'Chanchal is back, Chanchal is back!' Chanchal had been gone all summer.

He hoped that Ajit would drop him off and leave, but also knew it was ridiculous to expect that. Mrs Fletcher came out of the house. She didn't speak but watched the turbaned men on the footpath, a hand over her eyes to shade them from the afternoon sun.

Ajit strode over and bowed briefly. Now all three children watched, gawking at the men. No longer abrupt, as he'd been with Chanchal the past two days, Ajit introduced himself and Uday warmly. Mrs Fletcher offered them tea and they followed her into the house. The middle child, Rose, had baked a tea cake that day with her mother, and this was offered around. Chanchal listened uneasily as his uncle told Mrs Fletcher about his banana plantation, his plans for the family's future and the potential for farming around Woolgoolga. Like Chanchal, Uday said little, occasionally making a funny face at one of the children. When Mrs Fletcher told Ajit that his nephew was no trouble and the best boarder she'd had – quiet, cleaner than she expected a student to be, reliable with the rent – Ajit interrupted. 'That's good to hear, because he's disappointed us.' Mrs Fletcher took the hint and sent the children out to the back garden.

Chanchal tried to protest, but Ajit held up his hand. 'He was running around with a girl and we've had to bring him back,' said Ajit.

Mrs Fletcher frowned at Chanchal, clearly surprised.

'I won't be seeing her down here I hope,' she said. 'If I do, you'll be out on your ear.'

Humiliated, Chanchal thought – Maybe I should move house, and sat with his head bowed.

'This is our address,' said Ajit, painstakingly writing his details in English. 'Please let me know if you think my nephew is getting into any sort of trouble, and I'll come down.' With the cake finished and the tea drunk, Ajit rose to go. Out in the street he lectured Chanchal sternly.

'What you did was wrong, Chanchal. You'll come and work with me in your holidays, and you'll not be contacting her in any way.'

His supervisor, Professor Turner, had found him this converted garage with the kitchenette in Princes Hill, just north of the university on a street that bordered the Melbourne Cemetery, and only a couple of blocks from Princes Park. Mrs Fletcher had helped him in his first days by pointing the way to the Queen Victoria Market and other places of interest. There was a little of India at the market – it was crowded with people and animals, fruit and vegetables. But while Mrs Fletcher was friendly, he understood that he was meant to keep his distance. He didn't eat with the family, and she'd scold the children if they followed him into his room.

An hour or so after his uncle's departure, Mrs Fletcher knocked. She was short and freckled and her hands holding a folded cotton rug were small and pretty with a plain wedding ring – even though Mr Fletcher hadn't been around for years, according to the children.

'I hope you won't be missing your girlfriend too much. Don't pine. It's bad for your studies. You need to concentrate.'

Chanchal was numb, and assented in an uncharacteristic mumble.

She looked around the room, which was still stuffy from being closed for so long. 'I've got a little rug you can have,' she said. Chanchal nodded his thanks listlessly, and took it. 'Your uncle's a nice man. He invited the children and me up to stay for a holiday.'

'That is nice,' Chanchal agreed, and then, partly to hide what really had happened between himself and Ajit, and because he thought it was probably true, he added, 'He's very kind, my Uncle Ajit.'

Mrs Fletcher went back inside, and Chanchal got out notepaper and pen. It wasn't good enough that Tejpal was checking on the animals, he'd need to write to the Carmichaels himself. They might even send him some of his wages. He'd write his address clearly for just that purpose. He wrote that he and Rafaela had needed to leave in a rush, but he hoped that his cousin had taken care of the animals satisfactorily, and he thanked them for his employment and their hospitality. But then he tore that letter in two, and started again.

Dear Clarissa and Bob,

I hope you have come back to the farm to find everything in order, and Bob, that your father is recuperating well. Rafaela and I left the farm separately without preparation, however my cousin did check on the stock.

I'm writing to explain that Rafi and I weren't completely honest with you, and that currently I don't know where she is or how to contact her. Could you please give me her address, if you know it, or pass on my address to her if you can?

My cane-cutting wages are hidden under the bedside drawers on the right, and I'd appreciate your sending them to me. I don't expect any payment from you for the work I did, having let you down.

My address is:

Chanchal Singh, c/- Mrs Fletcher

139 Morecroft Street

Princes Hill Victoria 3053.

Folding the letter and sealing the envelope, he thought – Where *is* she?! He wondered how angry she was. Maybe she didn't want to see him again. Perhaps, as his uncle had said, she was relieved to be free of him. He'd felt like that about Veronica. And this thought – that Rafi might feel about him as he had about Veronica, relieved to be getting away without an argument – struck him painfully.

He would give the letter a week to arrive, then he'd phone them.

Chanchal laid the rug on the floor and focused on its multiple colours: he'd not seen anything like it before.

Twists of cotton cloth were knotted with thread. He'd use it for his prayers. Perhaps that's what Mrs Fletcher meant him to do with it?

Then Nicholas came to the door with his mail. The longed-for and yet dreaded aerograms. Made of the frail paper usual for his mother Aparna's correspondence, the aerograms rustled in his hand. But there was another letter, too, ominously thick and heavily stamped. He opened that first.

Dear Chanchal,

I have enclosed a photo of a delightful girl, Mushti Kaur, whose family we recently met at the golf club. You'll see there is also a group photograph showing her standing third from the left beside her parents and brother and sister. They were visiting from Amritsar, which is why we've not heard of her before. We've spoken to the family and they are eager to discuss marriage, being very impressed with your education and prospects for university employment. Narbir Singh is an engineer, and all his children have been university educated. Mushti is in her second year of Accounting.

Bani and I have been thinking that if you could settle on a girl, we'd like you to come home to meet the chosen one during your mid-year break. It will be an expense, but well worth it.

Please let us know by the earliest mail what you think. She's very sweet, has good teeth (which you can't see in the photo) and is about average height. The family are disease and rumour-free!

Love,

Ma

It had started.

Immediately, Chanchal began on a response.

Dear Ma and Pa,

Thank you for making this effort of meeting with Mushti Kaur's family and sending me her photograph. I'm afraid, however, that while her facial structure is pleasing her skin is far too dark. I notice that all the family have dark skin. What would your grandchildren look like?!

Love,

Chanchal

Then he threw the photographs in the bin; muttered, 'Sorry, Mushti, it's not your fault.'

Between his parents, Mrs Fletcher and his uncle, he was trapped. If he were to disappear for even a night – and he thought hourly of returning to the farm – Mrs Fletcher would be on the phone to Ajit. Although his room had its own entrance up the side path, it was easy for her to look out the kitchen window and check on his whereabouts.

Disheartened, Chanchal reread his reply to his mother about Mushti. I'll write my summer holiday letter and post it separately, he thought. That way I'll distract them. He hoped that his uncle Ajit, being semi-literate, might not write at all. In which case they need never know what happened.

Then he thought – I miss her. How long am I going to feel like this? Was there even a single line of Wittgenstein that answered these questions? He placed the *Guru Granth* on the rug, deciding to read *after* he'd written the second letter. Contemplation would help.

Dear Ma and Pa,

The past two months have been hard work, but have also had their enjoyable moments. The cane cutting was strenuous and Queensland is a hot and humid state. I followed it with some fencing work in New South Wales, before meeting Uncle Ajit and my cousins Uday and Tejpal. Their banana plantation is impressive — the land fertile, and profitable. Ajit is highly organised, and has a small comfortable house which by Indian standards is a virtual palace. Uday's wife Neena cooked some delicious dhals and breads.

The pleasure I mention came from my daily birdwatching: I sighted and heard numerous koels, herons and mynas, but also birds unfamiliar to India, including a 'barking' owl, a rosy-crested pigeon, numerous babblers and ducks. I attempted to locate a lyrebird, but wasn't successful. I did see a wedge tailed eagle leave its nest to hunt. With so much bushland, forest and rainforest, rivers, coastline and lakes, Australia is a natural habitat for birds and other wildlife.

I am now back in Melbourne ready to work on my thesis again. I'll go to the university tomorrow and meet with Professor Turner.

Uncle Ajit has invited me to come up to his farm each holiday, an offer I'll certainly take up. He has also invited my landlady, Mrs Fletcher, and her three children. (As I said in an earlier letter, I'm not sure what happened to Mr Fletcher. Not all women here wear widow's clothes, and I don't want to intrude by asking.)

Love to you both, and to Nilima, Susheela and Sarla and my nieces and nephews,

Chanchal

20

RAFAELA STOOD TALL WITH HER ARMS BY HER SIDES, breathing evenly to keep the tears at bay, until the blue truck was parked and the girls had jumped out and there was lots of noise to hide herself in. Bob Carmichael wasn't with them.

'How are things?' Clarissa asked. She shook out her skirt which, in the heat of the drive, had stuck to her legs. She looked glad to be home. 'Thanks for staying on. Bob's mother's breaks aren't as bad as they could have been. His dad's a little better. So, fingers crossed.'

'The calf is doing well, but Queen Bee hasn't had hers yet.' Rafi was only repeating what she'd said the other night. It was as much as she could say. 'And Chanchal went through that load of timber,' she added.

'Is he about?'

Rafi turned away and pulled a bag out from the back of the truck. 'He had to go on to Melbourne,' she said, as casually as she could.

'Oh,' said Clarissa, surprised. 'Do your parents know?'

'I hope you don't mind,' Rafi lied. 'I rang them a couple of times to tell them how we were going.' Her voice felt stiff in her mouth and not breezy and cheerful as she'd intended. 'I'll meet up with him there. He finished the fencing and we thought he should go.'

'I'm sorry to have put you two out like that,' said Clarissa. 'I should have rung you more often so you could have said.'

Rafi shrugged. 'It's fine.'

'So now you have to travel down there on your own.'

Rafi nodded, then ran up the steps with the bag before Clarissa could ask any more questions.

Clarissa was as she remembered, but more so. She was all-embracing, her face confident and open and interested in everything Rafi had to say, standing tall with her bare legs tanned, toenails red, eyes open and about to see straight through to her secrets. Rafi both did and didn't want to talk to Clarissa; she barely knew the woman.

Thea and Amelia were at Clarissa to come and look at the calf, Thea clapping a hand over Amelia's mouth so that she alone could talk. Amelia struggled free. They'd grown in the few days, it seemed to Rafi. As she had.

It only took her a moment to pack her bags and then throw them onto the veranda. She'd already washed the sheets that morning to get rid of his traces, though hanging them over the clothesline she'd found a long strand of Chanchal's hair. Once Clarissa had rested, she'd ask her to drive her to town or to the bus stop. From the garden she could see Clarissa and the girls with the cows. The girls fetched hay, and Minkie and some others ate from their outstretched hands with the calves hovering nearby. Amelia was nervous, pulling her hand back each time. Clarissa rested her hands on her daughter's shoulders.

Rafi thought – It's just a matter of biding my time until it's all over. I'll have the child adopted. Live in one of those places girls stay at until it's born.

Hidden by the large sheet, she sank down onto the grass and cried. Then she wiped her eyes with her skirt and went inside to put the kettle on for Clarissa. But it was already boiling, steam puffing out, so she made a pot and took herself down to the paddock to call them in.

When Clarissa saw her bags, she told Rafi she couldn't leave yet as the train wasn't coming through for two days.

'I'll stay at the pub,' said Rafi.

'We can't have that. You stay on in the caravan.'

It was a relief, after all, not to have to go right away. Over tea and biscuits, and cordial for the girls, Rafi told her about the calf's birth. Amelia and Thea munched and gulped on either side of her, hanging off the edge of the table by their elbows, swinging their legs and asking questions. They couldn't be still. 'We've been driving for hours,' Clarissa said. Rafi liked them, she'd liked them from the first minute of meeting them, and felt herself relax a little. She touched Amelia's hair briefly when the girl spoke to her. Then they ran off to the chook pen, excited to be home again and not cooped up in hospitals and hotel rooms.

Clarissa handed over their dirty clothes. In the laundry Rafi lit a match to start the gas and began to sort the clothes into coloureds and whites.

Clarissa came and stood in the doorway. 'Tell me again your arrangements with Chanchal. Where are you meeting him?'

'Melbourne. I have it written down somewhere.' For the life of her she couldn't remember the name of a single suburb.

'Surely you know?'

The tub was filling noisily. Clarissa leant against the doorjamb with the light coming in behind her so that a halo hung suspended around the loose surface of her hair. Rafi thought – I'd need fine threads of paint for that.

'I'm getting forgetful. I should have bought some meat. Chanchal is a vegetarian. Do you think I could be anaemic?'

'Yes, you could be anaemic.'

Rafi turned to the tub and began to prod the clothes down with a long spoon.

On the way back to the house she picked up a dirty-heeled sock belonging to one of the girls. She looked about her blankly, forgetting what she'd come for. She thought – I could tell Clarissa everything. A woman like her will understand how this could have happened. But what *had* happened? Why had he gone without even saying goodbye, or leaving her a note?

That night she read Amelia a bedtime story. There was some comfort in doing this. She'd not come into the room while the Carmichaels were away, but now she looked about her at the girl's things before turning off the lamp. Everything was arranged for a child's entertainment and consolation: the small woven cane lamp that was Amelia's night-light, the yellow gingham curtains which, missing curtain rings, hung crookedly. A row of wide-eyed dolls sitting along a low bookshelf. From the family's travels Amelia had brought home a Russian babushka doll and a wooden Dutch girl in clogs with a stiff red skirt and articulated limbs. Rafi sat with Amelia until the girl fell asleep, feeling safe, as though if she didn't move, the pain wouldn't begin again.

When it came time to leave for the train station two days later, the girls clung to Rafi beside the truck, wrapping their bare legs around hers, ordering her to stay.

'I'll write you a letter,' she said. 'I'll visit.' That was a rash offer. Rafaela let their uninhibited dismay make it impossible to talk.

In the truck, Clarissa took an envelope from her handbag.

'Here's more of your wages,' she said.

'What you've already paid me covers it,' Rafi said.

'Take it. You'll need it.'

She could tell that Clarissa didn't think very highly of

Chanchal right now. And Clarissa was right; she would need the money. And Rafi was thinking less highly of Chanchal herself. Coward, she thought, to leave without warning. Without a letter, or explanation. And then to send his cousin.

Clarissa drove, an elbow out the window, silent now. Rafi turned slightly to look at her. Whatever she was thinking of was making her mouth fall at the corners and her back, usually so straight, slump.

Another mile passed, then Clarissa called out to the girls, who were riding in the pan, 'You okay?'

'Yes,' they yelled back.

At the train station, Rafi thought – Bravery can hide fear. That's what I have to do, be brave even though I'm very, very afraid.

Then, on the platform, she looked north up the lines of steel and wondered if she should, after all, return to Petal Bay. But it wasn't possible; perhaps it had been two weeks ago, but not now. How could she possibly tell them what had happened? Rafi could see her mother's disgusted, disappointed look as clearly as if she'd drawn it in a study for her next portrait. And there'd be the appalled glances of women in the street. The gossip of their neighbours. Sean staring over the fence. Her dad's anger. Rickie shaking his head. And at the end of all that, an unwanted coloured baby.

But she also dreaded taking her seat on the train. Rafi thought – I won't bawl, won't cry, as they walked towards her carriage. Clarissa helped the girls to step across the wide gap between the platform and the high metal step. They hurried. The train was leaving within minutes. The horn sounded.

This was Rafi's last chance to change her mind, to beg Clarissa to let her stay.

'Telephone if you've forgotten anything.'

'Thanks.'

Rafi waved to them once they were back on the platform, wincing as she smiled.

2I

CLARISSA DRIVES BACK TO THE FARM, NOT CONVINCED FOR A minute that all is right with that girl. The pair of them didn't make sense together, from the start. An Indian and his young Australian wife? Not likely.

She stops at their drive, and Thea clambers down to collect the mail. She moves off in the truck, the dog coming down the drive to meet them, while Thea follows in her own good time, the way she likes to.

Thea gives the spider in the box a poke with a dry old weed to make it curl up, then quickly takes hold of the few small envelopes, and bends to scratch an itchy bite on her leg. She doesn't notice that she's dropped one of the letters. It flutters down into the grass, white against the green.

That night, when Rafi's train is heading towards Albury, and Clarissa is again on the phone to Bob, half a mind still on the question of Rafaela's and Chanchal's sudden exits, a bit of a westerly comes up. Clarissa says goodbye to Bob, and shuts the girls' windows so their curtains won't flap and frighten them.

Chanchal's brief note of apology and explanation is carried by the wind into the long grass down by the road, where there's a ditch, and where no one goes.

22

As evening turned to night, Rafi sank down into her seat, unwilling to look around at the other passengers, though aware that there were very few. She could hear laughter from a woman and some men rising over the clatter of wheels, but those passengers were far behind her. She closed her eyes, nauseous from the drive to the station and now the movement of the train.

She thought – It's the pregnancy doing this. It's not knowing what to do. I'll have to see a doctor, or go to a hospital and they'll tell me what I have to do. Even if it's awful, I'll have to do it. When I've had the baby and it's gone, I'll be back to myself. Then I can do what I want.

Clarissa had given her a canteen, sandwiches and even a cotton blanket, which she wrapped around herself. Then, dozing, she sensed a man standing near. She could smell his beery breath. Was he close? She couldn't hear him, the sounds of metal and wheels and the rush of air was too loud. She was so tired. She thought – I'm dreaming, go away. Then she sensed him rise and retreat. After a few minutes more Rafi opened her eyes and, neck stiff with anxiety, swung a glance around the empty seats beside her. The noisy party up the back was still going. It had been a bad, bad dream. She thought – I don't want to be alone like this. And pulled the blanket tighter around her.

Some hours later she woke again with a start. Her mouth was dry and burning down the back of her throat. She checked her watch. It was two a.m. and she'd not drunk anything since boarding. She'd need to fill her canteen from the dispenser, though she didn't want to move. Stumbling sleepily down the aisle, gripping the seats to steady herself against the rocking of the train, she saw the men and girl were gone. She didn't wonder about their bags lying amongst the party litter, the beer cans and empty chip and cigarette packets.

The rumble of the train's wheels and engine was louder than the clang of the thick door, so they didn't hear Rafi enter the carriageway, though the girl saw her after a moment, saw Rafi's stare of fright. And the girl's eyes, glassy with drink and pleasure, didn't change in expression. Her pale sodden eyes held Rafi's. A smile strayed across her lips, her mouth half-hidden by her long hair, thick tendrils of which were falling over her shoulders. Perhaps she smiled at Rafi's shame. One of the men pushed himself slowly in and out of her, while the other man, standing behind her, gripped her small bare breast, raddish white. The girl's scuffed pump hung precariously from her toes and, in a strange act of composition, her naked arm reached languorously up, fingers curling towards Rafi: *come closer*.

Three cans of beer stood apart on the floor and then one fell over, releasing its smell of hops, the brown liquid chasing across the metal floor. The black-haired man looked up from the girl's neck and saw Rafi. She turned, heaved the carriage door open and ran to her seat. Grabbing her belongings, she pushed her way down into the next car then the next, afraid the men would haul her back to where the girl was grinding and humping. She flung herself down into a seat near some sleeping passengers, her back against the window so that she could see the men's approach and kick them away. She found herself retching and struggled out of the narrow space and down to the next set of toilets. Sliding the lock tight, Rafi steadied herself against the wall, vomiting into the bowl until her arms were too weak to hold her up.

She wept at having been beckoned by the girl, as if she knew about Rafi's shame, as if it were visible. Rinsing out her mouth, every limb shook. She thought – I don't know how to stop myself from crying. I don't know what to do.

The train wasn't moving. Were they at a station? She couldn't tell through the frosted window, so she scrambled up, her bags swinging and bumping behind her. Yanking open the exit door, Rafi saw how brilliant and numerous were the stars. She leapt, legs scissoring, into the giant puzzle of the night.

23

Some days she hates Carlo, will not share a bed with him, and comes into Rafi's room to sleep. Her four sons are no antidote to the terrifying loss. Where is she? Is she safe? Norma is waiting for a letter, a word or a sighting.

Lying on her back, unable to sleep, she relents. It's not his fault. She walks through the silence and the dark back to her marriage bed. Tucking her nightgown neatly along her legs, Norma folds herself close to Carlo. His rackety old breath is a comfort in the empty house.

24

THE RAIL PLATFORM WAS JUST A SIGNAL BOX, A three-walled waiting room, if it was even that, and a broken-doored phone booth. Rafaela dropped her bags on the empty platform and lay down with the blanket covering her and her head on her duffel. She didn't think she'd sleep, but she did until the light began to come up. Then she walked over to the phone booth. The handset hung loose, and Rafi's heart sank. But when she replaced it and dialled, a telephonist's crackly voice asked, 'What number, please?' Rafi read out the farm's number, waking Clarissa sharply at five a.m.

While she waited for Clarissa, Rafi sat beneath the trees. She read, she watched a family of magpies, ate the oranges she'd been given. She'd have waited two, three days for Clarissa, if she'd had to. There was no way she was getting back on the train – either direction – north back home or south to Melbourne.

Rafi had all day to think – I owe it to Clarissa to give her some sort of explanation. She'll expect it.

Clarissa took it easy with her. Didn't demand too much in the first half-hour. They just drove. Rafaela wound the stiff window right down. Her humiliation felt lighter with the breeze whipping her tears dry. The big seat was broad enough to sit cross-legged on. She felt safe in the truck, on the road, safe though she was with a woman she barely knew.

It was hard saying the words aloud. Rafi cleared her throat, wiped the tears that began to ease out yet again – said that Chanchal had left without a word, without even a note, before she could tell him she was pregnant. 'And what's more, we weren't even married. We had an argument and he went! I'd said too many times that I didn't want to be a wife, and eventually he believed me, I guess.'

'Why do you think you're pregnant?' asked Clarissa.

'I haven't had my period.'

'You could be late because of all the changes and the travelling.'

Rafi thought this over. 'I feel different. I feel queasy all the time.'

'That could be nerves,' said Clarissa. 'But if you are pregnant, you're not the first to have this happen to you – you know that, don't you?' And then, 'We must find him and let him know.' She seemed as surprised that Rafi hadn't thought of this as she had been when Rafi said she was pregnant. 'You've simply had a misunderstanding.'

For a short moment Rafi believed her – that it was all a misreading.

'No, no, it's more than that. The next morning his cousin turned up and told me Chanchal didn't want to see me again.'

'Really? How strange. That means he told his family about you . . . What should we do, then?' Clarissa frowned, pulled off the road under some trees and stopped the engine. 'Well, it's time to tell your parents. You'll need to go home. Simply explain everything to them. I'm sure they'll understand.'

Rafi wailed, 'They won't. They won't! They'll send me away somewhere out of sight and they'll never forgive me. My father gets so angry. My mother too. Don't you think I've thought of that?'

'Well, what are we going to do?' said Clarissa, more to herself, as if the 'we' was now she and Bob, not she and Rafi. 'Chanchal is obviously not capable of looking after you and a baby, wherever he is. Sending his cousin. What kind of behaviour is that?' Clarissa sounded angry.

'I'll have the child adopted and then I'll do what I left home to do, enrol in art school.'

'Adopt?' Clarissa drummed her fingers on the steering wheel. 'You know – well, I fell pregnant to a fellow I thought I was in love with. Long ago, in Sydney.'

'Is that Thea?' asked Rafi, shocked.

'No, not Thea. Before her,' said Clarissa. Though they were parked in the shade of a tree, the air was stifling. Was Clarissa red-faced from the heat or from distress? Rafaela put her hand onto Clarissa's. She thought – How feeble I am. Stupid and needy and useless to this woman. But then Clarissa took her hand and held it, as if it helped.

'A boy. It seemed wrong to give him his own name, but then I couldn't stop myself and called him Peter. I'd always imagined I'd have a son called Peter.'

'Where were your family?'

'My parents were on a dairy farm. They'd sent me to Sydney, to a hospital where others like me lived until the birth. Peter's father was a young man who was living in Katoomba for a month or so.'

'Does Bob know?'

'Oh yes. But no one else. Not the girls.' Clarissa covered her face with her brown, strong hands. She took a breath. 'It's the worst feeling in the world, wondering where your child is.'

But Rafi was adamant. 'I want to go to Melbourne and paint. I can't have a baby. Perhaps I should go to Sydney and have it?'

'No!' said Clarissa emphatically, and turned the key to start the truck up again. 'Hideous place that was.' A curra-wong landed noisily on the bonnet, beak clacking on the metal as it attacked a dragonfly. It was rapacious and the two women watched it solemnly. Then it flew off. Clarissa pulled out onto the road, saying, 'The dragonfly is a friend of the garden. I wrote that in a column once.' She wiped her eyes with the back of her hand, and they set off back to the farm. 'Let's go home, and you can have a rest and think things through.'

'What will Bob say, though?' asked Rafi. He had his parents to worry about already.

'I think he'll feel the same as I do, Rafi.'

Rafi closed her eyes and remembered a few of the times she and Chanchal had felt the same. Yet another tear leaked out as she let the road back to the farm travel beneath her. She'd let Clarissa and Bob fix things. Maybe she could stay with them until the baby was born.

A week later Bob was back from Sydney. Given that he'd be travelling up and down the coast for the next few months because of his parents' ill health, it seemed a good idea if Rafi stayed on to help Clarissa. Clarissa and Bob insisted she let her parents know she was safe. Rafi agreed, as long as she didn't have to tell them where she was.

She wrote:

Dear Mum and Dad,

I'm writing to let you know that I'm safe and well, and I'm sorry you've probably been worried sick about me. I can't tell you where I am as I don't want you to send Rickie or the others to find me like you did a month ago.

Please tell Rickie I'm making my own plans now.

Love,

Rafaela

They then drove into town to do the shopping and post the letter. 'No, you can't read it,' said Rafi, holding the envelope tight so Clarissa couldn't see the address.

Clarissa was wondering what she'd said. 'Nothing unpleasant? No accusations?'

'No! I just said that I was safe and well.'

'Did you say where you are, or what you're doing?'

'No.'

'I think you're being unkind, saying so little,' was Clarissa's response; her harshest words yet.

And then Clarissa took her to Dr Rowse, blithely introducing her as her niece.

'Your first?' he asked kindly as the needle slid in for the blood test.

Rafi winced, and mumbled, 'Yes.' She thought – Never, never am I going to let myself go through this humiliation again.

The phone call from Dr Rowse came, and Rafi was right. Against all the odds of her dates and the one and only time unprotected with Chanchal, her jumping from the bales, and then his disappearance, and her resolute vision of herself as an artist, she was pregnant. It didn't make sense, it was so damn unfair, but there it was.

Rafaela earned her keep. She was industrious. She minded Amelia while Thea was at school, giving Clarissa time to write her articles and even visit the State Library in Brisbane for a few days at a time to research a book on an early woman botanist. She helped with the farm chores and the cooking. With Bob, Rafaela learnt to stretch and seal canvases, and cycled, increasingly round-bellied, on *plein air* painting trips. They painted the barn in which she'd jumped from the haystack, but she didn't say anything. Nor did she mention to him the hole in the field, though they passed it many times. She ignored the sturdy new fencing that Chanchal had erected. She read from Bob's biographies, catalogues and artists' manifestos. She thought – I'm getting ready to go to Melbourne. Next year, I'll be there. She had Chanchal's money hidden away with the money she'd taken from home. More than two hundred pounds. What little she spent, she drew from the wages they'd earnt working for the Carmichaels. She tacked her drawings to the walls of the caravan. It didn't remind her of him anymore. She learnt how to drive the truck. She sat for her car licence and got it long before her stomach was too large to fit behind the steering wheel.

Clarissa was determined to make Rafi more self-reliant. While Rafi thought – I'm cocooned here. I'm safe here. And kept everything difficult at a distance.

She didn't go into town much. Didn't want a finger pointed at her: That's the girl who was with the Indian. Sometimes a thought crept through – My parents must miss me. Or – I want Chanchal to be with me, so much.

The pain of missing her mother, the even greater hurt of missing Chanchal, wormed through her. But she'd been winded by the drama of his going, and the details of her last days with Chanchal took on the characteristics of an album of snapshots with too many of the pictures missing. And then she began to dream – dreams big with meaning in that way of deep review that can come to a woman during gravidity – and she decided to return to the field where she'd flung his things, even as she thought – Why do I want to go there? It's black, it might as well be empty. I won't see anything.

She cycled out alone one winter morning. Knees on the dew-wet tussocks, leaning over the all-the-way-to-China hole, nothing was visible. Just as she'd expected. Nothing but the unforgiving darkness below. Everything that had been his was long swallowed by the black air inside. Putting her ear close she heard the same fibrous rushing silence as before; reverberations, perhaps, from a subterranean spring. With rain and the shrinking work of time, his turbans and shoes had fallen down to where the earth was molten and remorseless. Or perhaps they'd been caught in a spring and swept away. She rose slowly. She thought – It's just old air and dirt, and empty. But I'm not!

She was full, and happy, she realised. The taut skin of her stomach tingled, the dizziness of rising passed, she felt the kicks from within. I like this baby, she thought.

She stalked the fence line to find the break she'd used to get through only ten minutes before. They were allies now.

25

CARLO CARRIES AN ENVELOPE IN HIS GLOVE BOX. AT THE truck stops he pulls three photos of her from it to show the other drivers. Standing in the shade of a tree or a station awning, he asks the men to take a look, to keep an eye out for her. Some have seen Carlo's photographs already. She doesn't change. In each portrait she is black-haired and a little blurry. Her sun-squint and smile are the same each time.

He blames himself. They try to tell him, No, that's what some girls do. Run off. Sometimes the men talk as if these girls are wayward pets. Or as if it's inevitable that some daughters disappear.

When her letter comes it is a shock. Like a bolt from the blue. Norma is out playing bridge and he's at home in the afternoon when the post arrives. He doesn't recognise the handwriting, which is large and shapely. Is this a trick? Is this Rafaela writing to them? Norma will know if this really is her writing. What he understands is that *Rafi doesn't want to be found. She's free of us.*

26

BANI SINGH'S HEART MAY BE PLAYING UP AGAIN. HE FEELS sickly today, and stays resting in the armchair beside the fireplace, enjoying the heat on his face, but worrying it may be too strong for his heart.

He had a dream last night that he was cycling amongst hundreds of other cyclists, all riding bikes made by his company, the Ludhiana Cycle Company, but that he was travelling down a slope faster and faster, and his bike had lost its brakes. When he woke his heart was beating too fast. Then Aparna woke, acute to his sighs of distress.

Aparna is reading a letter from Chanchal and another from his half-brother Ajit, and then looks at him in a very agitated way. But she folds the letters away and says, 'Have you had your pills this afternoon, Bani?'

27

WHAT WAS ROCK SOLID WAS HOW A LAB WORKED, THE rhythms of the laboratory days, the separating, distilling and mixing; the pattern of the shapes of the lab even – the long benches studded with bottles and distilling glasses, burners, racks of test tubes, and his bench area and stool for writing up notes. What wasn't solid was himself. Chanchal arrived back at the university disconsolate, with little in the way of funds for the year and a pervading sense of having disappointed Rafaela and himself.

Another student, Richard, was at his bench, vigorously scratching his head. Chanchal went past him and knocked on the door of their supervisor's office, but Professor Turner wasn't in. The new term hadn't started and the university was quiet, with only a few postgraduates like himself and Richard around in the science labs.

'Richard, you're doing it!' Chanchal sang out from his side of the room. Richard had asked the others to let him know if he scratched; it was his nerves, he said. As a consequence his dandruff was rabid.

Chanchal's thesis was on the biochemistry of cellulose digestion by ruminants, examining a hypothesis he had devised with his professor concerning how ruminants converted cellulose into energy. Or to put it bluntly: what happened to grass in the gut?

Turner was himself capable of converting from cordiality to anger within minutes. Chanchal thought of him as a biochemical event made human. It made for a tense lab some days. When they'd first met, he'd said, 'Not that I'm saying this of you, given the high praise from Professor Julian and the scholarship, but I've found that past Indian doctoral candidates, wealthy chaps brought up by servants, have been less than satisfactory in the lab. I've had too many Indians here expecting others to do the hard yakka.'

This riled Chanchal. He knew for a fact that Turner had only had two other Indian postgrads; maybe one of them had been a disappointment.

'I'm not afraid of long hours, professor,' he'd said in response. But he had no intention of defending India by becoming Turner's lackey.

Routinely, at the end of the week, along with the other students, he'd show Turner the week's write-up notes. Turner could be complicated, but Chanchal was soon used to his needs. His professor was strict but knew his science. 'The outcomes, mate,' said Turner, tapping with his pen – always teaching and always keeping Chanchal at arm's length, completely the opposite of Professor Julian – 'the outcomes are only as good as your method.'

For now, Chanchal had to remind himself of what he

was up to with his work, and sat on his stool to read over the previous months' work, and to re-read the first clumsy draft of a paper he was co-writing with Turner. Then he heard the sound of footsteps approaching along the thick polished linoleum outside.

'Morning, Professor Turner,' Chanchal said loudly when Turner came through the open lab doors. Richard quickly brushed his dandruff off the bench. Chanchal thought – At least I'm not a nervous wreck like Richard. How's he going to make it through his doctorate in one piece?

'You look pale, Singh,' said Turner by way of greeting. 'You need a holiday.'

Chanchal gave him a small smile and followed him into his office.

Within a fortnight, the letter he had dreaded came.

Dear Chanchal,

I can hardly believe what Ajit tells me, that you ran away with an Australian girl. Is this true? I have to believe him. I haven't discussed any of this with Bani as he's not been well and has been needing to spend time at the hospital having more checks done on his heart. They've adjusted his medication again. So I haven't told him anything of what Ajit wrote: that he was obliged to leave his farm and drive for some days searching you out; and that he then immediately returned you to your lodgings in Melbourne. Can all this be correct? I have to believe it is, as why would Ajit write such nonsense?

And why would he want to share his concerns with Mr Chandra-Singh, who wrote the letter for him in Woolgoolga, given he's not that literate as you well know, unless it was all true and he felt it important we know?

He's assured me that you didn't marry the girl, and that she has gone from your life. I'd like confirmation by return post that you are not already married.

All this brings the matter of your marriage to greater urgency. Bani and I took your point that Mushti and her family were dark, though I think you're being far too particular. Now that I've had Ajit's letter, I can only say to you that no Indian girl will be as fair as an Australian, and to put that expectation out of your mind.

The enclosed photograph shows Mohini alongside her father and mother. An only child, they are concerned that she marry well and happily. She achieved high marks in her Education exams, is now a teacher, speaks English fluently, and as a younger woman trained in Indian classical singing. If you are interested, and please make an effort, I shall send you further details of her family. Quite frankly, I'm too tired to write any more now as I am so very disappointed in you.

At the letter's end she underlined her 'love' as if to say that he obviously cared less for her and Bani than they cared for him. She's right to recriminate, Chanchal thought.

She'd asked for an immediate response, and so he wrote:

Dear Ma,

I'm sorry to hear that Pa is not well and I'm thinking of him daily in my prayers. I'm very sorry to be adding to your troubles and understand that it must be a burden not to be able to speak to Pa of your worries about me.

I can confirm that I'm not married. Please don't worry any longer. I am on the straight and narrow and back at university, which is my sole focus.

For this reason, I cannot think of marriage right now. I shan't share with you any of my grief, but it's there.

(And I can't help noticing that Mohini seems quite old. Is she close to thirty already?)

Your ever loving son,

Chanchal

Chanchal walked down to the GPO on Spencer Street. He stood in line, looking about him in the dim high-ceilinged building. In front of him were old and young people, Australians and migrants. Some were office workers with business mail and parcels to send. Wherever she is, she can write to me here, he thought, and moved one person forward in the queue. He wanted to open the other letter up again and re-read what he'd written. But he knew well enough what he'd said, and the relief that came with writing his apology.

Dear Rafi,

I'm so sorry that you had to spend more days on the farm than you wanted to and that I delayed your coming to Melbourne. I've been selfish and irresponsible, and if you could see your way to being my friend again, I'd be very, very glad. I hope you can forgive me.

My Uncle Ajit insisted I leave with him, and is now keeping a close eye on me. But this is all beside the point. I care for you a lot, and hope that you have found good accommodation and a place to study. Please write to me, and let me assure you I won't pressure you any more about anything at all.

Sincerely,

Chanchal

At the top right of the page, he'd written his address at the Fletchers'. Whether she would think to come to the GPO, Chanchal didn't know. He tapped the letter to Rafi and the other one to his parents against his hand. Whether or not there was a letter for him from her here today, he'd post the one to India and leave the one for Rafi at the post office.

He wondered again if she was in Melbourne and, if so, whether she would come to the GPO. Maybe, by some act of fate, they'd meet in this very building. For a wistful moment, Chanchal imagined surprising her.

Another week passed. There was no response to his letter to the Carmichaels, and he held back from writing again. He'd done enough harm. He had already tried ringing but there had been no answer. If she wanted to find him, she could contact him through the university or the post office. If she didn't, he would respect her wish.

He went a few more times to the GPO, queued again, and wrote down his name so the young man at the counter could find any letter for him easily. But not once was there anything for him. Everyone who knew Chanchal knew where he lived.

He posted a second letter to Rafi, just in case the first had gone astray, again care of the GPO. But he was pessimistic about it, though he'd toiled over each unsatisfactory word. Perhaps she'd received the first letter, and didn't wish to reply? In which case, what should a second letter say?

Dear Rafi,

Did you get my first letter? If not, I'd like to say how sorry I am that I insisted you stay on the farm when you wanted to be in Melbourne. I was selfish and irresponsible. If you're in Melbourne, I'd be very, very glad if we could be friends again. I hope to be able to apologise and explain in person, or by letter if you prefer, everything that happened the day that I left. Please, please write.

Love,

Chanchal

He hoped the postal workers didn't read the dead letters. It shamed him to think of his missives being read by anyone other than Rafaela.

After a few weeks his friend Vikram heard he was back, and came to the lab in search of him. Vikram Kirpal was a biology student from Calcutta and the previous year they'd started meeting for morning tea in the cafeteria. Vikram loved cricket and would turn up with the sports pages under his arm. He'd then taken to VFA and immediately convinced Chanchal to come to the games with him on Saturdays at the Carlton ground. Before long Chanchal was as voluble as Vikram and the rest of the Saturday crowd. At the International Club they had met two sisters, Joanna and Robyn. Vikram now told Chanchal that he and Joanna had started dating after he'd returned from Queensland.

'I've been taking her out with the money we earnt,' laughed Vikram. She was a graduate and demonstrator in the chemistry department, but didn't earn much, and Vikram was rather proud of his flamboyant wooing. 'Now I've been offered use of a holiday house in the bush at Kinglake. But we need a chaperone. Could you come?'

'Why doesn't Robyn go?'

'She will, but she doesn't want to be the odd one out.'

Chanchal shook his head. What was Vikram really after? 'It doesn't sound right,' he said. 'Two couples alone in the bush.'

'You're not going as a couple, neither of us is,' insisted Vikram. 'We'll have separate sleeping arrangements.' Vikram was tall and lean with a sharp nose and twinkly eyes. He was very good at his science, though he gave the impression of being a lightweight. Right now he was looking at Chanchal pleadingly. Chanchal thought – I know how he's feeling.

'Okay, I'll come, but only because I want to do some bushwalking.'

'Yeah, yeah. Bring your binoculars.'

Having lost his first pair to the Carmichaels, Chanchal had needed to buy new binoculars, and another copy of *Birds of Australia*.

The arranged weekend came.

'How was your week?' Joanna asked him from the front seat of Vikram's borrowed car. She leant over to look at him.

'Good,' he answered. 'Nothing unusual.'

'Tell them about your visits to the abattoir, Chanchal,' said Vikram.

Twice a week Chanchal visited the abattoir near the Flemington Racecourse to buy fresh stomachs for his cellulose experiments. He'd cut through the cemetery early in the morning rather than take a tram to uni – he had to save money given that he was living solely on a scholarship – and get the esky and dry ice from the lab, then catch the tram to the abattoir. The meat workers knew him and passed the offal over without delay. It was very important that it be fresh. Sometimes rabbis were there, ritually bleeding their cattle and sheep.

Sitting alongside the other passengers on his way back to the lab, the heavy esky on the floor between his feet, Chanchal wondered that no one ever asked him where he was going with his picnic hamper. But now, given the opportunity to describe his routine to the girls, Chanchal baulked.

'It's all about blood and offal, and if I were to tell you, we'd all get carsick.'

The others laughed, and left it at that. The women knew he and Vikram were vegetarians.

They were awhile on the Heidelberg Road before it became another road that Chanchal didn't catch the name of. He'd gone on some drives with people from the International Club who liked to bushwalk, though he'd not met any other amateur ornithologists. Robyn and Joanna were locals, and Joanna told him about the old bushland areas and what had been cleared for the mixed farms in the area, explaining that they supplied many of the vegetables for the market wholesalers in town. Joanna had always been the friendlier of the two sisters, even before Vikram had started dating her.

When the road turned to dirt, they wound their windows up to keep out the dust.

'Wouldn't want a heavy rain this weekend,' observed Chanchal. 'We'd be bogged in.' Then they were driving on a rock-strewn fire trail up the mountain, through tall trees, and the air was singing with the warm day and the sharp smell of eucalyptus oil that he'd come to know and like a great deal.

'Eucalyptus oil in the leaves of the trees,' Robyn explained. Chanchal thought – I won't tell her I know all that. She was friendly but it was clear that she didn't expect they were going to be close friends, let alone anything more than that.

The shack was actually a house set back a little from the bush. It had a frail veranda and, inside, an open fire-place and small kitchen. There was a toilet some distance away. Each of the two bedrooms had metal bunks. A note at the sink asked visitors to fetch their own water from the creek for cooking, and recommended boiling it. They walked around the place, Vikram congratulating himself on his friend's generosity. 'Luxury, ain't it,' he said in an Indian-Cockney voice.

'I think it's all right,' Joanna said, bouncing a moment on her bunk to test the mattress.

'What he means is that this holiday shack is better than what most Indians live in,' said Chanchal. He and Vikram put their bags in the second bedroom.

They were going to have a barbecue that night, so they trailed through the bush picking up kindling for a fire, Vikram and Joanna together. Chanchal didn't mind to begin with, but then, as he and Robyn returned to the house and there was no sign of the other two, he thought – I could have been here today with Rafi and the other two if I hadn't mucked it up on the farm.

'Do you know how to light a fire?' Robyn asked. Chanchal smiled at her – he didn't want to seem morose.

'Not one of these,' he said and considered for a moment telling her he'd been brought up with servants in a house with electricity.

She placed the kindling and scrunched paper amongst

a heap of carefully placed stones. She sat on her haunches and said, 'This'll do well.' Then she started wrapping potatoes and corn in foil and cutting up onions. Vikram and Joanna arrived with a huge bundle of kindling and Chanchal thought – All they did was walk further afield and get more kindling. He'd assumed they were up to more than that. When he had some time alone with Vikram, his friend said, 'I want to ask Joanna to marry me.'

Chanchal felt a stab of jealousy. 'But you've only known her a few months. And what about your parents?' Then he thought – I was far more impetuous! Why am I saying this?

'She's the one for me, Chanchal. Don't you think she's great? But I'm worried she won't want to marry me. And maybe mixed marriages don't work?'

'You could be happy together. You're – what do they say here? You're mates.' Vikram looked relieved.

'If she says yes, that she'll consider it, I'm writing to my parents.'

Called awake by the whipbirds and a butcherbird just outside the window, Chanchal rose early the next morning. He left the shack and quietly walked into the forest, binoculars in hand, planning to find both the male and the female of the whipbirds. The male made the whip sound, the female the two high-pitched tail sounds right at the end. But he couldn't summon the patience. Standing amongst the trees, swatting at a fly, he thought bitterly – How is it that I thought of Vikram as a bit of a fool, when really it's me who's stupid? Stupid at everything except science.

After some months, another of the heavier envelopes arrived from his mother.

Dear Chanchal,

Thank you for your regular letters: it has been a relief to read them and know that all is going well for you in Melbourne once again. I have let Uncle Ajit know that you're much more settled now. We were very proud to hear that your paper is to be published. Well done. Bani simply said, 'It's as much as I expected, the first of many publications and promotions!'

Now I'm very excited, because Dr Pradhan Gaur-Singh, the brother of our state Minister for Railways, has heard of our search, and has intimated that one of his daughters might be a suitable match. I've managed to procure a photograph of the young lady from the mutual friend and cousin who has put us in touch. It's very exciting to think that you could be marrying into a ministerial family. Her name is Manak and she is twenty. An auspicious name, I feel, as it means ruby, and rubies are my favourite of the gemstones. She has an excellent disposition, and is studying law, her debating team at college having won many awards. As you can see, she is very petite and reasonably fair. During the summer they holiday in Shimla, where they have property.

Please arrange to have a photograph taken of yourself alone, and another one of you standing alongside Professor Turner in front of the university gates, if he'd be so kind, and send them to us immediately with a friendly note. If you and Manak like each other once you're corresponding, I'm sure the two families can combine forces to find you an excellent position at the Punjabi Agricultural University as soon as you return. We only hear impressive things about the new university.

Much love,

Ma

28

NORMA ADJUSTS THE VENETIANS IN THEIR BEDROOM TO LET in more light, then kneels in front of Rafaela's glory box. What should she do with it all? She takes out the fine linen tea towels that she stitched with the wildflowers of England. She takes out the scallop-edged pillowslips and lays them on the bed. Should she give them to Julie? The wedding is two months away.

She confesses to Carlo: I don't feel like being generous yet.

29

THE BIRTH WAS AWAITED BY THE TWO WOMEN AT A LOCAL motel. It was early in the rainy season again, almost a year since the flood which had swept Chanchal and Rafaela from their train. Clarissa brought Rafi into town ahead of her due date because of the rain. The roads might well become impassable.

Despite the talks and diagrams and Clarissa's warnings, the birth dumped Rafi like a freak wave. Drenched in her labour, Rafi paced and groaned in a hot room at the hospital for a day, the midwife coming in and out, giving sips of water and slivers of orange to ease her heat. Outside it rained, sometimes so loudly the room reverberated with the pounding of the water and her heaving moans. She was wearing her wedding ring, the one Chanchal had bought from the hock shop with the gypsy ruby in it. It'd always been loose and the ring slipped about on her finger. Rafi panted and gritted her teeth and worried that if it fell off it would be lost and then how would that look? She touched it more than once, and the midwife asked her would she like to take it off and Rafi yelled 'No!' Then in the harum-scarum of the last hour of the birth, when the midwife put down her knitting and telephoned Clarissa to come in from the motel, a chink of a bright thought broke through. Her baby was about to be born.

After all that trouble, the baby slithered out shockingly, painfully fast. Rafi was awed by the child's speed and her squalling, wet voice. She had a name for her ready, a name full of daylight: Chloe. When the bluish white cord was cut, thick as a plait of her own hair, Rafi reached out to take her. But had to wait. The midwife was rubbing Chloe dry, ready for weighing and swaddling.

Given her, Rafi loosened the wrap and slipped a finger into her baby's small, pale-skinned fist and felt her daughter clench tightly for a moment. Then her fingers let go, and spread out. She had tiny moon-slip fingernails. 'My girl, the sweetest girl of all,' she whispered, gazing at Chloe's newborn, crumpled face, smelling her, taking her in.

When Clarissa came, soon but not soon enough, Chloe was asleep, hidden and curled up. Rafi gave her the baby to hold and thought – Mum and dad will never see this. Might never meet Chloe at all.

She began to weep and Clarissa and the nurse exchanged a sympathetic look. Clarissa gave Chloe to Rafi, saying, 'Get some sleep now and I'll go back to the motel. I'll come again in a couple of hours.'

That evening, amidst the noise of the visiting hours, Rafi whispered to Clarissa, 'She's not very brown.' Clarissa frowned at her. 'I'm being realistic,' Rafi whispered. 'It's not that I wouldn't love her anyway.'

'So we can stop talking about adoption?' asked Clarissa.

Rafi nodded. Still, what a relief that she wasn't dark. She thought – Everything is going to be so, so, so much simpler.

Back at the farm, Bob and Clarissa sat with Rafi as she fed the baby and in a quiet voice suggested Chloe take the Carmichael name; that Chloe and Rafi both take the Carmichael name. Rafi looked at them, a little dazed. Thought – Why are they being so kind to me?

'We need to think about this in practical terms. What's Chloe going to do when she starts school, for instance?' said Clarissa.

The way Bob said it in his rough, relaxed voice, it sounded so easy. 'We could register her at the courthouse this week. The clerks don't know us from a bar of soap.'

Bob pulled out Thea and Amelia's birth certificates. Using them, the three adults examined what personal facts were needed and then tossed about a few honest men's names. Rafi came up with a story that she could tell about Andrew Carmichael, a cane cutter, aged twenty-six, who was a cousin of Bob's from Queensland. Clarissa came up with a Brisbane address. That was all they needed to know about him. Bob took the paperwork into town along with the midwife's form, and returned that day with a birth certificate and Chloe's new name. It was that simple. There was nothing of Chanchal documented and there was barely a trace of him in Chloe. Only Rafi knew he was there in the curl of her ear and in her slender fingers and toes. Perhaps a glimmer of a foetal, soft-boned memory? His muffled footsteps crossing the farmhouse floors, the gentle impression of his voice whistling through the amniotic sea, then swimming away.

This second burial of Chanchal gave Rafi some night-time grief, but in the briskness of day it really was easier. Time and sun might brown her daughter, she might develop his lush mouth or shapely legs or have too-thick, resolute black hair. Perhaps she would love to read, excel at science, be kind and seem loyal. Perhaps she would one day leave her mother without explanation. Seen altogether, it was easier if Chloe looked like her mother and spoke like a Carmichael, though so much was lost.

But lost, thought Rafi, the day you walked out on me, *coward*.

The Carmichaels settled themselves around the new child. The two girls were playful, and Clarissa helped Rafi with that myriad of chores and affections a baby demands of its elders.

Rafi and Chloe must stay, Clarissa and Bob said, until Chloe started school, leaving the question open as to what could happen then.

'But I don't want to wait that long before we go to Melbourne,' said Rafi. 'And she'll be marked out if she goes to school in town. Someone will say, hey that's the girl who had the Indian dad who took off.'

She had just turned twenty. She thought – In five years I won't be able to wrench myself away. The place was idyllic in so many ways. She calculated the years. Five years was a quarter of her life.

The talk went on intermittently over that first year, with Rafi still determined to leave. I'll go to Melbourne and find a job, she told herself. I'll be where I set out to be.

Then, out of the blue, Clarissa said, 'I wrote to your mother letting her know you're fine.'

They were washing up the breakfast and lunch dishes, Clarissa at the sink, Rafi drying, while Chloe played on the floor. The day was hot. Amelia was having an early bath. Bob was in town doing some accounts and would pick Thea up from kindergarten on the way home. The house was quiet but for the sawing hum of the cicadas.

Rafi was silent. How could Clarissa have done this without asking her?

'I've suggested it to you more than once,' Clarissa said. 'One letter isn't enough.'

'You wrote to my mother? But how did you find their address?'

'I went to the GPO when I was in Brisbane last

week. It turns out Mollino isn't a common name. You've mentioned Mimosa and the map showed that Petal Bay was nearby.'

'Well, that decides it. We're going to Melbourne,' said Rafi, putting the tea towel down and picking Chloe up.

'You're leaving?' Clarissa peeled her gloves off and turned to Rafi.

'Why are you surprised? How could you do this?'

'You can't just not contact your parents. I didn't say anything about Chloe. They must be worried to death!'

Rafi could hear her voice was loud but she couldn't seem to get the wail out of it. 'But they'll find me and want me to come back. It's their fault I left in the first place. You don't know my father. I just don't want them to know. I don't want to be found.'

'I didn't say where you were living.'

'I don't believe you,' said Rafi. Chloe began to cry loudly.

'I'm sorry. This isn't what I intended,' said Clarissa. She left the room. Then she reappeared. 'You should have written. I stand by that. You're a mother yourself now. I expected you to gain some understanding about that. But you haven't.'

'Families are not all the same, you know,' Rafi shouted after her, neck straining, feeling like the bad daughter, not the good friend.

She went in a rush out onto the veranda, slamming the screen door shut, repeating 'there, there' as she roughly patted Chloe. Thought – Why am I so horrible? Why can't I do as she says? She didn't know why she was like this. What was this chunk of resistance?

Chloe whimpered and Rafaela felt the utter solitude in her comforting of the girl. In a matter of days there would be no one to help them. But perhaps this was what she *needed* to happen, to make her move on.

Clarissa and Bob tried again to persuade Rafi to stay. But the rift, to Rafi, was vast. Clarissa said, 'Please, Rafaela. Melbourne is so far away. What about Sydney? How will you cope on your own?'

'Sydney's too big. Melbourne is where I've wanted to go for two years now.'

'Leave Chloe with us, then,' said Bob. Rafi shook her head at this ridiculous suggestion.

'We'll drive you down, help you get set up.'

'That's kind of you, but no, we'll go on our own.'

At the station Rafi tried again to explain. 'You know I've always wanted to keep going. It's not all your doing. This time is as good as any. I really want to do this.'

Clarissa and Bob didn't answer. They'd already said Chloe was too young. She'd have no family now but Rafi.

'I'll write to them myself. Not now, not soon. But I will write to them. And to you. I'll write every week.'

'Promise?' asked Clarissa sadly.

Bob picked up Thea and Amelia so that they could kiss baby Chloe, then turned back to the truck before the crying started.

'Promise.' Her breath shuddered when she took it in.

On their first night on the train, in the sleeper cabin purchased with a small portion of Chanchal's money, Rafaela dreamt of the decent sun-bleached Queensland fibro that had been her family home. Then she dreamt she was hovering high above a city. Generous with her sunlight, showering the throngs below with cloud bouquets and sun-tipped gold dust; her fingers tipped with vermilion – vermilion! what a glorious colour to dream of – she was ready to paint the town. Red, the dream was full of red. Rafi twirled, held aloft by hot air, her skirt billowing out over all the crowds who passed below. Or so she dreamt.

It was 7.14 a.m. when they alighted. Leaving the station she looked about her: this was to be her town, then. The wide sludgy river, the soot-grey stone buildings, nearby a row of dark shops, a low bridge. And it was to be Chloe Carmichael's city too, daughter of Rafaela Ellen Carmichael. They seemed to be in a gully at the bottom of the city, where debris clogged drains and cluttered the corners of unused doorways. Vagrants slipped past. A woman with a grimy face offered a kiss to an old man. Passing beneath a studded-iron railway bridge near the hotel she'd been sent to, a train rocked overhead with noise so loud and steely her ears felt pain. Ambushed,

Chloe cried. 'They didn't say the city is noisy,' Rafi said to her, though she couldn't be heard. The city was *loud*. Why hadn't Chanchal warned her? Or Clarissa? There were smells too, of transport and fish, of rotting oranges and dogs. Inside the ageing hallways of the forty-room hotel, there was a dust and phenyl smell. On that first morning Rafi retreated into Chloe's warm neck. She buried her face in her baby's soft pungent skin to escape the anonymous smells of their room.

Rafi thought – Melbourne has to be better than this. This was the Olympic city. She found her way with Chloe to the National Gallery that afternoon. She thought – So here it is, this is why I came. She walked from a Frederick McCubbin to a Tom Roberts, thought – Is my mouth hanging open? Was startled by the simple shape of the Blackman rowboat. Thought – Are those Tucker shearers black? They reminded her of Clay and Tom and Albert. They'd have a laugh if she told them all that had happened.

There were so many Italian artists. Tiepolo, Toscani, Modigliani – a longtime favourite. Rafi struggled to reconcile their pictures with what she knew of Italy: her father and the cane fields and the Italian cutters and sugar mill workers around them.

Then, just as Chloe was losing all patience with the large rooms and her small stroller, Rafi found herself before a Rembrandt. Here she was, between Europe and the Carmichael kitchen, here in Melbourne with him. Here he was again, fleshy and kindly and red-nosed. She thought – I must paint my self-portrait. Call it 'Rafaela Arrives in Melbourne'.

His hair curled out from beneath his cap, and his round eyes were small and dark, but my, how Rembrandt's eyes could *see*. She lifted Chloe up to view the painting, and said, 'Look, there's our friend Rembrandt.' She'd done the right thing to leave, to take Chloe with her. She'd come to the right place.

She boarded a tram with Chloe asleep, and then another tram, and they criss-crossed the city. Each time they waited for one at the stop in the middle of the road, she gripped Chloe close, afraid they'd be run down. In St Kilda she drank coffee at a cafe and felt very cosmopolitan. She briskly walked the windy quarter-mile pier, the stroller clattering its simple rhythm over the grey boards. At the kiosk, she held Chloe up in her arms so that they could drown their eyes in the grey-green sea below. A shag plummeted through the salty air into the swell. The wind whipped salt mist across their skin. The horizon lay far away, an edge dimly visible and not yet propitious.

The next day other trams took them past spacious parks and distinguished houses with manicured gardens, rows of terraces, windowless factories, grocery stores, weed-strewn vacant blocks, kids playing footie down glimpsed lanes, stomping in puddles and wetting their shoes, traffic jams and clusters of people waiting at traffic lights, their umbrellas overlapping like netted black fish.

Travelling up Swanston Street, they passed the University of Melbourne. Rafi pulled the cord and hurried them off, then dawdled past the university gateway. Young students swung past, confident and happy. None of them looked at her. She noticed this, and thought – To them I'm just a mum, not one of them. The buildings were large and austere. Rafi turned back towards the city. There was a fruit cart and she bought bananas for herself and Chloe. It began to rain again. The cool drops were nothing like the warm rains up north. Scores of people briskly walked the streets, skirting puddles, running to tram stops and trains. Other mothers pushed their prams under the shelter of awnings and into shops. On her way back to the Grand Central Hotel through the wet streets she mistook a man for Rickie. She felt herself blanch and shrink back, unsure what to do, how to hide herself, how to hide Chloe. She stopped short, causing a lady to bang into the stroller, then relaxed when the jaunty young man whose lips were pursed over a tune became himself again and was drawn down into the train station's dark belly, taking with his whistle her fading reminiscence.

And there it was, Rafi realised; that sneaking half-hope that she was going to be found.

Out of the rain and back at the Grand Central, a woman stepped through the gloom of the hallway to Rafi's room as she was changing Chloe.

'Hello, love, I'm Husky,' she said. Her voice crackled, as if she'd lived hard and loud, swilling beer and puffing on cigarettes in pub singalongs. This was the woman Rafi had heard singing in a rich and raspy voice from the bathroom. She scared the hell out of Rafi, but at the same time seemed generous and kind.

'You should go up to Carlton and find yourself a place to live. You don't want to stay here much longer.' Husky was decisive. 'I'll look after the baby.'

Rafi hesitated. She didn't know anything about the woman.

'I've had four of my own. She'll be fine for half a day.'

Rafi wasn't going to argue. They needed somewhere better than this to stay. She needed a kitchen of her own, for one thing.

The next morning, Husky lifted Chloe from the stroller that Rafi wheeled across the hallway and, cradling the child in her freckled arms, looked as competent as Rafi could hope for, given the circumstances. Chloe placidly examined Husky's sun-stippled face.

'She's fed and I've changed her. She'll be ready for her sleep in an hour,' said Rafi.

'Know the routine well,' Husky said cheerfully.

'Then I'll be off,' said Rafi, needlessly rearranging

the spare nappies, pilchers, Chloe's bottle, her teddy and books. She'd hadn't left Chloe in the care of anyone but the Carmichaels before, but she had to take up Husky's offer.

Out on the street alone, arms light without her daughter in them, hands loose without the stroller handles in her grip, Rafi hesitated. Thought – Which way should I go? She took a deep breath, and stepped off the kerb.

She noticed a woman on the small bridge. A grim stone wall ran along each side. The woman, whose grey hair was pulled back in a bun, stood looking down into the eddying brown water. With her feet tucked into the wall's narrow cavities, the broad-backed woman was unnervingly high above the low balustrade. She could easily topple over. The closer Rafi stepped the more the woman looked like her own mother. This can't be true, she wouldn't be here, Rafi thought. She ran to her, ready to grab hold of her thighs, to save her. Turning, the woman uttered a cry of fright as Rafi leapt forward. She shook her off as if Rafi were a madwoman, pointing to the water below, saying, 'Look. Look!' Her bags of fruit and vegetables had fallen into the river. That was a relief. Apples and oranges bobbed in the current beside cucumbers and a lettuce and – were they lamb shanks? Rafi put her hand over her mouth to hide her laughter. Lamb shanks, ruddy and thick-boned and still in the mesh of the bag. The woman explained in an Italian dialect similar to her father's how she'd lost the bags. 'I was taking a rest, just looking into the water for a rest. I put the bags on the wall.'

Rest was a curse. Rafi thought – There are probably very few foolish things she's ever done, and none for a long time. She was reminded of her own mother's frugality. Wasting food was a matter for regret and recrimination. Vegetable peelings, dripping, a half-rotted apple; they could all be used again, the spoilage trimmed off and the saved pieces stewed with sugar and cinnamon or composted beneath the fruit trees.

'Where did you get the fruit from?' asked Rafi. She looked like the kind of woman who knew a good grocer.

'From the market. Come with me,' she said. She set off back towards the city, walking fast. Her legs were strong, like Rafi's mother's, though the hairs flattened blackly beneath the stockings. Her thick dry hair was threaded with silver and braided around the back like her mother's light brown hair. They hurried up past the Railway and Administrative Offices, a building of grey-blue fretted stone. The woman's black vinyl handbag swung in time.

Rafi kept pace, her own hair flapping loose from the bobby pins. She thought – I'm sure to learn something useful, and followed her along what looked like a short cut, up a cobbled lane, past a Greek cafe and a white-shirted waiter smoking in the doorway, who eyed Rafi with feigned disinterest, then past a cleaner on her knees washing a bluestone doorstep. She hoped Chloe would soon be asleep and that Husky wasn't talking too loudly to lodgers in the hallway. They passed a pharmacy, a cake shop, a post office. She thought – I've a few letters to write. She wasn't used to these fast, hard surfaces, not at all. She remembered the softer dirt roads in Petal Bay and the splatter of mud rimming her ankles after rain, and the early morning frost on the grass at the Carmichaels' farmhouse. She remembered the aching shock of hitting the floor of the barn, the pain shooting up her feet. She thought of Chanchal and the lighter-coloured soles of his dark feet lying on the bed. She thought – He makes me so angry. So angry. A tram approached and the woman leapt on to it, gesturing to Rafaela to follow when Rafi hesitated. Rafi thought – I'm really going to need my wits living here. And then, spirit surging back – No, I'm doing fine. I've made some pretty mighty mistakes, Chloe's living proof of that, but so far I'm managing fine.

They rounded a corner, and then they were off the tram, and made their way down a wide street to an intersection of five roads. The junction was as wide as a country town crossing, easily big enough for trucks and carts. An old part of the city, Rafi figured. There was a long stone and brick building. Above an entry sat a painted relief of a merino ram, his wool tightly curled and his horns short and proud. The two women pounded down the footpath towards it, the older woman fearlessly cutting through the busy traffic as Rafi darted nervously behind. People came and went, their shopping in string bags and bulging floral shopping carts. They walked straight in and Rafi found herself by a table of pig's heads, alongside aisles swinging with long carcasses of beef and mutton. She dodged dawdlers and tight throngs of women scrutinising the butchers' meats, who yelled aloud their specials on thick chops and stewing rabbits. A fishmonger slapped down large, shining black mullets in a row. Then they were outside again in the open air of a huge metal hangar dense with fruit and vegetable stalls – hundreds of them – the woman tirelessly moving through yet more packs of shoppers. She smiled at Rafi, as if to say, I told you, but then as a hundred people pushed their way around her, Rafi lost her guide, who merged into a dozen other women.

Rafi felt lost, thought – I feel like a kid who's let go of her mother's hand. But that also meant freedom, and these plenitudes of people and fruit, the raucous crowding of it, animated her beyond anything she'd known before or expected of the city. Passing bags bumped her. A wheel ran over her toe, a heel scraped her ankle. She was in the way but she saw herself from above, cartoon-like, a supergirl, black inky lines frolicking across the world globe as it spun through its cycles of dark and light, of need and amenity, of desire and satisfaction. Rafi thought – I'm going to draw this: Rafaela arriving in Melbourne, amidst the crowd. She wished she had her sketchbook with her, and vowed to keep pad and pencil on her all the time from this day on.

'What's this place called?' she asked a bony man who was stacking and rearranging Granny Smiths and Jonathans, polishing each apple with a frayed tea towel.

'Queen Victoria Market,' he said, as if she should know.

Finding a crate, she sat down to rest. She looked around her. Checked her watch. She'd been gone a bit over an hour, not that long really. She'd planned on three hours. She thought – We've got to get away from the Grand Central. It felt evacuated and forgotten down that end of the city. This was where she wanted to work, here amongst the throngs. Didn't matter she'd be selling vegies again.

She went back to the apple seller and said, 'You wouldn't need someone to work here, would you? My last job was selling fruit and veg.'

He shook his head, said, 'That bloke over there might need someone.' She went to the stall he'd indicated, three stalls away, and asked the man there, who in turn suggested another stall run by a Chinese couple. They seemed to listen with interest but then said they already had someone.

There were seven or eight aisles alphabetically ordered, and each aisle held thirty or so stalls. Rafi began working her way down the aisles, with many of the stall-holders shaking their heads even before she could ask her question. But Rafi was determined. Work like this she could do even with Chloe. She saw other babies rugged up in baskets, toddlers playing behind the vegetable displays around the feet of their parents. One child slept in a small hammock made from a knotted sheet.

An old woman explained that they were family businesses, mostly, and didn't employ other people. 'And anyway, it's too cold in winter. You don't want to work here, it'll wither you up. You start early, the rain and wind come in.' She showed Rafi her knuckles, gnarled and red and sore. Blurred by cataracts, her gaze was cold through the white across her eyes. The woman reminded Rafi of bad-tempered old biddies back home who muttered and grouched at bus stops and shop doorways, who clucked *tsk tsk* at impetuous girls who strayed. She said thanks, and got away.

Squeezing through a doorway she entered a cooler, aromatic section. The brick hall was suffused with red, the red of salamis and bacons and sausages, of labelled tins of tunas, of brown and red beans, and slickly oiled capsicum, red-waxed cheeses, smoked red-orange haddocks and herrings in oily tomato sauce, and the brackish, black-red of horsy bratwursts, kranskies and mettwursts. Rafi bought a bratwurst roll. It looked almost rude, so fat and tasty, so deliciously wrong of her to be eating her lunch while walking. Then she noticed the red and white of an ASSISTANT WANTED – EXPERIENCE PREFERRED sign fronting a delicatessen towards the back wall.

Keeping out of sight, she finished her roll, wiped her hands and mouth with a handkerchief, reapplied her lipstick. She checked that her skirt was straight, smoothing it down over her hips.

The manageress looked as if she would agree with her mother about a good many things. She wore an exacting houndstooth dress, but went without an apron. Silver buttons coasted down her broad bosom and waist and spoke of other engagements later in the day, of chats with a friend over a dry sherry, of dressing for dinner. Rafi sidled up, waiting her turn to speak as the manageress chatted familiarly to a customer. She was elegant and severe, and like Clarissa enticed Rafi with her air of certainty and of living in her own atmosphere. Rafi breathed in the aromas. The food hall had aromas galore. Rafi thought – I want this job. Not that she knew anything about it. It was the triumph of the cured meats, of salt over sugar, the seductive aromas of curing, of spices and condiments and tenderising, of food as art, that thrilled. This red glowing hall smelt of transformation, of life reinvented and savoured. She had already done her time behind the greengrocer's counter back home. She wanted more now. Ambition sizzled inside her. Salamis, liverwursts, shiny, briny olives, cheeses aged with mould and speckled with pepper and just cut sun-yellow rounds, tins of delicacies stamped with foreign alphabets from exotic lands: Lebanon, Greece, Italy, Russia, Turkey.

When her moment came, Rafi enthused about the beautiful foods displayed. Mrs Gould seemed charmed. Rafi straightened up and used her best voice, clear and full.

And then Mrs Gould offered her the job, just like that.

Rafi asked, 'But could I bring my child, my baby?' There was nowhere else for Chloe to be other than with her. Mrs Gould wasn't as put-out as Rafi had feared she might be.

'I shall have to ask my husband and he won't be back until much later today. Can you come back?'

Rafi paused, held back the tears, felt them sting as they wobbled at the rims of her eyes. 'I've just arrived and don't know anyone who could keep her. My husband, Andrew, died in an accident. He was a cane cutter.' She paused. 'One of his arteries was sliced through by the knife, before our baby was born.' She almost saw the blood-red leaves of cane and knife. She slid her wedding ring along her finger as far as the joint. It had become a bit of a nervous gesture.

Rafi wasn't a fool, of course; she'd wondered how it would be this year, next year, standing alone in the park, pushing the swing, helping her girl arc away and up and back, until she was dazed with the lonely weight of the child. Just one more push. No husband to take a turn at it, no man to lie beside and tell the story of her day to. Rafi sensed the hard edge, was right to want to grind the stone down. She now had modest plans for a sound life, and she knew she had to lie.

'I hope he wasn't alone?' Mrs Gould asked.

'A mate tied a tourniquet,' said Rafi.

'I was in a camp during the war, and shared many deaths,' Mrs Gould said bluntly.

'I'm sorry,' said Rafi. She couldn't think what else to say.

'But wait, let's see,' Mrs Gould exclaimed, leaning sympathetically close. 'Is it a boy or a girl?'

Mrs Gould squinted through her glasses, pinching up her nose. Rafi let go of her breath.

'A baby girl. She's very happy and healthy and almost never cries.'

'A girl!' Mrs Gould exclaimed. Rafi nodded, sharing the pleasure. 'How lovely. We'll get a crib for her, something to put on the floor beneath the counter, and I'll find a rug. Babies are no trouble.'

Boldly, Rafi touched Mrs Gould's arm in thanks.

Her anxious voice gave Rafi the hope that Mrs Gould was also disappointed by delays, the possibility of Rafi being deemed unsuitable by Mr Gould, too encumbered, morally questionable, her story of her late husband implausible. Rafi imagined the worst. Was a young woman in tight straits to be forgiven for an excess of language?

'Perhaps I could come tomorrow morning about the same time and you could meet Chloe?' But by then

Mrs Gould would have had an entire evening to reconsider.

'I love little girls, you see,' she said, 'but Mr Gould is not quite so adoring. Babies are easy to love, I tell him, it's when they get older that they're trouble.' She laughed at her joke.

Then Mrs Gould took down the sign. The job was in the bag.

Jogging back up the long street, eager to return to Chloe, Rafi wanted to be certain that all would be right between herself and her girl. She thought – If I apportion to each day a few good things, a play in the park, tasty food or friendly talk – then it's going to be all right. Chloe will grow up into a fine young woman who loves mortadella. Rafi laughed to herself. The grass on this other side was going to be very green.

Within a few days, and with Husky's help, Rafaela had found them a place to live, just in time to start her new job at the delicatessen the following week. Ruby Fleiss's cottage was in Carlton, where Husky had suggested she look, as it was affordable. Ruby's house was divided into two. The front garden, the furnished front bedroom, bathroom and a small kitchen were to be Rafi and Chloe's. Mrs Fleiss – 'Call me Ruby,' she said – had the back garden, a bedroom, a large parlour and kitchen. It was cheap and wasn't too far by foot and tram from the market, though they'd need to rise early. Very early.

The first night that they slept there, Rafaela dreamt she was standing before a huge stone wall, as small and useless as a pebble. When she woke, she thought – That's right, there are pebbles beneath the poplar tree in the garden here. She shook the dream off. It was only natural to worry when there was change.

30

'Damn, it's hot,' says Clarissa to the road, levering the jack up and down to get some space underneath the tyre. Their old truck has blown a tyre and here she is, miles from the farm, having to change it. And there's no shade. She drops it and stands upright, looking across the field at the cattle. They start to run a little when a larger truck comes thundering by, and instead of stopping to help, the guy yells an obscenity at her. 'I was *dumb*founded,' she rehearses telling Bob. 'He didn't stop, but swore. What's this place coming to?'

Clarissa thinks of Chanchal. Rafi had told them about an incident in which he had a pie thrown at him from a passing truck.

Prising the tyre off, she rolls it to one side. They're heavy tyres. The next driver to come past will surely stop.

She can't help but think, not for the first time, that Chanchal would have thought an Australian girl like Rafi was a bit of a prize with her paler skin, her nice voice, and on her own. She'd never said this to Rafi, but perhaps he'd been after her precisely because she wasn't a Sikh or an Indian girl, and that the whole thing was a bit of a ploy to have some fun with her. Putting a wedding ring on her finger without marrying her, then pissing off – that really took the cake.

31

THE MID-YEAR BREAK CAME AND WITH IT AJIT'S INVITATION to Mrs Fletcher and the children, and to his nephew Chanchal, to come to Woolgoolga for a fortnight. With Melbourne bitterly cold, they all looked forward to Woolgoolga, where it would be balmy and warm, perhaps even warm enough for Nicholas, Rose and Lizzie to swim.

Joan Fletcher took a bedroom with her children, and Chanchal shared with Tejpal. The holiday went well. Neena and Joan liked each other, and Joan was happy to work alongside her packing the bananas for market when she wasn't at the beach or otherwise occupied with the kids.

That summer the Fletchers again spent time with Ajit's family, accompanied by Chanchal. Chanchal thought – Mrs Fletcher is becoming a part of the family even though she's not a Sikh. It cheered him, uselessly cheered, given that he'd lost Rafi, to see that someone in his family, other than himself, had befriended a woman who wasn't a Sikh.

The building of the *gurdwara* had begun and Ajit suggested that Chanchal work on that project rather than at his plantation. Chanchal was pleased with this. To be building Australia's first Sikh temple was honourable work for sure. Now when he laboured he was with other Sikh men of the town, and the talk was of the *gurdwara*, Punjabi politics, the discovery of the Chinese road in Ladakh, local politics and, of course, women. The men were very interested to know of Aparna and Bani's arrangements for him in this matter. They themselves were arranging marriages with Punjabi women, or had already returned with a Punjabi wife. But these Woolgoolga settlers were semi-literate, and so, impressed to hear from Ajit that his nephew had the offer of a minister's niece. Advice came, beginning with the observation that it was a good thing he'd forgotten about that Australian girl. Chanchal didn't say – Not for one day have I forgotten.

This Manak, one said, would do stellar good to his career. No, said another, the girl's family would always think less of Chanchal for being less wealthy. She was too short. How wide were her hips? Too educated. A debater? She'd harangue him, argue every point until he lay down exhausted, hands over his ears. No no, no, her family were energetic and intelligent: good stock to breed from. Hurry up and marry her! He listened and responded when he needed to, attempting to bring some sobriety to the discussion. He said, 'Let's just build this *gurdwara* wall.' He quoted from the *Granth*, 'The rich are proud of their riches, but not a straw goes with them at death.' That brought some laughter from the farmers, and Chanchal

was well liked for working hard and providing such entertainment.

He knew he must write and say no, or write and say
yes. The offer was tempting: a minister's niece. Yet he
despised nepotism and the cronyism that some other
countrymen found use for. He had sent a photograph of
himself and Professor Turner to his father and mother, but
had begged off any decision with the argument that he
could concentrate only on his studies. Marriage arrangements were distracting him from his work, he said.

For the trips to and from Woolgoolga he and the
Fletchers sat up in a six-berth cabin. He kept an eye on
their things when she took the children for a wash; they
played cards, talked and slept, found themselves bored,
told jokes, made up rhymes. Other travellers looked at
them askance: the turbaned Indian in the white shirt with
the tanned and freckled Fletchers, their hair a reddy-
blond colour. Clearly unrelated, so what was their arrangement?

Having put his Wittgenstein down for a year, he'd
taken it up again to remind himself of the philosopher's
proposition that the expressiveness of language foreclosed
precise expression; he thought this seemed to suit his
predicament. He read again: 'A picture held us captive.
And we could not get outside it, for it lay in our language
and language seemed to repeat it to us inexorably.' He
thought – This is my problem with Rafaela exactly. I have

a picture of her, of my feelings for her and my failure, and I'm doomed to repeat this to myself. Until – what?

What was going to end this misery of missing her and wishing he'd done the right thing by her? He'd never know what happened; he'd finally given up going to the GPO.

'Mrs Fletcher,' he began, during an hour on the trip home when the children were playing with some others in a neighbouring cabin, 'you probably know that my parents have arranged for me to meet a young Sikh woman from a well-connected family.'

'Yes, Ajit told me,' said Mrs Fletcher diplomatically.

'It's just that two things bother me. One of them a great deal. I can't forget the Australian girl I was in love with. And I don't like the idea that my career could benefit from being married to a government minister's niece.'

'Does that mean you would marry the Sikh girl if she was poor?'

Chanchal laughed. 'No. I don't know what to do, it's as simple as that. I don't even know if I want to return to India permanently or not. I thought I did, but now I'm not sure.'

'Have you been in touch with the Australian girl?' it occurred to Joan to ask.

'No. I don't know where she is.' He paused. 'I've thought of looking for her, but between you and Uncle Ajit there's been no opportunity.'

Mrs Fletcher said nothing for a moment.

'I'm not easing up on you now, Chanchal. So don't take off, because I'll be on the blower to Ajit immediately.'

'I realise that,' Chanchal said. He thought of the art schools he'd contacted. 'I did ring a few places in Melbourne, but each time I was told they'd not heard of her. I think they were put off by my accent and thought it strange that I was calling in the first place.'

'Yet you must be tempted by the marriage proposal.'

'I am. Though not for the reasons you think. What tempts me is the idea that, if I did have the ear of a minister, I could use it to do good in the Punjab and for India. The country needs scientists like me. We Sikhs like to do good.'

Now it was Mrs Fletcher's turn to smile. 'I'm glad to hear you sounding confident for once.'

'So maybe that's my answer, Mrs Fletcher?'

She was a very kind woman, he thought.

'Perhaps it is. This marriage could work very well, for you and others.'

32

OUTSIDE THE CARLTON COTTAGE, THE DAWN LIGHT WAS shrouded by fog. Rafaela needed to rise early, much earlier than Chloe, so that she had some time to herself before they prepared for work. She looked out through the curtains, and there was the winter fog circling the house. Even with her slippers on, Rafi could feel the poxy linoleum was icy all the way to the kitchen. She turned on the bar heater for warmth, and the oven too, and sat working on a small drawing of the cottage she'd been doing for some days: enveloped in a black shadow to one side, with some wintry light coming through the leafless poplar tree, and a bird almost indistinguishable amongst the tree's branches but with a faint shadow showing on the ground below. She thought the bird was probably a crow. The foggy morning was perfect for the drawing, and Rafi again looked out the window. It was a sombre picture with the deep shadows and the black bird.

She drew, and waited for the kettle to boil. Her eyes itched with tiredness. The gas seemed to be firing almost uselessly, then when she poured the boiled water too quickly into the teapot water splashed and burnt her hand. She dropped the kettle onto the bench and the bang rang out loudly in the quiet. She listened for a sound from Chloe.

Their flat was too small for her to paint in, the smells too strong and the oils too easily reached by Chloe, so she'd returned to pencil and charcoal. She didn't mind. Pencil suited Melbourne with its flatter planes of colour.

Once she'd had her tea and toast, she put the paper and pencils away and went to wake Chloe, turning the light on in the chilly bedroom and carrying her daughter to the warmer kitchen to have a quick wash and get dressed before eating. She rugged her up in the stroller and by quarter to six they were off, walking to their tram stop. Chloe suffered all this silently, but cheered up when they got close to the market, because out of the dozens of workers coming down the five streets many knew her, and said hello or sang her a song or offered her a treat, such as a warm bun picked up at a bakery on the way.

Goods trucks had been driving in since two in the morning. In the cold of the winter morning, a winter that had come fast after their arrival in Melbourne from the farm, they passed through avenues of noise to reach the locked delicatessen. There was the racket of the wooden roller doors opening along the market's pathways and carts with metal wheels being pulled from trucks to stalls, hammers wedging open wooden boxes. Wood and coal smoke drifted from the kerosene-can fires lit by the vegetable-stallholders outside. The high ceilings boomed with shouted orders, greetings and complaints between haggling wholesalers and retailers. Rafi didn't always understand what was said and didn't need to. There wasn't a single person in the market who could understand all the languages spoken.

So it hadn't been a bad morning really: she'd got some work done in her half-hour alone, and hadn't brooded on being lonely. Some days she wondered how it was that she'd managed to leave or lose so many people. Her family, the Carmichaels, Chanchal – all gone. Though Mrs Gould had promised they could have time off at Christmas for a long holiday at the farm. A second cousin from Israel, the only person left of Mrs Gould's family, was coming to pay a visit and would work with Mrs Gould at the deli.

While Rafi began unlocking the shop, Chloe went to say hello to Helena across the aisle. Having just started to walk, Chloe's trips across the aisles before they were crowded with shoppers were adventures in themselves. She liked to try and do a run, too, though the workers in the deli hall knew not to let her get far. Amongst the Greeks and Italians she and Rafi fitted in; both were olive-skinned and Chloe not much darker than her mother. No one thought anything of it. Chloe was as round and cheerful as a young child should be, and Rafi had never been questioned about Chloe's provenance beyond what she'd originally offered: that Chloe's father had died of an injury while cutting sugar cane.

Rafi wrestled with a lock, pushing all her weight down and twisting a bolt that was stuck, hurting her thumbs and the sides of her palms with the metal. 'Grease it,' Helena called out, finding a tin of sewing oil to lend her friend. The oil ran thinly across the locks, which now slipped out easily. Rafi rolled open the shutters, laid out Chloe's thick wad of play mats, her boxes of books and crayons and toys, talking all the while to Chloe as she unpacked and arranged the cheeses and meats in the glassed-in counter that she'd assiduously cleaned the afternoon before. 'Helena!' Rafi sang out. 'Where's that tea?' An hour after they arrived they always took time to make a pot of tea and sit down to drink it while Chloe had warm milk and cheese or a sandwich. It was important to have this break before the hordes arrived, and because Rafi was always flat out with the work and Chloe, Helena made the pot. She was in her early forties, Rafi guessed, and had never married, but despite Norma's warnings about unmarried middle-aged women, Helena didn't seem to have become neurotic, or even peculiar. She did have scars on her arm from being in a fire, but these were only of interest to Chloe. Helena was a straight-forward Greek woman who liked her cards and the horses on Wednesdays and wasn't in the least interested in the arts.

At nine Mrs Gould would come in, so that by late morning Rafi and Chloe could take another break and Rafi would get Chloe out of the building for a stroll and her lunch.

All their days were the same, save Mondays and Wednesdays, when the market was closed.

Her landlady, Ruby Fleiss, occasionally babysat and then Helena and Rafi would go to a club above a Greek restaurant near Little Collins Street to play cards. Rafi had first thought – Is it hereditary or coincidence, or something more dire, like fate, that I'm playing bridge and canasta on Thursday nights with the clocks ticking away in time with mum's game up north? Rafi played confidently and Helena and she partnered well, and the club had something of a glittering atmosphere to it, with chandeliers hanging low and many of the women dressed to the nines, some in fancy costume jewellery and a few in real gold.

Apart from the odd outing with Helena, her social life was limited. Rafaela would occasionally share a cup of tea with Ruby while Chloe played in the back garden on an old swing left over from Ruby's own days of mothering. Her husband had passed away and her children were grown and had moved to other states. Ruby herself worked at Myer in the haberdashery department and had done so for many years. Ruby's arts solely encompassed opera, which Rafaela was reluctant to tell Ruby was her least favourite kind of music from what little she'd heard on radio through the adjoining wall of their kitchens.

Working such long hours, starting early and even working on the weekend, Rafi hadn't found a way to meet any of the mothers far up the street, though she knew they were there. They were like folk from a neighbouring village who might or might not share the same island language.

In a slump, she thought – When we first came here I promised myself I'd be cheerful and tell jokes and laugh a lot and this would be how we lived our days together.

It had seemed simple enough to begin with, but what an effort week after week. Getting up at four-thirty and working, cooking, washing, folding, reading stories right through till seven-thirty at night. By eight-thirty she just fell flat on the bed exhausted. And then, after six months or so, Chanchal began appearing in her dreams – at least she supposed it was him, for who else could it be? And he was as unfathomable as he'd been at the end when he'd gone. She started waking in tears and didn't like it one bit, hurrying to the cold kitchen to sob where Chloe wouldn't hear her. The effect of the dream was to make her wonder where he was each day. She wanted to forget him, while Andrew Carmichael had begun almost to seem real in the telling. On mornings like these she wouldn't be up well before Chloe. Chloe would climb into the bed with her and wake her by talking and stroking and rearranging her loose hair. Ever-forgiving Chloe, sleep-knotted hair black and curly, like her grandfather's. She'd want to go swimming at the City Baths, or to a park, and Rafi would hook an arm around her daughter and draw her close. Though often her nappy would be soaked and halfway down her legs and she was cranky with hunger and there'd be no conversation or cuddles, just tears, and Rafi would slip out of bed and throw on her clothes from where she'd dropped them the night before. The fact was that as often as Chanchal appeared in her dreams, black hair streaming behind him as his figure ran from her, she didn't have the courage to return to the university and search the corridors for him, or even to ask someone about him. And where was he really? Perhaps he was back in India. How much of his story had been true? Quite possibly, very little. And now here she was wearing his bloody ring because of Chloe, a ring she'd never wanted in the first place.

As that first winter drew on, seemingly without end, Rafaela's spirits sank. She wasn't used to the cold and the dark and the rain and the long, long hours of work. When she wasn't working she just wanted to sleep and instead of taking Chloe to the park on their days off Rafi could only be bothered to drag herself to the cemetery down the road. She dreaded each new day, all twelve hours of it before Chloe went to bed that night.

The cemetery wasn't *so* bad for Chloe, Rafi told herself, as there was a grove of small trees with nicely placed branches that Chloe could climb. And all children should have trees to climb, especially if they didn't have creeks, cousins or a father to play with.

Bob Carmichael had written and asked why she hadn't sent a drawing for so long, so Rafi sketched some gargoyles to show how her drafting had improved. But it was dull work and she had to get up every few minutes to lever Chloe up, or down, or follow her somewhere. In the older sections near the east gate the gravestones slouched rough and uneven on the mounded beds, falling this way and that, inscribed with Hebrew dates. Walking through, Rafi saw some bones lying around and wondered, dog bones, or dead people? She thought about the war, and what bad things had been done to people, to women like Mrs Gould, whose family in Europe were pretty much all dead. It was as if these bones, old bones of Jews buried a century ago, had thrashed about in sorrow and come to the surface that way.

She squinted up at the sky and thought – It'll be dry for a good couple of hours, we'll take a tram to St Kilda and walk on the pier. Have a hot chocolate, then by the time we're home she'll be ready for dinner and bed.

She was pushing the stroller down the street toward the number 16 tramstop when right beside them a car collided with a tram. Rafi held Chloe tight as the tram turned the car towards the gutter. The car squealed and a front corner crumpled, but the tram kept going, the driver oblivious to the crack of metal. Then he heard conductor's shouts from the rear end.

The car's driver was upright, though his side of the car was mangled. Rafi ran over. 'Are you all right?'

The man shook his head, though there was no blood that she could see. He was tall for the small car and his knees were close to the steering wheel.

'Can you move your feet?' she asked. He didn't answer but just looked out the front window. 'Wiggle your toes, then.'

Now he turned to her, looking at her gratefully. She thought – He must have thought he'd lost his feet in the metal. The war, again. Not fifteen years past. Some young men were still like that.

'Now take your arms off the wheel,' she said. His hands fell into his lap, kneading each other. The tram passengers were disembarking, a few milled around the car, but most walked off to find another tram. The tram driver leant his head in past her and Rafi stepped back. Chloe loudly demanded to be released from her stroller, kicking her legs in frustration. 'Up! Up!'

'What were you thinking of, mate?' said the tram driver.

The car door wouldn't open when she tried it so she went to the other side, Chloe on her hip, parking the stroller by the kerb, but the window was shut and the door locked or jammed.

'You can climb over the seat and get out,' she said.

He did that, and once he was on the footpath and she

could see he was walking fine, Rafi thought – I'll go, he's in one piece, he's fine, Chloe weighs a ton. I'm too tired for this. They'd never get to St Kilda at this rate.

'You're okay then?' she asked, placing Chloe back in her stroller.

'Thanks so much for your help,' he said. He pushed his hand up through his fringe and looked at her.

'Don't thank me, really,' she said.

The tram driver brought out a notepad and, after giving him her address, Rafaela and Chloe left.

The very next week the not-injured driver was saying 'hello' across the deli counter. Rafaela didn't at first recognise him, though she returned his hello through the gap in the counter's display boxes of sweets and marzipan fruit.

'My car's a write-off,' he explained with a smile. 'Does that help?' He held up his hand and wriggled his fingers.

He'd been ashen-faced last week. Now he looked robust and confident.

'Of course. You're all right then?' she asked.

'I was in a bit of shock. But now I'm shocked at what it's going to cost me in repairs.' He smiled, shrugging. 'I own half the car, but I have to pay for the whole repair. My friend is very annoyed.'

He said he remembered her from other visits to the deli hall. It was strange that she was then at the accident, because at the time, he thought he should know her name.

And not knowing her name made the accident seem worse than it was.

'Do you usually have such complicated thought processes?' Rafi asked, though not severely. 'My name's Rafaela.'

'I'm Alex.' He reached his hand over the candied fruit for her to shake it.

There were a few customers and she didn't want to stand talking, so he moved off with a final thanks.

'Found an admirer, have you?' Helena teased the next morning over their cups of tea.

'What?' Rafi wasn't thinking of anything, just half-watching Chloe eat her cheese sandwich with gusto.

'The fellow yesterday chatting you up.'

'He was doing no such thing. I gave him some help when he ran his car into a tram last Wednesday.'

'Hmm. Did he ask for your phone number?'

'No, and anyway I don't have a telephone, as you well know,' laughed Rafi. She rather liked the idea that he might admire her.

'Did you see the leather bag he had over his shoulder? Full of paperwork. He must be a student. Or better still, a professor,' added Helena. She thought she was being very funny, and Rafi smiled at Helena's pleasure, not her joke.

Alex did admire her, and was soon back. He'd chat with her once a week when he came by for salami and olives, then one day, he asked about her husband.

'Does your husband work here as well?' he said.

Startled, Rafi said, 'No,' then added, 'he's passed away. Died in an accident.'

'I'm sorry to hear that,' Alex said, abashed.

Sometimes, when she was offered sympathy she wanted to respond, 'Don't be sorry. *Please* don't be sorry.'

The next week Alex asked her out. She thought – Aha, over the week he's thought about what I said and got his courage up. She wanted to go, but she'd need a babysitter.

She hardly ever asked Ruby for babysitting really, so when she saw her that same evening leaving the house she dashed out after her, catching her up at the corner store, to see if she'd be free the next evening.

'Going out with Helena?' Ruby asked.

'No, someone I met recently has asked me to see a film.' She stopped there.

He took her to the Astor to see *I'm All Right, Jack*, and Rafi found herself laughing so much – Peter Sellers was acting the part of a union shop steward – that she almost brought herself up with the thought – When did you last laugh, Raf? Really, *really* laugh? Did you laugh with Chanchal?

She couldn't remember.

From there it was off to dinner at a cafe in St Kilda. But what was irresistible, Rafi was to confide to Helena on the following Thursday, in a voice she made sound worldly and amused, was being taken to a Communist Party meeting, St Kilda branch. Helena clapped her hands to her mouth to stop the loud laughter.

For all that, Rafi had enjoyed the outing with Alex Levy, journalist. The CPA meeting, after the film and dinner, *was* a little arduous, and Rafi had wondered at Alex's intentions – especially as he'd resigned his party membership that night, protesting the cumulative impact of the invasion of Hungary, Stalin's revelations about Khrushchev and more immediately the Victorian state secretary's support of China. The hall was cold, the floor needed a thorough sweep and some of the youngish women in the room appraised her with less-than-friendly glances. And after Alex had said his piece, briefly, he got up to leave to an unfriendly silence. It hadn't been a pleasant exit.

By then it was very late and she wanted to get home. She'd been up since before five, and could hardly speak for tiredness. They caught the tram back up through the city together and as soon as she was home and had said good-night to Ruby, she fell into bed.

But the next morning, tired as she was, she woke up happy. Glad that a portion of happiness had come back. What an exquisite word *happy* is, she thought, stretching. Happy is the sort of feeling Chloe has daily – not me. It's much more than the alleviation of worry.

It wasn't Alex Levy himself, so much as having spent an evening doing what should be done in a city: meeting people, going to town, eating out, coming across the unexpected and the unimagined. That's what had made her feel happy.

'Thank goodness he's resigned then,' said Helena, smirking.

'I wouldn't have minded going to a few meetings and finding out what it was all about,' Rafi said, and she meant it. 'Don't get too excited. I've a young child. I'm a widow.' Rafaela sipped at her tea, thinking. 'I'm not looking for romance.'

'Did you ever want to get married, Helena?' Rafi asked after a moment.

'No. I like to be independent, and I never ever wanted to have to wear black.'

'I didn't want to get married either,' said Rafi, glancing at her friend to see her reaction. If she could say this to anyone it would surely be Helena. 'I was in love, but I didn't want to get married.'

'Ah,' said Helena, and nodded solemnly with understanding.

33

WHEN RAFAELA TOOK THE CARMICHAEL NAME AND CRAFTED her lie about her husband bleeding to death in the cane fields, she'd not foreseen how complicated the story was going to be. People wanted to know about Chloe's dad and how he died and how they'd met in the first place. She couldn't even invent stories about him for Chloe, for fear Chloe would come to repeat them and that everyone would be at her to know more. Though if she showed just a hint of grief they left her alone. She missed Clarissa and Bob's confidence.

Ruby Fleiss knew one of the women from way up the street that Rafi hadn't felt robust enough during winter to search out. Ruby had known Penny as a girl when Penny lived in Drummond Street; now she was a mother of two and a part-time social worker. Ruby hinted that her boarder was lonely and she worried the child didn't spend enough time with other children. She said that Rafaela was taking her husband's death hard, and didn't like to talk about her past. Perhaps there were hints about her past that Ruby didn't want to spell out to Penny. Sometimes, through the adjoining wall, she'd heard Rafi crying. An aunt, Mrs Carmichael, rang her every month or so on Ruby's phone, but the girl didn't receive any visitors nor much mail.

Once again, news of Rafi was travelling.

'I've got the picture,' said Penny, nodding sympathetically, anxious that it was in part her fault, as she'd known of Rafi and her daughter, but hadn't walked the five hundred yards down the street to introduce herself and the children.

Penny carried 'lonely' back with her to her friends, who all lived at this other end of the street, laying 'lonely' out on the wide kitchen table. In the hour before Rafaela arrived with Chloe for a visit, Penny, Karla and Anne regretted that they'd done nothing to welcome their new neighbour. Their callous mistake; as Penny said, 'We're not a clique, we don't ostracise.'

They'd not felt the need for a fourth; they were used to each other and there were already more than enough kids around, said Karla, who had four, only two of whom were at school. She said, 'I've had it just about up to here with the hissy fits and toilet training.'

'Then stop having babies,' said Anne, the droll one. 'And, you forgot making soup of the dog's dinner.'

It wasn't as if they hadn't smiled in passing; they hadn't seen her all winter, with their children just a bit older and Rafi on a different timetable. Penny reminded them in an awed voice that Rafaela was out of the house with her daughter by five-thirty almost every morning. A groan of condolence went up.

'What, she misses the Saturday game?' asked Anne.

Penny took a deep breath, a habit familiar to her friends. 'Here we go,' muttered Anne, 'the social worker effect.'

'Do you think it was death we were afraid of? Her bereavement?' She looked at Karla and Anne. 'Death is a terrible divide between the living.'

'It didn't really cross my mind,' said Karla.

Anne glanced about to see that none of the children were in the room. 'You don't really think he died, do you? Haven't you thought for even a minute that it's pretty unlikely?'

'No.'

'Look,' said Anne, trying to find a kinder way of being blunt to her friend, the still naive social worker. She actually did feel sympathetic, though she didn't look it with her severe bun and throaty voice. 'It doesn't make a shred of difference if she was ever married or not. But I don't believe she's a widow, not for a minute. She's a young unmarried mum like a lot of others, trying to do the best she can.'

Rafi knew they'd have talked about her first. These women were going to be different from the unaffected lot she was used to and at ease with at the Vic Market. These were going to be the kind of women she might come across at the gallery or, for that matter, at Alex's St Kilda CPA meeting. She was terrified, but also keen. And then she had to smile. She'd just realised that this wasn't the first of these experiences for her, oh no – she'd struck out on her own before.

Rafi and Chloe resolutely walked the couple of blocks to Karla's house. A magpie swooped when they passed its nest, and Rafi ducked. Then they arrived at the hopscotch squares chalked out in front of the house. The front door was open. It was spring and the air was fresh and clean, the street trees gleaming after an early morning sprinkle.

Chloe didn't speak but put her arms up, pleading to be held tight. Calling out with her curly-haired, suddenly-shy girl on her hip, Rafi faintly heard the chatter of other children from a room off the hallway. Then the gang pounded down to look at the newcomers, a half-dozen faces coming to a halt at the doorstep. They were like large family dogs, a muddle of sizes and colours, not predatory but way too boisterous. Chloe hid her face as they edged their way in. It was a strain. Rafi knew the women wanted to ask more than they did, and that they didn't need her and Chloe half as much as she and Chloe needed them. She didn't even want to spend time chatting, because conversation led to enquiry and enquiry led to lies. And really, she wasn't bloody interested in their home-by-five husbands and cosy, rosy futures. As they sipped their tea, Karla mentioned that until

'56 – said as if Rafi should know what 1956 meant apart from the Melbourne Olympics – she and her husband Ted had been members of the Communist Party, Carlton branch. Ted had even stood as a local candidate, up until the Khrushchev fallout, when so many members had resigned in protest at the revelations of Stalin's atrocities. Rafi wondered why on earth Karla was telling her this, except to see what side of politics she was on. Penny saved the moment by telling her about the other children; who was at school already and who was not.

Rafi thought – I'm not going to say a word about Alex. They'll leap on me. If we get personal they'll start asking about Chloe's dad.

As it was, she and Alex Levy had been out only a few times since that first night, partly due to Rafi's reluctance to ask for the babysitting when she still preferred Helena's card nights. She also didn't want to give Alex the wrong idea.

'Do you ever play cards?' she asked Penny. They were now out in the back garden, Rafi encouraging Chloe to make friends with one of Karla's girls. There was a thick vigorous lawn and huge tubs of geraniums and laburnum, and other tubs of parsley and nasturtium. A faded blue canvas wading pool leant against the fence. The damp sandpit was full of toys.

'Yes, bridge,' said Penny. 'I sometimes play at a club.'

'Not the one in Little Collins Street? I go with a friend once a month.'

'Yes, that's the one,' said Penny. 'We could play here together sometimes now that we're four.'

'Once Chloe is a bit more confident I'd like that.'

Standing alongside Penny, Rafi thought that it really was time to get rid of her long hair.

'Where do you get your hair done?' she asked. Penny's auburn hair, an unusual and beautiful colour, was cut in a bob that reminded Rafi of Clarissa. More than a year had passed since she'd decided to get her hair styled.

What best did she remember of that first afternoon? Chloe wriggling in one of the cardboard fruit boxes that were lined up as a make-believe train; Chloe tooting as the eldest boy, just home from school, pushed her recklessly along the floor. Chloe looking so beautiful with her black curls and a gleam in her eyes and a wide smile. But also, these rowdy families, so many children together, five boys and four girls. Rafi was reminded of her own brothers, who were also Chloe's uncles. In all likelihood, Chloe also had young cousins by now.

Then overnight half the children came down scratching, fevered and weepy with chickenpox, and Chloe and Rafi had to stay away. It went on for weeks. Rafi thought – This is dreadful, she has no one to play with. They were both lonely without their new friends.

The children recovered after a few weeks, though one of the boys had bad scarring on his forehead. Rafi didn't like feeling that she needed them more than they needed her and Chloe. For their next visit, she packed a sketch-pad, her good paper, and pencils.

'Look who's had a haircut!' said Karla, opening the door. Rafi's black hair was a foot shorter and swung above her shoulders in a blunt sleek line. 'It makes you look older, in a good way.'

Rafi laughed. It wasn't too bad looking older, given she was only twenty-one. Older gave her authority. As the hair had flopped to the floor at the salon, she'd remembered dropping Chanchal's turban down the hole. It was as though she was cutting him out of her life. Then she thought – No, he's already done that for us.

When they were all sitting down around the table, Rafi pulled out her paper and pencils and said, 'I draw some-times, and thought I might draw a few of the children.'

Chloe was playing with Anne's daughter Sarah, so she started with them. They were loose sketches, but Rafi worked to get a likeness of Anne's youngest at play, a sense of young Sarah's weight and posture, her intense concen-tration as she put the dolls to bed on the floor. She did a few of the girls, following the game through its gestures. She sat down against a wall, close to them, and managed to sketch a quick portrait of Sarah. She'd been studying her face for the last half-hour so it wasn't too hard. Yet sitting there, she thought – We sat like this on the veranda at the pub. Pencil stilled, she remembered the pub veranda with him on it, leaning against the post, remembered rising and the way he touched her hand with his before they walked off.

A tear came to Anne's eyes when Rafi gave her the page. Sentiment was unusual in Anne. 'I love it. Thank you.' She showed the drawing to Sarah and Chloe, but they were uninterested. Not Karla and Penny. Karla said she knew a good framer and Anne should have the page framed. Rafi thought – I've started something here.

That week she wrote to the Carmichaels.

Dear Clarissa, Bob, Thea and Amelia,

Chloe's friends are over their chickenpox and luckily Chloe didn't catch it. Chloe missed her friends a lot for the weeks they were sick. Funny that one end of the street can get it while down my end, we didn't.

We're really looking forward to summer. Melburnians say there can be heatwaves around November, but the air isn't humid, it's bone dry. Chloe is asking me already when we're leaving to visit you. To be honest, she only has a vague memory of you all. She does remember the cows!

I did some sketches of the Carlton women's children, and Penny and the others liked them so much that Karla is going to ask her framer to put my contact details alongside one of the images in his studio. I may get some commissions.

Bob, you'll be interested to know that after doing these portraits of children on the move (can plein air be done indoors?) I went back to the NGV and looked at the Francis Bacon Study *from the* Human Body, *and felt my drawings to be so cluttered. His body is very simple, strong and simple, with the figure's back to us, and in front of him there is what seems like a sheer 'curtain' (imagine vertical browns, greys and black) but it also suggests something abstract: frailty or vulnerability.*

(I've suggested to Penny etc. that I could do some portraits of the children while they sleep, so that I can draw them while they're still. The only other time is when they're being read a story, but even then they all wriggle, shift and talk!)

Counting the days!

Love,

Rafi and Chloe

To some extent, Clarissa had withdrawn from Rafi. She was friendly and warm, and they spoke each month, but Clarissa didn't offer advice or admonish her any longer. Perhaps she knew that Rafi didn't always tell the whole truth. She said she'd written to her parents, but she hadn't. She said she'd looked for Chanchal, but she hadn't. She'd hovered around the university gates a few times. The place scared her. And the thought of him angered her. Who was he really, the Chanchal that she'd spent a few weeks with, or the Chanchal Singh who'd left her without a word? She dreamt about him still.

Bob was still generous with his mailings; sent her clippings and occasionally a book, or his thoughts on the artists that she'd viewed if he knew their work.

For this reason, Rafaela spent some time on this letter, particularly the paragraph in which she described the Francis Bacon painting.

34

WALKING BACK INTO THE LABORATORY AFTER THE MONTH working in Woolgoolga on the *gurdwara* and the plantation that summer of early 1962, Chanchal was clear about what he was to achieve in the next six months before the winter trip to Woolgoolga, and the six months after that. He wrote a list, and taped it to the inside cover of his workbook.

This year: focus on CAREER and PERSONAL QUALITIES

1. Finish experiments and start writing up thesis by September.
2. Work <u>at least</u> an hour longer each day = extra day each week.
3. Learn touch typing, starting this week.
4. Continue bushwalks and birds with the Bushwalking Club – clears mind, provides exercise.
5. Write to ma and pa explaining intense concentration required now but interested in discussing marriage to Manak later – discussion <u>not</u> to be begin until end of the year, please.
6. When thinking of Rafaela, stop. Do not dwell on the past.

7. Do not mope. Do not be self-indulgent. Do not be wretched. Be welcoming and cheerful with others.

The talk was that the Australian-trained Colombo graduates were seen as the innovators back home in India. The American universities had high-tech labs, but these weren't available in India, and as a result some of the American-trained scientists struggled; they'd got soft. Chanchal began to draft another co-authored article with Professor Turner and a colleague, based on their work on ruminants. He purchased his typewriter and his learn-to-type manual. Mrs Fletcher heard the typewriter keys of an evening when she was washing up the dinner things; rushing, then pausing, then the click and swing back of the carriage, and then more pounding of keys.

Vikram and Joanna were engaged and the marriage was scheduled for later that year, with Vikram's family coming out from Calcutta for it.

Professor Turner had said he could stay on another two years on a work contract before returning to India to complete his Colombo Plan bond. It was a great opportunity. But did he want to stay? He was lonely and would continue to be lonely. Then again, what was it going to be like at the Punjabi Agricultural University? If indeed he got a position there. And if he *didn't* marry Manak, what were his long-term prospects going to be, if in fact he wasn't able to effect a serious research program? Perhaps marriage to Manak would bring some peace of mind and ease this loneliness. Chanchal's thoughts were in a spin.

They continued to spin when, shortly after he'd written his list, another aerogram arrived from Ludhiana, the first paragraph written by his father, Bani.

Dear Chanchal,

Your typed letter arrived. Well done — I am told that typing is like bicycle riding, that once learnt you don't forget it. Are you using a Remington? The Godrej Prima Company is manufacturing typewriters modelled on the Underwood brand, and they sell them all. Work hard on your next article. Typed, it's sure to impress.

Yes [wrote Aparna], as Bani says it was quite exciting to see you have learnt to type and with all your fingers! You were always dexterous as a boy. I must tell you, though, that your sisters thought it very funny, and made us laugh with their 'inventurous' descriptions of your typewritten love letters to Manak. On this humorous note, please tell me this: what are we to do? You cannot simply say, I won't discuss it until the end of the year.

Congratulations again on your new skill, my talented son.

Love,

ma and pa

35

WHEN RAFI GOT HER FIRST PAID COMMISSION TO SKETCH some children living in South Yarra, she thought – At last! Someone wants to pay me for my art.

Nothing changed behind the deli counter, though. She was still slogging it out, getting the two of them up before five. And she'd be doing that for how long? Here she was, heading towards her mid-twenties, concluding that trouble was so very difficult to undo. When she thought about how far she'd journeyed, the thousands of bitumen and railway miles of it, Rafi decided she should be writing to them. The one letter, well over a year ago, was not enough. Clarissa was right, and she was wrong. But what could she say? How on earth could she explain Chloe, and would she do it with more evasions and lies, or would she do it honestly? How much did she have to say for her letter to be honest? Her father would keel over with a heart attack if she wrote what had really happened.

The pull of these opposing gravities was exhausting. She didn't want to return to Petal Bay. Ever. But how else would Chloe meet her uncles and cousins and grandparents if she didn't return? She thought – It's as if writing to them is the same as being made to go back. But it's not. It's not.

She received more commissions. She painted head and shoulder portraits, again starting with the Carlton friends and their children, painting straight onto boards a bit smaller than the sitters' faces. She wanted them to be inexpensive to paint and frame because most of her clients weren't rich. She didn't charge more than four guineas. It was pocket money, but at least she was painting. The sociability of the sittings, the surprise of hearing a life story, of going to a new street. When Chloe came with her it was a bit chaotic, but there wasn't anything she could do about it.

The axioms she'd grown up with had gone out the window, and Rafi now thought – I don't have an education or a husband, but I'm in the right city at the right time.

Helena trotted off every now and then to one of the fortune tellers that worked at the market, hoping to hear some good news about her next bet, while Rafi tossed about at night wondering about their future; in the immediate future Chloe was going to Princes Hill Public School when she was old enough. But Rafi, she'd just work and paint and work and cook and tidy and worry and work until Chloe was old enough to leave. For what? Nurses' college? Marriage? No. She'd save up enough to send Chloe to university. Every guinea she earned from her painting she put aside for Chloe's education. If she could, she'd save up enough so that they could both go to Europe, too. She thought – But me, I'll end up thornier than the blackberry bushes and rolls of rusting fence-wire back around the farm. The longer I don't write a proper letter to mum and dad, the thornier I'm going to get.

Then Karla came up with a contact who could rent her a first floor flat right at the market. Helena and Rafi went to look at it during a break while Mrs Gould kept an eye on Chloe. They picked up the key from the administrative offices, and found the door to the building. It was a heavy door, and behind it a set of dark and dusty hardwood stairs led up. But inside, the rooms were brightly lit. Previously it had been a sewing workshop. The wooden floors were marked by nail holes and other indentations from where the machines had been clamped down in rows. Two rooms that could be bedrooms, and a bathroom, were partitioned off with glass and maple-wood sheets from the large work-room and kitchen. A bank of tall windows looked out towards the open-air stalls near the hangars. The place was much roomier than her half of the cottage in Carlton, and cheaper, and Rafi couldn't have found a place any closer to work than this. She and Helena walked around it excitedly. Penny and Karla and the others would still be only a tram ride away.

Rafi and Chloe moved in. Alex and Helena and Penny's and Karla's husbands helped; she had so little stuff they were done in a few hours, though Helena stayed to help her wash the place down. She got down on her hands and knees and washed and waxed the wooden stairs leading from the street. Alex went in search of a ladder and when he'd put a stronger globe in the stairwell light the entry-way came up nicely.

The three of them stood at the bottom of the stairs admiring Helena's handiwork.

'We Greek women really know how to scrub,' she joked.

'Look, there's even a brass letter slot,' said Rafi. She lifted it and let it swing back with a short bang. There was something exciting about having her own door and stairwell and letter slot. This place was going to feel like a home.

The first night, she settled Chloe into her new bed and her new room. Chloe jumped up and down on her mattress, excited that she was now out of a cot. Rafi caught her and hugged her; felt the soft brown skin of her legs. 'Rub noses,' she said, and they lightly rubbed noses. 'Cheek to cheek,' she said, and they gently pressed cheeks. 'Butterfly kisses,' she said, and they fluttered their eyelashes together. The night-time rituals were to be treasured. Rafi threw another pillow on the bed and started on Chloe's story.

'The noises and smells here will be different to our other home at Ruby's place,' she said, when she turned the lamp off. Light from the main room came in through the glass of the partitioned walls of Chloe's room. She and Helena had tacked sheets up to darken it until Rafi made curtains.

'We're not going to live at Ruby's place anymore, are we?' said Chloe.

'No, that's right. We live here now.'

'Good,' said Chloe matter-of-factly.

The noises *were* different. Rafi slept lightly, listening to the produce trucks come in at two, the drivers' voices rising in strange grabs of garbled words; the garbage trucks arriving, heard the thuds of the metal bins being thrown back down; a car backfiring; the clinking jostle of bottles bumping together from the milk delivery vans.

Soon she also noticed the draughts and the dust that came with them, and sometimes at night the scurry of mice, and spiders' webs in the mornings, and from the lanes below the squeal of a rat bowled up by a stray cat. But she had already grown to like the sounds of Melbourne traffic, the sound of a sense of direction and destination, and these new sounds became a part of that.

Chloe had space to run, play, build, draw; there was so much space Rafi asked some of her sitters to come to her. For a while she moved into a thick, painterly oiled-canvas kind of dreaming. Slick-textured and shadowy. She woke one morning and thought – My only opportunity to master painting is going to be in these dreams. In my dreams, I'm a genius! In real life I do small portraits.

Then she had the idea of using the perspective of their height above the markets for a series of paintings. She spied on the workers and shoppers from her windows, setting up an easel beside her. She began on a series painted onto rectangular boards, wider than they were high, of the crowds below, the people individual, but also streams of pattern and colour. 'Still a kind of *plein air*', she wrote to Bob – 'I have to be quick, as everyone's on the move along with the light shifting on the roofs opposite.' She painted strutting young men – intrigued by those that reminded her of Rickie and there were quite a few of them – and women big and round with pregnancy (she'd think about some – Poor you, you don't want this next one do you?), women pulling shopping carts and children by the hand, and thin old women shuffling back to their fruit stalls. These were working, unassuming people, used to long days. She drew a widow with a thick charcoal so that she disappeared into the black of her dress and stockings, eyes flashing white in the dark of her grief. Rafi thought – Chanchal hasn't died but my bereavement is as angry and as heartfelt as hers.

Penny considered her a trendsetter now, working and painting and raising a child on her own as if it were a choice she'd made. But it was so hard and everyone's marriage looked as easy as chops in comparison. Rafi knew that these married friends of hers had arguments and shared stony silences and shouted hysterically sometimes. But to be intimate, even acrimoniously: she envied that. She surveyed the men walking below, and the men she knew. She couldn't imagine being a family with any of them.

Once she'd moved house, Alex Levy began to drop by once a week or so. Other times there was a bit of a party at Karla's or Penny's, with almost a dozen of them there – two dozen, if you counted the children. A few Sundays they went fishing. One night he took her out to dinner at the Little Vienna in Acland Street and she had goulash for the first time. It was a knock-out dish. Half the restaurant had it on their plates. Alex was originally from Germany, some village outside Berlin, but he didn't say much about his family and Rafi was more than happy not to talk about families. She had her silences, and he had his. Alex was Jewish and his family had been killed during the war while he'd been in Wales on a boys' walking holiday. A telegram came from his father telling him not to leave; and that was the last thing he'd heard. He still hoped the Red Cross might locate a cousin, perhaps in Canada or America. That much he'd told her. It wasn't a lot.

Rafi suspected Alex felt constrained by her having Chloe. Or that's what Helena reckoned: that he hadn't made a pass at her because of Chloe being about. There was also the fiction of her widowhood to keep their evenings subdued. The biology of it all; she thought – I'm so choosy, it's a like a fatal flaw, a bad gene inherited from my family. What's the point of being loyal to Chanchal – who wronged me – when it's a waste of time, my precious youth, and what good sense I've learnt so painfully, to want what isn't possible?

Chanchal had taken off, while here was Alex Levy, handsome with his floppy brown hair and bright blue eyes, attentive, on a wage and liked by Chloe and all their friends. He was educated, he was witty, good-tempered, but she didn't want to venture even a kiss.

One night, just as summer was hotting up, the air dry just as Rafi had been told it would be, Alex came over to lend a hand cooking dinner: meatloaf with the carrot grated fine so Chloe wouldn't know it was there. They ate heartily, even Chloe, then Rafi bathed her in the tub while Alex talked to her through the partition. Parliament had adjourned and political news was thin, but a couple of days earlier a state minister had disappeared while sailing in New Zealand.

'All kinds of people go missing for no obvious reason,' he said. 'Families and, in this case, two nations are left wondering why, and whether the chap's dead or alive.'

Every scrap of the man's past was being gone through for clues, as well as other disappearances and murders completely unrelated. Kidnap had been ruled out. In the struggle to find a new angle, Alex said he hoped to interview someone who'd intentionally disappeared.

Because he was in another room, he couldn't see Rafi pale. She thought – I'm one of those people. Someone who 'intentionally disappeared'.

'What sort of person would leave without a word, without giving any hints?' said Alex. 'They can't all have been kidnapped or murdered.'

'I guess not,' agreed Rafi. She sat at the edge of the tub and watched Chloe play with her toys. She was clean enough now, but liked to play until the water was cold.

'The only guy I could find who'll talk to me is one of the great-coat vets who sleep in the Gardens with the bats and the possums.'

'What's wrong with him then?' asked Rafi.

'I was hoping to find someone who's set up a new, well, a more functional, life for themselves.'

She thought – This has been in front of me the whole bloody time and I've not seen it. *I'm* like a missing person. But I'm also missing out on I don't know what.

'Time to get out,' she said suddenly to Chloe, who looked at her surprised.

In the same way she'd been too afraid and angry to write to her family, Chanchal hadn't written to her. He could have, through the Carmichaels, but he'd chosen not to. He had no reason to be angry with her, but perhaps he'd been afraid of everything he'd said. Everything he'd promised. Chloe spurted water at Rafi's face. She looked so sweet with her black curls stuck to her face and her cheeks pink. But annoying nevertheless.

'Don't!' said Rafi, wiping it off.

That's why he didn't write to her.

Chloe began to splash the water vigorously.

'Stop that, Chloe!' She lifted her from the bath and

wrapped her in a towel, glad that she had the squirming girl in her arms as she went past Alex.

How tired she was of her deceptions. She was shackled. She'd tied herself in knots of what she could say, and what she couldn't say.

As she struggled to get Chloe's nappy on in the bedroom, she called out, 'Alex, your story might bring some families back together.' Chloe was crying piteously that a nappy pin had stuck her when it hadn't. Rafi frowned at the thick nappy, tugging the corner across to pin it.

'I'll read Chloe's story tonight if you like,' said Alex.

Rafi started on washing up the pans and plates while he read to Chloe, and she was glad of the quiet. She thought – He's drawn to families, like Penny's, and to making one with me. He wants us to be a family. He needs a family.

The fact was, no one close to her had died, and she knew nothing of real grief. How could she ever justify her lies to Alex? His whole family had been killed by the Nazis, while she'd walked out on hers.

She'd asked him to get a small bottle of rum before closing time for their dessert: bananas, brown sugar and rum wrapped and baked in tin foil until shellacked. Baked bananas were simple. She held the bunch in her hands, rum to one side, considering how many she'd bake. She would eat one, but perhaps he'd like two or even three? Then she thought back, back to the sound of the banana tree scraping against the house, the shadows swaying outside her girlhood bedroom window. She felt the cool of the lino beneath her feet as she watched those shadows and listened to the scrape and groan of the tree along the wall.

Girlhood. What a faraway place that was, and stolen from her by Chanchal. And frilled with easeful memories. The smell of her own bare salty shoulders after running along the beach. Shelling peas with her mother on the back veranda steps. The longing to hear those leaves again, even the snap of the pods; Rafi had to shut her eyes. They were stinging with tears.

'Should I close her door?' Alex asked, coming out.

'I'll give her a kiss first,' said Rafi. She lay down beside Chloe and patted her to sleep. She thought – I want to go back with Chloe on a sunny, breezy spring day and have her hear that banana tree and run on my beach.

Back in the kitchen, Alex was dribbling the rum over three of the bananas. He turned to her and touched her hair. 'The cut suits you,' he said and Rafi, sensing he was about to embrace her, moved away to the other side of the bench and picked something up from the floor. She thought – If we were to marry, going back to Petal Bay would be a great deal simpler than going back without him.

'Wine?' she asked, pouring a glass for him and a half glass for herself. Alex lit a cigarette and went to sit on the couch with his drink.

He deserved a loving family. Could she and Chloe be it? He was kind and diligent and she really did like him. For a lot of women, that was more than enough.

He got up and went over to one of the windows and leant against it, hand shielding his eyes so that he could see through the glass to the markets below.

'Do you often see people you know from up here?' he asked.

'Yes. And people I think I know.'

'What do you mean?'

'Well, I'll see someone who looks like an old friend, but who isn't.'

'Have you ever seen me?'

'When I knew you were coming over.'

'Were you pleased?'

'Of course! What a question, Alex.'

He was frowning. 'Chloe looks a lot like you, but I've often wondered what her father looked like.'

'I packed away all our photos a long time ago. I don't like photos.' And with a sweep of her hand she gestured to her painting table. She moved to the kitchen, half-heartedly wiping the sink. Alex was sometimes melancholic, though not usually so intrusive. She scrubbed the stove top, thinking about how selfish she was, never having even touched his arm when she knew he was remembering his family. She thought – Would he like to talk about them? Perhaps he would: his mother and father and sister. Not a big family. She thought – Memories are as solid as tombstones.

He wanted her, that was clear. He came up to her and wrapped his arms around her. Then he let her go. She hadn't returned the gesture.

'I'm here every week, wanting you. Waiting for Chloe to fall asleep and hoping that this time, something will be different.'

'I'm not ready,' she said. 'I've been thinking about it, but . . .' Rafi left her sentence unfinished.

'When then?'

She thought – He means my mourning for Andrew Carmichael.

She walked nervously across the floor and slipped open Chloe's door to check her blankets were on. Everything she said made her lie worse. 'I don't know, Alex.' It occurred to her that the names Andrew and Alex both began with the same letter; pure coincidence. And evasive thinking.

'She likes me,' he said of Chloe, 'and I like her. She's a sweet child.'

Rafi poured more wine into her glass to stay on the move. He'd make a wonderful father to Chloe. Chanchal had told her all marriages were arranged in India. But then he'd told her that he wanted to choose who he married and that he wanted to marry her. Well.

'She does like you. I can see that and it's really lovely.

But I just don't feel ready yet to move on. Memories, feelings, stay with me.'

'I have memories too,' said Alex. 'I thought we understood each other the better for it. Perhaps it sounds a bit grim, but I thought we had some understanding because we've both lost family.'

Rafi twiddled the ring on her finger round and round. She knew that whatever she said at this point was going to be awful. There was no way to avoid hurting him. 'There's stuff I've not told you,' she said.

Alex suddenly changed pace. 'I know,' he said. 'Let's go to bed and sort it out.' He had an arm around her and his hand on her hair, but when she said, 'No, you don't know,' he stepped away. 'Right, you just want to be friends,' he said, and walked out of the flat.

Rafi thought – Deceit isn't too strong a word for what I've done. But it had been their survival.

She slowly undressed in her glass and maple-wood bedroom. It was incredible that a few days ago she'd reflected on her good luck, the blessing that she was Chloe's mother, that she had friends like Alex Levy, a place like this to live. A job. Flat on her back in the dark, with the honeyed tang of fruit and the rum in her mouth, she thought – My good fortune needs a lot of work. I've been too careless.

Alex's truth had punched a cavity in her. She didn't like her story about Andrew Carmichael. Chanchal was as good as dead, but he *wasn't dead*. She'd need to tell Alex about Chanchal. Start at the beginning.

Alex was back at two, tapping at the door then letting himself in because she'd forgotten to lock up. He was in her bed, waking her, saying, 'Tell me,' before she could even scream with fright. He was almost in tears, as though still grateful for that small courtesy she'd done him by talking to him after his car crash. That wasn't much to be thankful for. He'd repaid her in so many ways.

Stroking her, cigarettes and whisky on his breath, shirt untucked, he placed his hands on her thighs. Her nightie always worked its way up. Was that why women wore them? She pulled it back down and sat up, fully awake. Alex was in her bed.

'Alex?'

'What?'

The flat was very dark. Outside, the Friday market was beginning. She could hear trucks moving around.

'Chloe's father didn't die. He left before she was born, before he even knew about her. I'd run away from home, and we met, and you can imagine the rest. No one I know has ever died.' She let out her breath. 'So I made up a story that would help Chloe and me get on with things. I didn't want her called a bastard.'

'You've been waiting for him,' he said.

She thought – Yes. Waiting for someone I couldn't even speak about.

She found his hand and gripped it. 'Your whole family died, and in such a terrible way. I'm so sorry.'

She felt with her other hand for the bedside lamp. 'I'm sorry that I didn't tell you the truth long ago.' He kept his hands over his eyes because the light was so bright.

'Can you turn that off?' he asked. 'Who else knows?'

She turned the light off. 'No one in Melbourne. My friends at the farm. Clarissa isn't really my aunt. She and Bob Carmichael kind of adopted me and Chloe.'

'What about your parents?'

'They don't know about her. They don't even know I live in Melbourne.'

He breathed out in a rough way. 'Rafi, all this time I imagined you burying him. Giving your husband a decent burial. I've envied you. Because my family were thrown in a pit.' She could hear from his breathing he was trying not to cry. She touched his head, stroking it. It was the only thing she could think to do.

'I know. Mrs Gould has told me a lot about what happened.'

'Everything you say about why you did it makes sense. But why didn't you tell me what really happened?'

'I didn't think I needed to. Then, it seemed too late. We'd known each other too long. But I hated the lying! I've never been able to say how I really feel about anything.'

'It's been almost a year,' he said. He rolled onto his side, facing her. She guessed he was staying the night. What would she say to Chloe about him in the morning?

They were quiet for a while. She could tell he wasn't asleep. Then he put his hand on her hip, his fingers playing along the worn flannel of her nightgown, and she wondered what it would feel like.

'Would you like a pillow?'

She thought – I've been afraid of men before, of my dad's criticisms and his anger, and Sean when he was trying to drown me, and then those horrible men on the train. I was afraid of that weird guy with the dog. But I don't need to be scared now.

She rolled to face Alex and took his hand away from her leg and held it. She liked the feel of his palm. Chloe's hands were often sticky or grimy. 'Let's not do this,' she said. 'I don't want to end up pregnant.'

He rolled onto his back and she heard the clink of his belt buckle as he rummaged. 'Can I change your mind?' Alex asked gently. 'I've got a sheath.'

She thought – He can't have been as drunk as I thought. His hands were surprisingly firm on her thighs. They kissed and his mouth tasted of whisky, and then to her surprise she was as urgent about it as he was, hungry to feel him. Alex couldn't see her smile, for now it made sense how much trouble she had got into, because if it was this nice with Alex, whom she didn't love, then no wonder she was still in love with Chanchal. No wonder she couldn't let him go. She was glad to feel that man-pulse again, that earth beat, his long salty exclamation. And with that thought, she burst.

They lay, legs crisscrossed, holding hands. She had taken in too much air and couldn't stop hiccupping. Alex was laughing at her.

Thank god she'd been able to tell him something truthful. And he'd spoken about his family and all of a sudden they actually knew something about each other that was true and real.

'I'm glad we've talked, Alex. You're a real friend.'

Alex kissed her languorously in the dark.

'I need to sleep if I'm to be up in two hours,' she said after a while. 'But could you do one thing? Turn on the light and check that the rubber didn't break? Would you mind?' Chanchal had more than once described her as being practical – yes, she was. She had to be.

36

SHE AND ALEX SLEPT TOGETHER A FEW MORE TIMES, BUT Rafi always asked him to leave before Chloe woke, and Alex, knowing that she had Chloe's father on her mind, began to stay away. And then it was early December and time for Chloe and Rafi to leave for their holiday, before the Christmas rush, and Rafi was glad to be leaving him and Melbourne – not that she regretted either, but to be on the road again, that was exciting.

She couldn't arrive without having written to her parents. It was difficult and humbling, because with each line she thought of Alex and others like him, who couldn't write to family. It was impossible to guess how the letter would be read. She hoped she was expressing herself well. She didn't think so. She wanted the letter to be warm, but it wasn't. Each time she started it, it came out firm. Not unloving, but not particularly loving either.

Dear Mum and Dad,

I hope the letter I wrote a year ago reached you safely. I was living then in the country in northern New South Wales, but now I'm living in Melbourne, where I've been for most of the year. I think of you both every day and know that I must have worried you sick by disappearing. I didn't mean to worry you, I just had to go.

I work at a delicatessen at the Queen Victoria Market (you've never seen such a variety of foods from all over the world!). I'm in good health, and I guess there's so much else I could say I don't know where to begin. I've made some good friends and have also been earning money through painting portraits — just as you suggested I should, Dad.

I love you both, and I'm sorry for not writing much, much sooner.

Much love to my brothers, and please write back,

Rafaela

So that there'd be no mistake, Rafi wrote her address on the sealed envelope neatly. She imagined them passing it around. They'd not be pleased, but at least they'd know that she was safe. And maybe Rickie or her mum would write back.

On those quiet evenings when she went over her household budget and totalled everything she'd spent for the month, a habit Helena had insisted she get into, and had made sure she had paid her bills and rent in advance and put more aside for Chloe's education, on those nights Rafi's satisfaction was a little like the one she felt on sealing and stamping the envelope. It was like a white flag, this white envelope. A peace offering, a kind of surrender. An apology. It was good to say 'I'm sorry' even if she wasn't going to say 'I was wrong'. She'd not seen that subtle difference before. It was something to think more about.

She thought – I've turned a corner here and it'll be good for Chloe. Checking that Chloe was fast asleep, Rafi ran barefoot out of the flat and around onto the street where the tall postbox was. She listened as the letter lightly thwacked the others beneath it.

'Do you remember coming down to Melbourne on the train when you were a baby?' Rafi asked once she and Chloe were settled into their sleeper and the train had begun the long journey to Linden.

'Yes,' said Chloe emphatically.

'You can? What do you remember?'

'Don't know,' she said, perturbed by this contradictory experience of memory and forgetfulness.

'Well, I remember that you liked me to hold you up so you could see out the window.' With that Rafi picked Chloe up, though at more than two years old she was getting rather heavy.

'I remember the cows.'

'At the farm.'

'Yes.'

What excitement at the station when they arrived. Thea and Amelia standing with a balloon each. Chloe refusing to look at them. Clarissa and Bob with their own broad smiles. As soon as Rafi saw Clarissa she had to give Chloe to Bob. 'I've missed you so much!' she said, hugging

Clarissa tight. It was true, all of a sudden so true. Clarissa and Bob – and Chanchal.

After a couple of weeks, Rafi biked to the hole, taking a string with a weighted hook on it. She'd only kept his notebook and the picture she'd drawn of him that he'd asked to keep but had then left behind. She wanted to see if there was anything else she could retrieve. Chloe would want to know more when she was older. So she lay on the ground and dropped her hook down and up and swung it about, but it didn't catch on anything except the sides of the hole. Perhaps there was a spring down there, and it was water coursing that she could hear when she had her ear to the earth. Chanchal's things had been washed away, after all.

    She cycled back to the farm. She'd been too impetuous and now she had so little to offer Chloe of her father, so little family, or history, for when Chloe was old enough to need it.

37

Dear Chanchal,

   I think we've been very understanding of your youthfulness and we've supported you financially as best we could, although you know with Bani being unable to work as he used to we're not as well-off as we were when you left four years ago. So I feel justified in complaining. I have explained to you that Manak is a lovely mix of the old and the new and the least you could do is start writing to her. If you find you can't communicate then we'll let it go, but a couple of letters must be exchanged before we pay for you to come back to India to visit with us and her family.

   I miss you so much, Chanchal. Couldn't you please be less unbending? I don't understand how you can say all you can think of is your work. This is your family's future we're discussing.

   Perhaps you could send clearer details of the offer Professor Turner has made for next year: after all, Christmas and New Year are only weeks away. Specific information would be helpful. Has he offered you some work over the summer? Will you be working with Ajit, or will you be coming home?

   Susheela has arrived with the children, so I'll seal this aerogram now and get it in the post. Bani is unchanged; his health is not good. Your nieces and nephews are fine.

   In Nanak's name,
   Love,
   Ma

When he finished reading, Chanchal put the letter down and lay with his pillow over his face. Typed or hand-written, he didn't want to write to Manak.

Some days he couldn't remember what his doctorate was about. He was in that end-of-PhD miasma, the thick fog of theoretical details that needed refinement. Exhaustive detail was required, and that was exhausting. Sometimes the tips of his fingers were sore from bashing away at the typewriter.

Underneath his pillow his small world was dark, while he longed for the moonless black of the open countryside. He wanted to be somewhere so dark at night that he'd not be able to see his own hand. He missed the birds around the farm. He wanted to listen out for barking owls. See an eagle soar high again. Chanchal took the pillow from his face and sat up. From his list of career and personal qualities, he'd been able to do the tasks that required the hard work, but had lost the knack of grace.

These last months had involved a series of repeat experiments to confirm earlier results and the revising of his written thesis and the following up of lost citations and other tedious chores. He'd then handed in the draft document to Turner to read before final revision and readying for examination.

'You should accept this contract position in the faculty before going back to India,' Turner had said again a few days earlier. They were in his office, and Turner had offered him a seat, which was unusual. Chanchal sat on the edge of the black chair, still not sure of Turner's purpose.

'The choice is entirely yours, *Dr* Singh,' said Turner, smiling grimly as if he was both relieved and pleased to have got his student this far. The university hand beckoned.

'Thank you,' said Chanchal, shocked by Turner's confidence in him. 'Thank you. You know I've been considering a position at the Punjabi Agricultural University – nearer to my family. My father is not well. Each time I hear from my mother, his heart problem seems to have worsened. It's a lot to think about.' His eyes wandered over the professor's family photographs. He knew the faces of Turner's children, and even the shrubs behind them, quite well now, in real life. They were much grown. Looking at them, he thought – Yet I don't know my own nieces and nephews. My sisters' faces are vague to me.

He wanted, sometimes very much, to be amongst his own family again.

Vikram and Joanna kept urging him to take more time off, and to come out with them. He hadn't been to a Saturday football game in months, or a bushwalk, or anything much. So Chanchal walked round to Vikram's flat, the one that Vikram would soon be sharing with Joanna. Vikram had landed on his feet, that was certain, and he deserved his good fortune. He was thoughtful and hardworking and now he was also very happy. They were keen to have children so that Vikram would be allowed to stay as a permanent resident. He joked he was soon to start making Aussie babies.

Joanna wanted to get their fruit and vegetables for the weekend, so the three of them set off with string bags. For himself, Chanchal bought a small pumpkin, half a dozen potatoes and a bag of apples.

'That's not enough,' Vikram said, frowning at Chanchal's incomplete assortment.

'I'll come down again. I can't get interested in cooking this week,' said Chanchal. They came out of the swell of people, but instead of making their way home, Vikram insisted they visit the tool shop. This was Vikram's favourite shop and he'd tell whoever would listen about his plans to build shelves and a table for the flat. Once he'd finished his inspection of the saws and hammers, Joanna suggested they get something to eat, some soup perhaps. As they left the small shop, Chanchal saw a black-haired woman through the glare of light on the windows. Out of the doorway, he saw indeed it was Rafaela. His breath caught, and he stepped towards her to call her name. Then he saw who she was with.

'You go, I'll catch up,' he said.

'What are you doing?' asked Vikram.

'Bathroom,' Chanchal muttered, watching Rafaela, shrugging at Vikram.

She was only a few yards away, and if it hadn't been for the noise of the crowds around them he might have heard her very words. The shape of her face, her smile – what he could see of it – even the contours of her crouching body in its cotton jacket, were unmistakable. She was bent down in front of the pet stalls. He wanted to rush to her, but couldn't move for the shock he felt. Her hand rested lightly on a squatting girl. A man was close beside them, waiting for them to finish; tall, thin, brown-haired.

Vikram and Joanna passed alongside, and because the pathway was so crowded with Sunday shoppers, when the little girl stood up Joanna almost bumped into Rafi.

He'd been away from Rafi for three years, and the girl could have been only two or three years old. She was waving goodbye to the caged animals. Kittens, puppies, budgies and rabbits were on sale. Then she walked away, hand in hand with Rafaela and her father, kicking at litter on the asphalt, trying to stamp on something without letting go of her parents' hands.

This was Rafi's child and husband; her family. He felt sick, seeing right before him how he'd failed to achieve that with her. Promises, and more promises he'd made to her, all broken as he'd let his family and circumstance take control. She must have met her husband soon after she left the farm.

Chanchal thought – During Partition my father sat on a floor ready to be killed if that would save us. What could I ever do to equal that?

She had made it to Melbourne and had landed on her feet. That was good, he supposed, trying to be generous. Chanchal stepped back into the shop for a moment to recover himself.

When she moved off, he followed. They didn't go far.

He watched her rifle through her bag outside a tall door until she found her keys. An odd place to be living. Her husband held the door open for them. He and the child went in, while Rafi turned around and went back towards the big hall. Perhaps she'd forgotten something.

Chanchal turned away, face hot with anger at himself. Aware that he was sweating, he wiped his hands on his trouser legs. He was so hot all of a sudden!

He found Joanna looking around for him at one of the entries to the food halls.

'Where have you been?' she asked. 'Vikram thought you'd taken ill.'

'No, just bumped into someone I knew.'

'Here's your soup,' she said. 'Who'd you bump into?'

'Just someone.'

'Come on, Chanchal, give me a clue,' said Joanna, keeping an eye out for Vikram.

'Look, I'm going to head on home. I think I'm just fagged out from all the work.'

He gave his soup back to her, and scrabbled in his pocket for the money to pay for it, but she shook her head.

'Sorry, Joanna. Let Vikram know I'll catch up with him at uni tomorrow.'

He started back towards home but as soon as he came to the barber's shop a few blocks away, he stepped inside. He passed by it most days. The barber didn't hide his shock when Chanchal sat down in the chair and pulled off his turban. There was his thick hair, wound up in a bun that knotted at the front.

'You want a ladies' salon,' said the barber. 'I don't cut long hair.' He stood well back.

Aggravated, Chanchal tried to speak lightly. 'They'll send me back here. Come on, give it a go. You can't expect me to sit with the old ladies getting their rinses.'

'S'pose not.'

Arms crossed with distaste, the barber watched as he unwound his hair into thick kinked lengths down his back.

'Why're you doing this?' asked the barber, gingerly touching the Indian's hair with the tips of his fingers, loosening it.

'Professional reasons mostly,' Chanchal lied. 'For work.' The barber liked Chanchal's answer. When he took up his scissors, his hands became confident again. He worked quickly. Chanchal watched himself coldly in the mirror, saw his dumb features that could so easily turn out a promise, a romantic turn of phrase, the quotes from his *Heer Ranjha*. What on earth had he thought he was doing?

Partly cut, his hair hung in uneven hanks, flopping about his ears and face. He thought – I wish it was my neck he was severing. My hair, my family, my history with Rafi, going, going, gone. At least he could put an end to the hair she'd thought so highly of.

Everything was all so inextricably entwined. Rafi had loved his hair. Manak or another girl chosen for him would need to love him like this. Shorn. Penitent. Westernised?

The barber cleared his throat. He was done. She was gone. Chanchal's hair was respectably short, well above the collar of his shirt. The barber relaxed and with a soft brush carefully flicked away the short loose hairs fallen on Chanchal's neck and shoulders.

'You've done a good job on your beard; nice, even growth there. What do you want to do with it?'

He'd not been beardless for almost ten years, not since he was about sixteen. 'That too, everything off.' Chanchal tipped back his head and shut his eyes as the hair was lathered, shorn and shaved clean away. When he sat back up, bare-skinned, he could tell the barber was good. There was not a nick or a graze along his pale cheeks or neck. He could feel the sweat sitting coldly on his skin, down his sides and under his arms. He wiped his hands again on his pants.

'Thanks, great job, mate,' he said.

He'd see if Manak really was a mix of the new and the old when they met later in the year. He'd not be staying in Melbourne now. He couldn't bear to be in the same city as Rafi. He just had to get through these last weeks of work.

Back in his room, Chanchal looked at his face in the small wall mirror. His short black hair was stiff with grease. He thought – What have I done? I'm a Sikh. And a heavy scared feeling settled on him. He looked naked and ugly. His cheekbones were more accentuated than they had been as an adolescent. He looked like someone else. Without his turban and beard, what did he add up to really? Chanchal examined his shoes, his arms with the shirt on, then quickly took everything off, throwing them on the floor; trousers, shorts, even his bracelet, and stood naked in the room, and thought – This is all I am. Skin, bone, brain, a mouth to talk with, penis, feet, eyes, chest hair. This is all. He was inhabiting a borrowed, hairless body.

He picked his clothes up from the floor and slowly redressed, sliding his *kara* back onto his wrist.

He thought over what he'd seen of Rafi and the man and child. Tears stuck in his throat and his eyes watered, but he knew he was also embittered, and that was worse, to know he was embittered by jealousy. He should have been happy for her, pure and simple; no need now for remorse, only for celebration of her.

He had much growing to do. But that *could* have been him with her.

He had his new shaving kit, bought from the barber. He put it to one side. He heated water for a small bath and washed his hands and face, rinsing off the cloying smell of the barber's aftershave. Sitting on the floor he opened the *Guru Granth*, and his heart beat a two-step of fear. He was crawling hair-naked in a tunnel. He could still be a Sikh and have done this. But he had to do something to assert that, and this was it.

This was his warrior day. But was he a swordsman blinded by the ignorant waving of his arms and weapon? Was he just wielding force, without aim? He thought – Am I just a bloody idiot who can't do anything much well, except some science?

Wherever he opened the book he'd find himself spoken to, he was sure of it. He closed his eyes and let the pages turn, then touched one with his finger gently, and opening his eyes read, 'We display scholarship, discipline and purity . . . With stones tied around our neck, how can we swim across the ocean? Those in whom the One dwells, says Nanak, they are wrapped in serenity.'

Chanchal crouched on the floor, arms around his head, missing Rafi, wishing he was different from the man he was.

38

MELBOURNE WAS BAKING HOT WHEN THEY GOT BACK FROM the farm, and on the train home Chloe had fallen ill with a virus. She coughed and wheezed and it sounded like bronchitis, and Mrs Gould had to find a replacement for Rafi the day of their return. That night when the city was asleep and silent and there was still an hour to go before the trucks came in, Rafi awoke sweating with the heat and worry. She could hear Chloe's wheezy breathing through the partitions. She went to her and crept her hands over her daughter's face and neck, feeling for signs of fever. Bent low, she listened to her breathing.

She straightened the bedding, then tiptoed away, lying stiffly in her own bed. She thought – What if I have to get an ambulance? Who can help me? Other children have fathers and grandmothers and aunties to say – She's fine, she's not getting worse, or – Don't worry, I'm here to help. She and Chloe were a family of two. If Chloe were to die there would be just one. If both died there would be none.

The next morning she took her to the hospital, after ringing Penny and Clarissa to let them know. Chloe hadn't had a serious illness until now.

The hospital loaned a nebuliser to her and showed her how to break open the nebule of ventolin and pour the clear liquid into a canister attached to a mask that was then placed over Chloe's nose and mouth.

They were both afraid of the machine, a small, heavy, green metal box. Turned on, it made a racket. Chloe's fear of the noise and the rigid plastic mask had her whimpering. Alex's family was killed by a different gas, Rafi reminded herself. This gas was expanding Chloe's breathing passages. But the other; she imagined his parents' bone-deep terror as the chamber filled with gas. They would have known that they were going to die naked that hour when the others fell down beside them. How terrible to see your child crying, bending, expiring, and surely without the resignation that Chloe now tiredly exhibited as the vapour opened up her lungs.

By the third day Chloe had improved enough to fight her off, swinging her head away, tearing at the mask, coughing and crying her protest. On the floor, her back against the couch, Rafi held Chloe's arms as she pleaded with her to stay still. Each time they had this battle of limbs and yelling until Chloe capitulated. Startled by Alex's loud 'hello', Rafi looked up and saw his apprehension. He held out her key by way of explanation as to how he came to be inside.

'I knocked, but you didn't hear me.'

Across the noise of the nebuliser and the bare expanse

of room, she said, 'This is what we have to do.'

She wondered at his coming, but had barely a minute to think about it. They hadn't seen each other since Rafi and Chloe had left for the farm.

'I have to breathe this so I won't cough,' Chloe said through the mask, now that she had an audience.

Alex sat on the edge of the couch, and lifted the cushion hiding the nebuliser. 'Is it helping?'

Chloe looked to her mother, her black hair tangled and sweaty from pillows and tears.

'Yes it is,' said Rafi.

Alex made tea while Rafi read to Chloe until at last the ten minutes were up. Chloe disappeared into her room to find a toy.

'I think you should look for him,' Alex said after a pause. Rafi had not told him Chanchal's name.

'Let's just forget about the other nights,' he said when she didn't answer. 'Unless *you* really don't want to forget about them.'

Rafi shook her head. 'I'm not going to forget.'

'How was your holiday?' he asked.

She smiled at him. 'Thanks. We had a wonderful time. But she fell sick on the train home.'

'Penny rang me and said you'd been to the hospital.'

Alex lightly put the tip of his shoe over hers, then she quickly lifted her foot over his and they made a game of it, the kind of game that Chloe wouldn't look askance at.

'He was a student at the university,' she said, stopping the game.

'But it's just down the road.' Alex looked at her, surprised.

'Mama,' Chloe called from her room with a small cough. Rafi lifted herself from the floor. 'Have you inspected the doll's house?' she asked brightly when she was in Chloe's room. Chloe knelt down to rearrange the chunky little wooden beds and chairs and dolls. Her face was still very pale when she looked up and said, 'Found it.' She had been searching for a very small doll.

'What's his name?' Alex asked when Rafi had sat back down on the couch.

'Chanchal.'

She thought – Does Alex do this sort of thing often for his work, with the same brisk voice?

'Is that an Indian name?'

'Yes. He's a Sikh and was here as a Colombo Plan biochemistry student. He'll have graduated by now, gone back to India to complete his bond. You know about those, don't you?'

Nodding towards Chloe's room, Alex said in a low voice, 'She can't look much like him.'

'Yes and no.' Her daughter was exquisite, but how much more beautiful might she have been if she'd had a little more of Chanchal showing? Rafi thought – I'll only ever be able to guess at what they share. A matter of weeks

I was with him. Less than that. She hadn't known him very well. His leaving proved that.

'Why not use the phone? Ring the university. Ask for him.'

'Don't make it seem uncomplicated. *Please* don't be the journalist and find him yourself.'

'I'm more the rejected lover when I'm with you.'

'You make it sound very matter-of-fact,' said Rafaela. Chloe came out, walking tiredly.

'What is so complicated about making a phone call?'

'Are you hungry? Would you like some lunch?' Rafi asked her.

She thought – What *was* so complicated?

Chloe draped herself across her mother. 'When is Alex going home?' she asked, glaring at him, her head on Rafi's lap.

'Please don't be rude. He's our friend.'

'It's okay.' Alex stood up. 'What say I come back this evening? Would that be a better time?'

'Early evening?' She stroked Chloe's forehead, which felt too hot again. 'I'll have to go to bed early tonight.' Rafi looked at Alex and smiled.

He looked at her uncomfortably. 'I'll put the key back on the way out. You didn't mind me using it, did you?'

'No.'

Alex left, but was back in a minute.

'I found this in the hallway below the mail slot,' he said, giving her a folded letter.

For a moment she didn't recognise her mother's handwriting. 'I've visitors arriving any moment,' she said to him in a hushed voice.

When Alex had gone she re-read the note.

Dear Rafi,

Thank you for your letter. I've come down to Melbourne to see you for myself — it's been too long. Rickie and I knocked a while ago, and we'll come past again in an hour or so. If we miss you again, we're staying at the Grand Central Hotel near Spencer Street station.

Love and kisses,

Mum

Her mother had come all this way to see her, and had ended up at the horrible old Grand! Rafi took Chloe back to bed and distractedly read to her until she was asleep. Then she did her hair and face. She studied her face in the mirror, her shiny bobbed hair, thought – How modern and mature I now look! She hurriedly tidied the flat. She was so nervous that when the knock came, it gave her a fright. She ran down the stairs and opened the door.

Her mother stood alone on the step, gloved hands clasping a handbag as if guarding herself. She was thinner and taller and less the trucker's wife with her lipstick on and her hair swept back.

'We thought it best to surprise you,' she said. 'Just in case you were going to run away again.'

Had she always been like this? Her bright violet-blue eyes didn't lie.

'Oh I wouldn't have done that.' She'd forgotten how beautiful her mother's eyes were.

Norma held back her tears, the bag her only ballast. Behind her, shoppers passed to and fro, women towing children and old mums and dads in need of care. Rafi remembered the squat woman she had chased up from the dank Yarra River through the city streets and back ways here to this market on one of those first crazy days; the Italian woman she had thought to save from drowning. She'd lost her that day amongst the market crowds, mistook her for a dozen other women. Back then, she'd still been the motherless mother of a fatherless girl.

Then Rickie threw down his half-smoked cigarette, stubbing it out with his foot. Rafi hadn't seen him standing at the corner of the building. He sauntered over after Rafi and Norma silently kissed, then, grinning, pulled his sister into a fierce hug. Released, Rafi embraced her mother again, pressing herself to her tightly.

'Come on up and I'll make us all tea,' she said at last.

'I won't come in just yet,' said Norma stiffly.

Rafi frowned, and moved back onto the step uncomfortably. 'Come on, please come in and talk properly.'

'Rickie found a lovely tea shop nearby,' Norma said.

'We could go there. Of course, you'll be coming to visit us, won't you? I don't expect you to come home for good, but you will come back with us for a visit?'

'I have to be at work,' said Rafi. 'I wrote in my letter about the delicatessen. I'd have to arrange a holiday.'

'Yes,' said Norma, as if she had forgotten that Rafi had a job.

Rafi looked at Rickie, wondering if they had come all this way just to take her back with them. She wouldn't go. She hadn't done all this just to dutifully hop on a train with them as if nothing had changed.

'Well, off you go to get your coat then, and we'll have that tea,' said Norma. 'Can we do that?'

'Actually, I can't leave the flat. Please come on up, and when Chloe wakes you can meet her – my daughter.'

Norma shook her head, as if she was refusing to hear what she'd heard. 'I knew something like this must have happened for you not to write or come home!' Tears welled in her eyes again, but Rafi took her hand and squeezed it hard and that seemed to help.

'Congratulations,' said Rickie lamely.

'Oh, for goodness sake, invite us in then,' said Norma. 'It's been long enough. I'm shock-proof now.'

Ushering them ahead of her, Rafi noticed the way Rickie touched his mother's elbow supportively, and wondered if he'd always done this. Hadn't she noticed that he was a kind son, or had he become one since she'd disappeared?

'How's dad?'

'He's fine. Older, of course. Misses you, as we all do. He's had terrible trouble with gallstones.'

'But he's all right?'

'Oh, yes, just complaining a bit. Every time he comes back he tells me how his gallstones are. Since we got your first letter he has been much better, and he was so happy when you wrote to us this time.' She looked at Rafi as if calculating what more could or should be said. 'He cried on the porch after we read your letter.'

Rickie turned away, embarrassed. Rafi was speechless, crushed by her mother's revelation. She thought – I can't think of a thing to say to that, other than sorry.

She put the kettle on, and with her back turned laid out the teacups and saucers, milk, sugar and a plate of biscuits, listening to them moving cautiously about the flat, taking it all in.

'I'm sorry, mum,' said Rafi, still facing the sink. It was too much, all too much.

'Don't, or I will cry.' Norma shook her head again, as if trying to shake something off.

Once Rafi had sat them at the table with the hot tea, she said, 'Chloe's father disappeared, of course. Ran off, as they do.' Why hadn't she just told everyone that from the start? Just *said* it?

'I knew you weren't old enough to go out into the world alone.'

'Who knows,' Rafi groaned, then remembered a word of advice Penny had given her for when Chloe was to start at kindergarten; that she must help the teachers understand what a wonderful person Chloe was.

This seemed good advice for right now.

'You really are a painter, then,' said Rickie.

Rafi smiled weakly at him.

'Yes. We've done remarkably well, Chloe and I. She's a wonderful little girl. Happy, beautiful. Healthy, most of the time. She's been very sick the past week, though, with bronchitis and fevers.'

Her mother was looking at her strangely, not really listening. 'Don't start me off on what's changed. You haven't heard our news yet. You'd be surprised.'

'I'm sorry for not writing sooner,' said Rafi. 'For all the fright and the hurt.'

Norma took a sip of her tea, blinking her tears away, then said, 'Well. You had to go. At least you were sensible enough to take the money.'

'Yes, I had to go. I did – I had to go.'

'Now, let me take a peek at my grand-daughter.'

As she rose with Rafi to go to Chloe's room, Rafi took Norma's arm and said, 'Chloe doesn't know about her dad. So please don't talk about it.'

Norma looked at her, whether in disapproval or disbelief or relief, Rafi couldn't tell.

'Mum?'

'She's *your* daughter,' said Norma.

Her mother sat at the end of the bed and watched her grand-daughter sleep.

'I missed you so much when she was born,' said Rafi, but this seemed to make her mother angry, for she whispered accusingly, 'She's even more olive than you were,' as if Rafi had left Chloe out in the sun, hatless.

Rafi drew her out of the room so that Chloe wouldn't wake.

Back in the kitchen, Rafi focused on asking about the family, and for a while the conversation was easier. When Norma went to the bathroom, Rafi asked, 'How are mum and dad really?'

Rickie hesitated, finding where to start, jigging his knee under the table. There was something about him, and about her, that made her feel older, not younger, than her brother.

'We all spent more time at home, even when mum was still boiling at us for not finding you. At first we thought you had drowned, but then when we saw so many of your clothes were gone, we figured no, you just didn't want to be around. So I went over to Julie's to see what she knew. At first I thought Julie had made the story up, and then I thought she was saying Sean had something to do with you disappearing. Anyway,' and here Rickie seemed a little sheepish, 'one thing led to another, and now we're married!'

'You and Julie?' Rafi laughed. 'I always thought you'd marry a city girl. But no, I think Julie is your match after all.'

'You know, Sean Bullen almost died,' Rickie said. 'The day you ran off, he nearly drowned, and now he has brain damage. Just packs bananas.'

'Oh my god,' said Rafaela, remembering her struggle with him. 'Oh my god. I pushed him under the water.'

'Look, he was pissed.'

'The poor guy. Is he okay?'

Rickie shrugged. 'More or less. All round, it was a pretty low time.'

'Thanks for coming all this way, Rickie.'

'You're sensible to wear that ring,' Norma said, returning to the table, taking Rafi's hand to look at the scratched band. 'Chloe *is* a nice name! Does she have a middle name?'

'Ellen,' said Rafi. She had given Chloe her grand-mother's middle name just as she had been given it. 'Chloe Ellen Carmichael.'

Norma smiled, but was surprised by the surname. 'Carmichael? But, who is she? Where's her dad come from?'

'She's not a stray cat,' said Rafi. 'Her father is from India.'

'Oh. A cowboy Indian, or a coloured Indian?'

'Jesus, a black?' asked Rickie, looking at Rafi in shock. 'With a name like Carmichael?'

Rafi couldn't speak she was so angry. And scared that Chloe might wake and hear what she should rightly be told alone. 'From the country of India. I don't want to talk about it now,' she whispered.

After a while, Chloe came out of her room quietly, looking sleepy.

'You'll never guess who has come to visit us, Chloe. This is your Grandma, and this is Uncle Rickie!' Her voice sounded way too bright.

Stunned, Chloe looked from her mother to these new people.

'Norma is your grandmother and Rickie is your uncle.'

Then Norma said, 'Don't you know who I am?'

Chloe curled up on Rafi's lap and said, 'No.'

'I'm your mama's mummy. Your grandma.'

Chloe looked up at Rafi and asked, 'Is she?' Rafi could see she was going to be asked many more questions as soon as they were gone.

'Yes, and do you know she found us all by herself! She and Uncle Rickie have come all the way from Queensland to meet you. On a train.'

Norma smiled, and then, remembering she had Minties in her handbag, gave one to Chloe. Rafi felt uncomfortable for a moment about what she'd just said, for it contained yet another, if small, lie.

'I've got a big family!' Chloe then announced, shyly intrigued by Rickie and now wide awake, and excited by the lolly. Rafi thought – I've done the right thing by writing to them. Norma offered her handbag for Chloe to look through, and all three of them were stunned when Chloe repeatedly called Rickie *Uncle* and Norma *Grandma*, and taking *Grandma* by the hand led her to the couch and handed her a storybook and asked to be read to.

Rafi thought – Here is my mother, struggling to accept these enormities. So forgiving, yet so appalled.

Rickie and Norma stayed only a few days, as Rickie had to get back for work. Rafi wondered whom she could ask to mind Chloe, who was too sick to go sightseeing; Rafi wanted to take her mother and brother to at least a few places, like the National Gallery, and the Botanic Gardens and St Kilda. Ruby offered, and Rafi found herself feeling excited to be able to introduce Ruby to her family. At last she had family again.

After Rickie and Norma had left, during an hour when Chloe was rested and alert, Rafi got out a sheaf of drawings to show her. One by one she laid down her drawings of Rickie and Norma and Carlo that she'd sketched the last few nights from memory. Chloe studied them carefully. And then it was time to show her Chanchal, and she was glad Chloe was too young to ask her, Why are you showing this to me only now? She felt sick about it. Chloe was stunned that her father wore a strange hat, a turban. Rafi had started with the drawing of Chanchal sitting upright in the caravan. Looking proud and relaxed. Rafi then brought out more drawings.

'Long hair?' Chloe asked with a giggle. 'This long?' she asked, touching her shoulder, then her waist, then her knee.

'Not that long!' said Rafi.

Here it was: the drawing that had been her favourite, of Chanchal asleep on their bed at the farm, his black hair strewn over the pillow. The flood waters rising, then falling, his hair flooding across the paper.

Chloe spread the drawings out.

Alone on her bed that night, hearing Chloe dreaming through the thin partition walls, Rafi knew what she should do next.

39

'MAN, WHAT HAVE YOU DONE?!' CRIED VIKRAM WHEN HE SAW Chanchal the next day at the cafeteria. 'When did you decide to assimilate? Last night in your sleep?'

Chanchal nervously touched his bare chin. 'I'm not sure. I think I need to find out if this is more the way I want to live, or not the way I want to live. You know?' He took a sip of his tea, and pushed the biscuits he'd bought around on the plate.

'Yeah.' Vikram eased off. He knew the choices that had to be made: he'd made them. It was unlikely that he would return to India other than for holidays. His family would always be far from him, and his children with Joanna would begin life half-foreign in their own country. 'So how are you feeling?'

Chanchal thought – What a good friend I have. 'Oh, ready to wrestle with another ten thousand words and find twenty citations that I've lost.'

'You'll get there. Didn't you tell me a few days ago that Turner's calling you *Dr* already?' Vikram looked him over half in jest, half admiringly.

'I'm under pressure from my parents about this arranged marriage, I have Turner asking me every second day about my progress and do I want the job, and–' Chanchal stopped.

'And?' asked Vikram. Chanchal knew this was the moment Vikram and Joanna had been waiting for.

'And I'm sick of it. So I thought, I'm a good Sikh and I will see what I am as a Sikh in this country with my hair cut.'

Late that night, when he had finished his work, he tracked home through the graves along the paths he knew so well. He paced in his room waiting for the kettle to boil, touching his hair and his face. His beard would be growing back thickly and he'd need to decide what to do. To shave, or not? He'd had to get Mrs Fletcher to promise not to write to Ajit about it. When she'd seen him she'd clapped her hands to her face and said 'Oh my god' about six times. 'What about your father and mother when they see you?' she asked. Her face, behind the freckles, had turned pink.

'If I need to, I'll put my turban back on and grow my beard on the boat out there. I wouldn't for a moment want to give my father a shock.' Chanchal ran his hands through his crop. He liked the feel of it. 'You don't understand; it doesn't need to be permanent. It's hair. It grows. I just want to experiment with myself for once, instead of . . .' He didn't finish. Everyone wanted something from him!

He'd not asked Mrs Fletcher for any favours before.

Chanchal knew she wanted to do the best by Ajit. She liked his uncle and the family looked forward to their holidays in Woolgoolga. But Chanchal was the best boarder a woman could have. So she'd reluctantly agreed.

He thought – I should have told Vikram about Rafaela. He'd have laughed to hear that I thought about her for three years and it turns out she was married. Perhaps it will help to be laughed at? He took a swig of the tea he'd poured – it scalded his tongue. His heavenly sugary tea had burnt him. Vikram would say the gods were punishing him. From the cupboard he took out a bottle of whisky. This one bottle had lasted him a long time. He tipped out some of his tea and topped it up with the whisky to numb his burnt tongue and sore thinking. Then took a long swig straight from the bottle. He'd passed other men doing this late at night, homeless men they were, drinking from bottles under the trees. He wasn't homeless, just between homes.

'I've decided not to stay,' he told Joanna's sister Robyn from the phone booth on the corner.

He'd heard some coins jangling in his pocket and had thought of telephoning. 'I won't take up the department's offer.'

'Hang on,' she said. Chanchal heard her call out, 'Jo, something's the matter with Chanchal.'

'Nothing's the matter,' Chanchal shouted down the telephone, 'I'm just telling you I am going back to India.' But she was still talking to Joanna, and couldn't hear him.

'Where are you?' Robyn asked.

'I am obviously in a phone booth.' Chanchal thought – This is nonsense. It's an interesting experiment in intoxication . . .

'Okay,' she said, then away from the phone, 'Jo, he's very drunk.'

Chanchal waited for Joanna to get on the phone and when she did, he said, 'Populate or perish, Joanna.' That's what the Australian Prime Minister, their Robert Menzies, said.

Then he remembered, he was going. He thought – I'm not camping with the Fletchers for another two years. I don't want to live in the same city as Rafaela. The drinking had brought out an elusive clarity.

The cemetery was the closest park so it would have to do. Bats beat their way from tree to tree. There weren't many birds here; the trees weren't right. A possum hissed warily, and Chanchal growled back. He missed the cunning of monkeys.

He watched through the trees, waiting for Vikram. He needed to talk to someone or his head would explode. Why couldn't he have been with her as he was with his science: methodical, decisive and thorough? All the while he'd wanted Rafi. Yet he'd done nothing to find her. Not a single thing. He'd moaned and missed her and manhandled himself back to sleep, but not actually *done* anything.

When Vikram arrived, walking down the path and not through the gravestones, Joanna and Robyn were with him.

'What are you all doing here?' asked Chanchal.

Robyn had brought a rug, and they soberly sat down next to him.

'I wasn't going to come to a graveyard on my own at night,' said Vikram. 'We just want you to tell us what it is that is bothering you.'

'C'mon, spill the beans,' said Joanna.

Chanchal staggered to his feet, but Vikram tackled him to the ground, and Joanna sat heavily on his legs. 'Tell us about the girl!' they said, looking down at him, flat on his back and helpless under their friendly weight.

Chanchal laughed at this. He'd miss them.

When they released him, Chanchal found his wallet and took from it a piece of newsprint. The shipping times were advertised here and he'd found a freight-passenger ship that was leaving in two months.

Vikram studied it sadly. 'But you'll miss your graduation ceremony in May,' he said.

Chanchal shrugged. 'Maybe I'll come back for it. But it's time for me to go, friends. To leave this bloody, sunny country.'

40

CHLOE WAS SLOW TO RECOVER. RUBY TOOK TIME OFF FROM Myer and came down to the flat to look after her so that Rafi could return to work. She was flat out at the market with the Christmas shoppers. At home, though, a quiet month had passed after Norma and Rickie returned to Queensland, with a promise from Rafi that she'd visit with Chloe during the next year, around May if she could get enough time off. It was such a long trip she'd need to take three weeks, and stop off for a break with Clarissa on the way up.

But the worst *is* over, she thought – They know the bad, shameful, foolish things about me now, and all the good things too: Chloe.

When Christmas Day came, Chloe had her grandparents' and uncles' and aunties' cards and gifts, and more from the Carmichaels and Rafi's Melbourne friends. Alex didn't celebrate Christmas, but he did visit with a gift for Chloe, and then the three of them caught a tram up to Carlton for more gifts and food with Penny's family before heading to St Kilda for ice-creams. By late afternoon, when the sun wasn't so strong, Chloe was playing on St Kilda beach. It had been a stinking hot day, perfect for getting out of the house.

By mid-January Chloe was completely well. Rafi would take her on an early tram up to Karla's house for the day, then return to work. At four, when she left the deli, she'd go back to Carlton and bring Chloe home.

Alex asked her again if she had contacted the university.

'No,' she said. 'Chloe's been too sick, as you know.' And that was the truth of it. She'd decided to look for Chanchal. And she would. She and Alex hadn't shared a bed since before she'd gone to the Carmichaels', but he hadn't stopped being her friend.

'Pick up the phone, and dial.'

She even had a phone of her own now. And rather than walk into the university, how much simpler it was to find the phone number in the directory and dial it. So she did.

The secretary of the Biochemistry Department knew him.

'I'm not positive that Mr Singh is still in the building. Would you like to leave a message with me now, and I can find out?'

Rafi cleared her throat. She hadn't thought it through.

'Is this a personal call?'

'Yes – I'll call back.'

'Well, it's just that I believe he is leaving the department shortly. So you really should leave your name and number.'

Wet with her perspiration, the phone almost slipped

from her hand. She held it more tightly, listened to the silence, then heard his surprised and cautious, 'Hello.'

She hung up.

She sorted some of Chloe's colouring pencils back into their box, sharpening those that needed sharpening, and studied a portrait she was currently painting of a child from Yarraville, but couldn't think anything sensible about it. Then she telephoned the university again.

The secretary said he had left. 'May I leave a message?' In the small half-hour since she'd hung up on him, Chanchal had left. 'Could you let him know that Rafaela called?' She gave the woman her number then slowly put the telephone back down. She felt almost dizzy in this kaleidoscopic minute. Her heart was beating so fast. How long would it be before Chanchal returned to the office and got her message? He might choose to not ring her back.

Rafi went to the windows. Thought – I might have to wait days. She followed the trail of a bony-shouldered tabby across the shingled rooftops. A pigeon rose in nervous flight as the cat passed. She felt the vertical crease in her forehead; she was frowning into the grey light, her pupils shrinking, overlit and watery, as she gathered her patience for the next days of waiting. He might never ring, and then she'd have to face it. Twice rejected. If he didn't ring, she'd leave it at that. She could say – Chloe, he didn't know about you, but he didn't want to meet me again. I'm sorry. I tried.

She saw the layered rusty red rooftops beneath her. Felt her unshed tears. How long since she had last cried? How much she had cried that first hard, hard year here. The tabby cat leapt weightlessly to a lower roof. Rafi glanced down, and saw an Indian man with short hair. He was looking up at her and he too was frowning, and his face was unchanged from the day she had first spoken with him outside the library in Mimosa. They knew who they were and why he was here, waiting for her to come to the window. Chanchal took his hands out of his pockets and touching his heart opened his arms out wide, head upturned to her.

Rafi wanted to fall headlong into his arms. She would have to go down the stairs one at a time. She had not planned on this, and froze: how on earth had he arrived on her doorstep? She couldn't run down the stairs in her stockings. Where were her shoes? Rafi darted between rooms looking for her shoes, then to the bathroom mirror, and combed her hair with her fingers.

When she opened the street door, his hands were back down by his sides.

'Hello, Chanchal.'

'Hello, Rafi,' he said, feeling the greatest relief just in this simple exchange. He brought his hands together in greeting.

'How do you come to be here?'

'Well,' he started, his heart racing. His head was pounding.

'Would you like to come in?' she asked, for they hadn't moved from the step.

On the stairs she was conscious that he was behind her and must be examining the peeling paint on the walls, the back of her hair which she'd not combed. But when she glanced at him on the step that turned on the stairwell, his head was down. His black hair gleamed.

Chanchal was taking the stairs carefully. He thought – What will I do if the whole family is in? How will I manage to be polite and normal? Remember, you're here to say goodbye.

Their conversation was desultory as she made them tea. She could not think, was wholly conscious of how far or close he physically was to her, curious about his changed, more robust appearance, his smooth beardless unlined, *unhurt* face. She'd not seen his bare lips before. He still had poise: his shirt was white, his pants were grey and smooth. His Florsheims were creased, well polished. He still wore the bracelet. Wherever he looked she tried to imagine what he saw: her paintings stacked with their backs against a wall, her bench covered in paints, jars, oils, paper. Children's things: scattered Golden Books, Chloe's artwork pinned to the partition walls of the bedroom where she now slept, invisible and silent, a pile of teddies and soft animals that Rafi had thrown onto the single armchair. A busy life must be what Chanchal saw. Chanchal would guess she was a mother.

'This is an interesting place you have here,' he offered, but he didn't move about the large room as others did. He inspected it from the safety of the windows that had witnessed him minutes ago. They didn't say another word until the kettle boiled.

Chanchal wanted to ask when her husband would be back.

The steam puffed out furiously until she pulled the kettle away.

'How do you have your tea? It was black with two sugars, wasn't it?'

He came back to the table and they sat down across from one another.

'How do you come to live here?'

She watched his face, which seemed so innocent.

'Rafi?'

'I work at the Goulds' delicatessen, the one right at the back. Don't you know it?'

'I don't go to that section. There's not much I would buy there. I come often to the market though, just not into that building. It's odd that we've never met.'

'Why were you standing downstairs just now?' she asked.

'I saw you unlocking your door one day. And you rang me – didn't you?'

Rafi didn't answer.

'It was you who rang.'

She nodded, flushing. He continued. 'After the farm I came straight here. I'm about to graduate. And you?'

'I've been here two years. Living in this flat a bit less than a year.'

'Did you get my letters? I wrote to you care of the GPO.'

'No.'

Her hands were clasped around her warm cup, her shoulders hunched. Chanchal looked at her hands with some surprise. He recognised the ring he had given her, the same modest slip of gold, but thought it odd that she wasn't wearing a new one.

His bracelet clicked against the wood of the table – she had completely forgotten that sound. She stretched out her fingers.

'You're not wearing a ring, I see,' she said.

Chanchal stood up and from his pocket drew out the answering ring, tied to a circle of leather. 'And you're married now,' he said.

'Not at all! That's *why* I wear this. While you have finished your doctorate. Isn't that what you said?' He knew nothing, she thought angrily. 'Chanchal, you have a daughter.' Her voice was low and the words felt rough in her throat. 'I was pregnant when you left.'

She'd not had time to plan for his response, not

imagined the part where she was to explain who Chloe was. He said nothing, just sat looking at her. Perhaps he didn't believe her. 'She's asleep at the moment. She still has naps.'

'Does she know about me?'

'Yes, a little.'

Rafi put her head in her hands, heavy with the task of explaining herself. What could they say, other than to go over their various movements the past years, the dissolution of his feelings, the surprise of how close, but how separate they had been. She had told too many lies. And now to find he'd been only streets away! She began to cry. She didn't want to cry in front of him or in front of anyone, ever again, but the tears just came and wouldn't stop. Chanchal edged over to her, and patted her shoulder. He wanted to comfort her, but if her husband was to come home suddenly he didn't want to – no, that's right, she wasn't married. *He* was the father of her child. Where was the child? It was the girl he'd seen!

Rafi stifled her tears and, not looking at him, found a tea towel in the drawer to wipe her eyes with.

'Here at the market I saw you with a girl,' he said. 'There was a man with you. I thought he was her father. That you had married.'

'That must have been Alex. A friend. He might be over later.'

'I'm booked on a ship home.'

'Why are you even here, then?'

'I had to see you before I went. I've been thinking about you for years,' he said. He couldn't think what else to say. She was telling him he was a *father*. It was truly incredible. How could he be a father and not know it?

'I don't understand why you sent your cousin to ask about the cows.'

'The cows?'

'You sent your cousin to tell me you didn't want to know about me anymore. And he asked about the cows.'

'So you hadn't left?' asked Chanchal, confused.

'No! I told you that. I didn't leave the farm until after Clarissa and the girls returned.'

'So where were you when Ajit came?'

'I was off…' It struck her only now that she had been in the barn. 'Doing a drawing or something.'

All of a sudden Chanchal wished he hadn't come up to see her, he wished he was on the boat out already, ignorant and – yes, morose and bitter. He was too far from home. He couldn't do this anymore.

'Then my uncle has been lying to me for years. He sent Tejpal back to make sure the animals were okay. I was worried about that second calving. I didn't think anyone was at the farm. He told me you had left.' He ran his hands through his hair, trying to piece what he knew, and what Ajit had told him, and Rafi's facts, all together.

'What did happen to that second cow?'

'She had the calf. Clarissa was back by then.'

She could see he wanted to leave. Had she imagined that cat wandering the roof alone, leading her eyes to him? Had she imagined his arms opening to her just now? A last shaft of light flew across the floor at an angle. Illuminating nothing. It would be alight only a few minutes more before the sun sank beneath the roofs. How the years had levelled and cautioned her.

They faced each other, the breath between them rising hotly, indecisively.

'So the girl I've seen you with, is . . .?' He was having some trouble. 'She is my daughter?' he asked at last.

'Yes, that's Chloe.'

From downstairs there was a firm knocking. Rafi jumped.

'That's Penny. A friend with a casserole, of all things,' she said, worriedly.

'I'll leave then?' Chanchal was keen to go.

'Penny's just dropping off dinner.' Rafi ran down the stairs to let her in. She thought – You humiliated me. I didn't even have your Melbourne address when Clarissa returned. You left me, and now you want to again. He could bloody well deal with her friend dropping by.

Penny stood at the door with a bright yellow enamel casserole dish and a bottle of red wine on the step beside her. Her thick brown hair was newly trimmed in its short springing bob, and her cardigan, knitted in a deep orange angora, also looked new.

352

'My two have gone over to their gran's for tea, and Tom's keen to mark some papers, so I can eat with you if you like,' Penny said.

Rafaela picked up the wine. 'I've a friend over you've not met before. We can eat together.' She wasn't going to send Penny away.

When they reached the kitchen, her daughter stood sleepy and dazed just outside her room, looking at Chanchal, who was pressed close to the table. Silently, she stretched out her arm and pointed with a sullen, sweet smile at the dark and unexpected figure. Chanchal didn't move. 'Mama, he's here.'

Rafi stared. She couldn't tell if Chloe recognised him from her drawings. 'Yes, people keep dropping by.'

'Chloe is so dramatic,' said Penny, smiling at the toddler. 'He's here, he's here,' she sang.

Rafi took the wine and casserole to the bench, introducing Penny and Chanchal, and wondered if there was anything she could do; Penny was alarmingly ebullient and outspoken.

'Yum,' Penny said to Chloe, and swept her up into an embrace.

'Hello, Penny,' said Chloe, with a shy but don't-put-me-down smile. Her curls were matted in knots that hid her father's ears. An undone pyjama button revealed her soft sternum.

Rafi and Chanchal stood a few feet apart watching

353

Penny cuddle their daughter. Rafi was aware of his anxiety, his tightly folded arms. And of her admiration for her own daughter. It was good to see Chloe loved and indulged by friends. Rafi glanced at Chanchal. Did he feel a little of this? Penny slung Chloe back into her arms like a baby, and gently rocked her to and fro. Chloe's feet flopped in rhythm and she laughed. Penny carried her to the couch and they sat down, their backs turned. Chanchal glanced worriedly at Rafi, and said again in a low voice that perhaps he should go. 'No,' said Rafi, and this time he seemed relieved. They were almost stumbling about the space, fiddling with things, unable to part, but restrained by Penny's presence.

'How old is she?' he whispered. 'I mean, I know how old she is.'

Penny was watching their reflection quizzically in the windows. The light outside had faded and the interior lights had turned the glass into a mirror. The market below was shuttered up, the shoppers gone, the produce aisles silent.

'Chloe, are you hungry?' Rafi's voice was reedy.

'Very hungry.'

Rafi put the casserole on the stove and lit the flame. She wished the kitchen were untidy, for that would give her something to do.

All of a sudden Penny announced she was going. 'I forgot I've made another arrangement,' she said, and briskly showed herself out, leaving the casserole.

'Well!' said Rafi.

'Well,' said Chanchal.

'She looks like you,' he said, picking up a folded newspaper, slapping it against his thigh.

'You do believe me, don't you?' she said quietly, hoping the sound of the gas was muffling their voices.

'Yes, and I can see other family resemblances.'

'Your family?'

He grunted a kind of yes. 'I live on McPherson Street in Princes Hill. Do you know it?'

'That close?' said Rafi, for that put him only a few streets away from where they had first lived in Carlton.

Chanchal watched Rafi stir the casserole as it heated for Chloe's dinner.

My enduring love, my bountiful love, he wanted to say to her.

She saw his look, and her accusations slid off the edge of the world. The world was round after all. She took his hand.

'Is he staying?' asked Chloe suddenly, hands on hips.

'Chanchal is staying,' said Rafi. 'I'll just serve you the potatoes and not the meat,' she said to him.

Figurines from Chloe's doll's house were out on the rug in the lounge area. Chanchal sat at the table watching Chloe play on the floor.

Chloe began to include him in her story, and he answered mildly with, 'Oh, really?' and, 'That's a good idea.' All his suggestions met with rebuttals but he didn't mind. He told Chloe that his landlady had three children whom he'd made friends with. 'Your doll's house family is huge,' he said. The child didn't know who he was, yet he felt somehow she did know.

He couldn't imagine *being* her father: he was just acting like one for a few minutes.

Rafi thought, it's not so easy being alone with him. She delayed serving the casserole. They weren't alone as long as Chloe was still awake. Clearly Chloe did not recognise him from the charcoal sketches: his hair was short now and he didn't have a beard. He was simply another friend.

'I don't have to go,' Chanchal said suddenly.

'Yes, there's more than enough for dinner.'

'I mean, I don't have to leave Australia. I've been offered a job here. I'll take the job, if you like.' He gestured to Chloe, to Rafi.

'Then stay, if it's so easy to stay! Or go. You and I are the only ones to know.' She was telling him again that she'd not told Chloe that he was her father.

Rafi heard the scrape and creak of a chair pushed aside. Then Chanchal was beside her, his hands in her hair, kissing her.

'I have missed you so much,' he said. 'Every day. I said you were brave, and look at you. I was right.'

She wrapped her arms around him, not caring if Chloe

saw. She wanted Chanchal so badly. 'But why did you leave me like that, and not write, not come back?'

Chanchal sat down, his face in his hands.

Chloe went over to him and put her hand on his shoulder.

'It's okay, he's thinking of something sad,' said Rafi. 'But it happened a long time ago.'

Chloe slowly edged back to her game.

Chanchal was thinking – She has borne the child, she has carried my daughter inside of her and every day since. Alone.

'My uncle and cousins from Woolgoolga found us,' Chanchal whispered. 'They came to the farm and took hold of me and pushed me into the truck and drove off.'

'I did realise that you were never coming back.'

'My uncle told me they'd put you on a train back home, and that you were glad to be going.'

'Don't whisper,' said Chloe. They ignored her.

'They laughed at my plans that we get married. I thought how ridiculous I must have seemed to you.'

'How convenient,' said Rafi.

Chanchal winced.

'I'm sorry,' she said. 'I didn't mean that.'

Chanchal went through the kitchen drawers and found a carving knife. Then he sawed through the leather thong hanging from his ring. He slid it back onto his finger. 'I have always loved you, Rafi,' he said, taking her hand.

But she wound the ring off his finger and placed it on the table, and took her own off too and put it beside his.

'We're not married,' she said. She thought – I won't be foolish twice. Chanchal pushed his hands through his short hair. She hoped he might grow it again.

Then Rafi thought of his notebook and went to the dresser.

'Here,' she said, giving him the small book of his bird sightings and the drawings that she'd wrapped in a scrap of silk. 'I kept this for you. I even treasured it a little.'

'Thanks,' he said, looking at her wonderingly. Treasured? He unfolded a loose piece of paper tucked into it, and there was the portrait of him he'd asked to keep. Sitting upright, turbaned and bearded, in their caravan.

He sucked in his breath. He thought – That's the day I should have said, Get on down to Melbourne and I'll meet you there, no more delays. She drew this the night she fell pregnant. The first and only night without protection.

Turning the pages slowly, he went from his first days in Melbourne after arriving from England, to his notes from the cane-cutting fields. The wedge-tailed eagle. That was a magnificent bird. He turned the pages until he came to Rafi's first drawing of an ibis. He remembered that day so well. The strange drowned lands patched with feeding birds, insects in the trees, and then Rafi beside him, and him in somersaults of love. Her small exquisite drawings.

He'd felt each one was a gift. But really, he'd taken so much from her.

It was time to eat, and time for silence.

Afterwards, Chloe wanted a story, and though Rafi wished she'd just fall asleep, she knew Chloe wouldn't. They chose a book and she began to read, and then Chloe interrupted. 'Is he your friend?' she asked.

'Yes,' said Rafi. She listened to Chloe's silence. 'Is that okay with you?' she asked Chloe.

'Yes,' said the girl.

When Rafi came back out they sat at either end of the couch not saying much. She didn't repeat Chloe's question. He asked her about her painting.

'I've some more pictures that I drew on the farm, if you'd like to have a look.' Rafi brought out a sketchpad of her farm sketches of him. His long black hair filled half the thick-papered page, dangerous and beautiful like a river bursting its banks.

Chanchal didn't want to look at them. He gently folded the pages closed. The crumpled newspaper clipping with the shipping times was balled in his pocket and as he put his hand in, he felt it. She hadn't told Chloe he was her father. Why had she held back? He rose to say goodbye, straightening his shirt, gathering up the ring and the leather and looking about him for anything else he had come with. Then he darted about and finding a pencil and paper wrote his address down for her.

'You've got it now,' he said ruefully. 'Could I phone you tomorrow?'

Alone again, she wished she'd not shown Chloe her drawings. She tidied the dinner things away but didn't go to bed. She went to her work table and sorted through her paints, feeling glum that yet again she was here alone with Chloe and the question was still open. Why had he left? He could have insisted on staying. Leaning her chin on her hand, Rafi idly sketched him with his newly short hair. Then she crumpled up the page and threw it on the floor.

Rafi could hear her name being called, and in her dream walked to a phone that rang and rang, but then as she woke she realised someone was knocking on the front door and calling her name from the footpath below. It was Chanchal.

It had been simple: as he had walked away from her towards his place, he knew with each step that he was going the wrong way. He was as dumb as a donkey. So while his first urge was to fling himself at Rafi's door right there and then, he returned home instead, washed his face and hands and feet, and then sat on the floor and calmed himself. This was a time he needed intelligence and grace. He was not going to leave on the boat. He would not do or say anything to upset or hurt her or their daughter.

'I'd like to see you again tomorrow,' said Chanchal, standing on the bottom step of her building.

'I'd like that,' said Rafi, dishevelled in her nightgown. His coming back was the main thing. He was oddly upright and alert. 'Do you want to come inside now and have a cup of tea?'

There was, after all, much more to say. When she told him about the birth certificate and Andrew Carmichael, and how the Carmichaels had cared for her and Chloe and that Clarissa and she wrote still, every week, Chanchal was filled with shame. Rafaela's story was huge. 'You were so brave,' he said. Words were not enough. What could be enough now? His presence?

'I was actually very scared.'

She took him into Chloe's room, leaving the door open so that some light fell onto her. At eleven p.m. Chloe lay solidly asleep. Rafi drew back their daughter's tangled hair and motioned to him to come closer.

'She has your lovely ears,' she murmured.

Chanchal knelt down and gently ran a finger along the curl of her lobe.

Chloe scratched at it.

'She looks so much like my sister Shusheela, when she was young,' he whispered.

'Does she? And she has your fingers and toes.'

He'd need to send a letter tomorrow explaining he wasn't coming on the boat after all. Leaping ahead, Chanchal thought – How can I get us all over there? His family would fall all over Chloe in delight.

He held Chloe's long fingers in his own, and breathed in the sweet, unwashed fragrance of her hair.

Rafi wanted him to touch Chloe as a father should: to hold her hand on crossing the road, to offer knees for jiggling on, and a back to clamber up. What else could she show him of himself in Chloe? Rafi peeled back a corner of the blanket to expose Chloe's narrow foot.

'I shall ask Susheela and Nilima to send jewellery. Gold bangles and rings. They love jewellery.'

'You'll tell them who they're for?'

'Yes, of course. And my parents. Everyone!'

She wasn't sure if he looked daunted or excited.

'Ma and pa first, of course,' he said.

Chloe stirred and they left the room.

'She may not want me. I'm not the father she imagined.'

It hadn't occurred to Rafi that he might be afraid.

'She already likes you.'

He seemed a little reassured.

Chanchal came back the following evening, after they'd both finished work and Rafi had collected Chloe from Karla's house.

'Are you our friend?' Chloe asked.

'Yes,' Chanchal said. 'Rafi and I lost each other for a couple of years and that's why I've only just met you.'

Rafi again had to find moments when Chloe was noisy to ask the urgent questions she'd not thought of the night before. 'What will you do when your two years are up? You can't live in Australia any longer then, is that right?'

Chanchal had phoned Vikram during the day to check on the immigration rules. 'I can stay if I marry and have children. That would give me permanent residency. That's the law: you must have children.'

'You have three children in your house already,' said Chloe, back again, ears like the eyes of an eagle. She meant the Fletcher children.

She was his child. He and Rafi were her parents. He was her father! But what was to be done about the birth certificate that had this other man's name on it?

Rafaela whispered, 'Do you think I'll have to go to court because of it? Or to prison?' She'd broken the law; she would need a lawyer and money to pay for one.

Chanchal shook his head; he didn't know.

'You know what your prime minister calls this?' Chanchal asked glumly.

'What?'

'Miscegenation. You might not want a black for your girl's father. Not if it means prison.'

'I don't think they'll do that. And I thought the word for Indians was "coloured",' she said. '*You* might want to meet an Indian girl.'

'No, no, no. Let's not misunderstand each other again,' he said, squeezing her hand.

'As soon as you've had your sausages, it's off to bed,' Rafaela said to Chloe.

Chloe looked up and said she did not want to sleep. But at last, after dinner and bath and a story, she did go to sleep.

'You're not going to leave us and go back to India? I couldn't let that happen to Chloe.' Even with her daughter asleep, Rafi felt she had to whisper. 'When we tell her you are her father, you can never leave again. *Never*. You will have to meet my family, get clobbered by my dad and my four brothers.'

'I won't even be late home from work,' he joked. 'I do have to go back to India to fulfil my bond, though,' he said. 'So we'll all go. And you will meet my ma and pa. My sisters. Their children. Husbands, aunties and uncles.'

'But I don't want to live in India,' said Rafi a little urgently. 'There are beggars and disease everywhere.'

Chanchal gave her a moment to calm down.

'Okay, I know very little about the place. But I don't speak Hindi or Punjabi, or any languages that I'd need!'

'I realise that. But you know, I don't feel at home here either.'

'So we're square?'

'I think so,' said Chanchal, taking both her hands in his. 'I remember you at the library. I was a little scared of you because you had an intensity in your eyes that was completely different.'

She pulled him into her bedroom, where a large square mirror was hung. She put him in front of it, and her close beside him, shoulder to shoulder. Giggling, she said, 'Snap!' as though they were being photographed, and then Chanchal pretended to steal a kiss, and she called 'Snap!' but a little less loudly so as not to wake Chloe, and then they flung their arms around each other and he scooped her up with a groan. Breathless from laughing, they stood in front of the mirror, each looking at the other.

'We're like birds that pair for life, Rafi,' Chanchal said. 'That's us.'

'Yes we are.' She led the way back to the living room, and flopped onto the couch, reaching out a hand to him to join her.

'I loved your hair, and your gentleness,' she said. 'Remember when I washed your hair? I loved your sincerity, though I doubted it every day.' She moved closer to him on the couch.

'How could you have doubted me? I was proposing to you every second day.'

'Well, I did. And I didn't want to be married. I wanted to be a painter. And I was right to have doubted you. Look what happened.'

Chanchal winced. 'Yes, I was unreliable and weak. But not any longer.'

And then, in a rather agitated way, Chanchal stopped

her from kissing him and running her hands over him. 'Didn't you bring anything?' she asked.

'No, I most certainly did not. I won't touch you until you give me a proper answer. You shall have to die of longing if you don't agree to my terms wholeheartedly.'

Rafaela had already thought about it. She had woken that morning thinking – Marry me, marry me. And made sure she had a packet of the things in her bedside drawer. She'd actually bought her first packet, ever.

He had changed in many ways. She was glad he was less impulsive. She pulled at his shirt, untucking it to feel the skin of his stomach. Then he stroked her stomach and said she had a woman's body now, just that much softer. They lay along the couch as close as could be, until she thought – What if Chloe wakes up? and beckoned him to the bedroom, but he wouldn't follow. He was rebuttoning his shirt.

'Ask your question, then,' she said.

And so here they were, at the edge of their known worlds: her city, his city, the colours of Australia and India, the beggars of India if need be. Each thought of their daughter's happiness, of the three of them together at last, of the other naked – how they longed to be naked and skin to skin again! – and the dismay of their families. But they saw them later, too, reconciled to this new family, and all of them together, the Singhs and the Mollinos, the saried women swishing past the men in their stubbies.

'Listen to me,' Chanchal said.

'Mmm?' She looked at his ears. Chloe's were a small replica. And the shape of her head was his too.

'I mean really listen.'

'What's worrying you, Chanchal?' she asked.

'My father's health.' It was gnawing at him. How to tell his pa about Rafi and Chloe without giving him a bad shock.

'Can I suggest something? You should grow your hair and put your turban back on.'

'Yes, you're right.'

Chanchal smiled at Rafi and then took her hands in his again. He wanted to feel her, he so much wanted to feel her.

'Will you marry me?' he asked.

'Yes,' she said. 'I want to marry you, Chanchal Singh.'

And then Rafi smiled, because there was still divorce, illness, wars, death – no guarantees. 'It's certainly the most practical thing we can do.'

Chanchal ignored her cheek and, loving her, drew her close.

What was sweet and what was hard – Rafaela and Chanchal now knew both.

ACKNOWLEDGEMENTS

The help of others during the research and writing of this book has been invaluable.

In particular, Dr G.S. Sidhu was very generous with his thoughts and knowledge in relation to Sikhs in Australia, and his own experience of the Colombo Plan for Economic Development. In Woolgoolga, Rashmere Bhatti and Mr Teja Singh were also helpful, as was Dr Davinda Singh-Grewal in Sydney. My father, Dr Michael Messer, assisted with the topic of Chanchal's doctoral thesis. Administrators of the Queen Victoria Market Offices allowed me to read through the market's archives. Rosanne Squire, former Acting Director of Nursing at Lismore Base Hospital was generous with her memories and knowledge of rural women's maternity experiences in the 1950s and 1960s, and Peter Haigh of the Queensland Railway Historical Society answered my questions about trains patiently and in detail. Hugh Rasseby's memories of London orchestras and post-war boarding school education in India were extremely useful.

Many other people responded to my queries and need for information, including the late Dr Max Marginson, Dr Alan Jones, Jacob Messer, Tom Carment, Jane Hammond and Peter Hammond. Mary Hammond's paintings of women at the Victoria Market and Tom Carment's landscapes were a guide and inspiration.

Numerous books, archived newspaper stories, government reports, films and documentaries were critical to my research, particularly relating to the Indian, maternity and Melbourne themes. These included Marie de Lepervanche, *Indians in a White Australia*; Dr Raja Jayaraman's contribution to Jim Jupp, ed., *The Australian People*; Urvashi Butalia, *The Other Side of Silence: Voices from the Partition of India*; Sukeshi Kamra, *Bearing Witness: Partition, Independence, End of the Raj*; Gita Mehta, *Snakes and Ladders*; Nikky-Guninder Kaur Singh, *The Name of my Beloved*; Neil Yates, *Woolgoolga: History of a Village*; and Ellen McCaughery, Mary Hoban and Ruth Maddison, *The Victoria Market*.

Safina Uberoi's *My Mother India* and Kay Rasool's *Temple on the Hill*, both Australian film documentaries, enriched my research, as did a number of ABC Radio National documentaries set in Woolgoolga.

The phrase 'the straight and simple way of things', used on page 96, is quoted from a Charmian Clift essay, and the idea for a Rembrandt in the Carmichael's kitchen is drawn from another of her essays, both collected in *The World of Charmian Clift*, edited by George Johnston. The song lines Chanchal quotes on pages 99 and 108 are from *Songs of the Saints from the Adi Granth*, translated by Nirmal Dass, State University of New York Press. The various Wittgenstein quotes are from his *Tractatus Logico-*

Philosophicus and *Philosophical Investigations*. Phrases quoted on page 155 are from *The Name of My Beloved: Verses of the Sikh Gurus*, translated and introduced by Nikky-Guninder Kaur Singh, HarperCollins Publishers.

Parts of the manuscript were written while I was a postgraduate student at the University of Technology, Sydney. Thanks go to the university for its support during those early years, in particular to the kind and wise Glenda Adams and Joyce Kornblatt. The support of the Department of English, Macquarie University, is also appreciated. Thanks also to the hundreds of students that I've taught over the years for our many and varied conversations about writing. I've learnt a great deal.

Extracts of earlier versions have been published, along with the author's essays, as 'The Maternal Heroine' in *Cultural Studies Review* Vol 11, No. 1, March 2005 and 'The Making of A Man' in *New Writing: International Journal of the Theory of Creative Writing*, Vol 1, No. 1, 2004.

Both while they are growing and once they are done, books need readers. Mary-Ellen Mullane and Helen Doogue read, criticised, debated and re-read with insight and skill and I am enormously grateful to them both for their commitment over the years. Jane Palfreyman took the manuscript on, talked it through and gave it a home. Jane Gleeson-White provided detailed editorial comment, making shrewd demands on the manuscript that have been exciting and in all ways invaluable. Jessica Dettmann's project management and final edit were consummately professional. Thanks also to Ali Lavau and Meredith Curnow.

Lastly, I acknowledge the young women who boldly made their way from faraway cities to Melbourne in the 1950s, in search of work, art, love, education and conversation – my mother, Judy Messer, Mary Hammond, Peggy Bartak, Pat Miller and Ruth Berman.